A TREASURY OF
Short Stories

Favorites
of the past hundred years
from Turgenev to Thurber
from Balzac
to Hemingway
with biographical sketches
of the authors
Edited by
BERNARDINE KIELTY

SIMON AND SCHUSTER · NEW YORK
1947

CONTENTS

NINETEENTH CENTURY

EUROPEAN

1

OF OUR TIME

EUROPEAN

1

2

3

4

FOREWORD

ONE OF THE outstanding advantages of an anthology, as I have learned through many months of work on this volume, is the self-inflicted education of the anthologist. One individual at least profits by the orgy of reading and the library prowling. But it must be said that the purpose behind this particular book was primarily neither self-improvement nor teaching. It grew out of an enormous respect for the really good short story, with no other criterion than enjoyment, and from this touchstone it never seriously departed.

The first test in the choice of stories, and the most satisfactory in the end, was savory recollection. Nostalgically I sought out the old not-to-be-forgotten favorites. It was a treat to reread them, but it was disillusioning too. In some cases the discrepancy between young enthusiasm and mature consideration was without doubt a measure of early callowness. But quite as often the story itself proved too closely integrated into the mores of its own day and place, or too much restricted by a technique that had now become shopworn. The strictly regional story thus fell into the discard, most of the dialect stories, and many of the deliberately humorous. Mark Twain's stories, for example—not his novels—no longer seemed funny. Rereading Galsworthy's "The Apple Tree" was like looking at an old picture of an old beau. How could one ever have been so moved! "Marjorie Daw," by Thomas Bailey Aldrich, which once seemed so knowing, had become obvious and artificial.

In the process of the hunt, I called upon friends who in some cases unearthed precious tales almost forgotten. "The Rocking-Horse Winner," by D. H. Lawrence, was one that turned up; Frank Stockton's "The Griffin and the Minor Canon;" and "A Voice in the Night," the thriller by William Hodgson. But the most interesting discovery at this point was the extent to which people's tastes coincided—how many of the stories long remembered turned up again and again.

In the table of contents as finally evolved, I have to confess to frequent lack of logic and to many arbitrary decisions. Concessions were made to literary history, but very few, and possibly not enough for the well-rounded book that some readers may be looking for. There were certain authors, however, who, if slighted, would forever haunt one. What story anthologist would be brave enough, even if he wanted to, to leave out a Kipling, a Chekhov, an O. Henry, or a Sherwood Anderson? Nevertheless, many a well-known name is missing. As a general rule those authors have not been included whose novels—or other media of their art —are outstandingly better than their short stories. This accounts for the conspicuous absence of Willa Cather, one of our greatest novelists, of Sinclair Lewis, of Thomas Hardy, to mention only three. Yet inconsistently there is Balzac, novelist par excellence.

A penchant for the exciting has resulted in what may seem an overweight of mystery and horror, but in my judgment some of the best-written and the most effective stories of the past thirty years have been in this field: the higher the degree of imagination, the more eloquent, apparently, the word and phrase. I have also leaned toward humor. W. W. Jacobs and "Saki" and Bemelmans and Runyon are here for the fun they furnish, though all of them have written serious stories, which, given the chance, they would no doubt themselves have chosen. Passionate and fanatical though the Irish be, I have sidetracked their politics in favor of sentiment, and selected tales for the lilt of their English. I have indulged a woman's predilection for a love story, and have put in a number of tales that revolve about a child.

In some cases celebrated stories are left out because they have already appeared in several anthologies, among them "The Procurator of Judea," by Anatole France, "The Devil and Daniel Webster," by Stephen Vincent Benét, "The Turn of the Screw," by Henry James; less well-known stories by all these masters have been substituted.

The most difficult task was selecting among contemporaries. One feels unsure about the untried: first impressions are so often dependent on immediate circumstance, on local prestige, even on the state of one's digestion. In retrospect we recognize classics among stories unappreciated in their time. But today's popular success may wear as thin as Ravel's *Bolero*.

The physical limitations of what can be put between the boards of a book have also forced decisions. Because of their length it was unfortunately necessary to omit three great stories from twentieth-century Central Europe: Thomas Mann's "Disorder and Early Sorrow," Franz Werfel's "The Man Who Conquered Death," Bruno Frank's "The Moon Watch." I should like also to have had room for Pushkin and Gogol and Bunin, and for James Joyce's "The Dead." In fact, this mechanical difficulty has lopped off centuries. There are tales, in the Bible that logically belong here, and in the *Decameron* and in the *Arabian Nights*. But the short story, as we commonly think of it, is pretty much a nineteenth-century product, and as such it is here presented—a modern vehicle of expression starting more or less on its way with Poe, and descending, cut and trimmed and sharpened, down through the years to Faulkner and Hemingway.

Actually the short story is an ideal medium in a swiftly moving modern world. Unlike the novel, it hasn't the time or the space to tell all. By nature it is provocative, it tempts speculation, its last note carries over-tones of infinite suggestion. As Bliss Perry said, it may be "the merest sketch of a face, a comic attitude, a tragic incident: it may be a lovely dream, a horrid nightmare, or a page of words that haunt us like music." It is a song, not a symphony.

If there is any formula to be deduced from the considerable exhibition here displayed, it is a very simple one, a formula, as I see it, with two component parts. In the first place, in each story a situation, however subtle or dramatic or ordinary, is resolved: "something happens." In the second place, there is emotional impact. The author has had his moments of vivid experience out of which it has been given him, by his acute sensitivity and his exceptional talents, to carry over to us a miniature cosmos that reflects the full sharp excitement of his original vision. If the author is successful, as in these examples I believe him to have been, the reader himself is also involved. The reader is moved—to laugh, to cry, to exclaim; and the more completely the mood envelops him, the greater the achievement. Aldous Huxley may have seen a bright-eyed boy and sensed in him the infinite tragedy of the misunderstood, and so con-ceived a Young Archimedes. Stephen Vincent Benét may often have heard the timeworn strains of "I've Been Working on the Railroad," but the time it brought forth an O'Halloran with his Luck was the moment that counted. Sherwood Anderson surely remembered the look a girl gave him—of contempt and superiority—when he wrote "I'm a Fool."

The lives of the writers themselves, summarized here, turned out to be quite as dramatic as their fiction. It was impossible to do them justice in the space allotted, but here again I found the task rewarding out of all proportion: delving into contemporary criticism often irrelevant for my purpose, dipping into diaries and journals and letters, here and there picking up odd but revealing bits, many of which are included in these brief biographical sketches, at the expense, I'm afraid, of more factual detail.

This excursion down through the years has also afforded fleeting glimpses of history. Ephemeral and hazy, but nevertheless there, behind the procession of stories and in the background of the lives of the men and women who wrote them, are the changing culture and modes of thinking, to a certain extent the politics and the immediate education, of each succeeding generation, as these various influences have affected the articulate members.

The best I can hope then is that the reader will have as thoroughly satisfactory a time—picking up this book for recreation—as the compiler had in the process of her so-called work.

BERNARDINE KIELTY

NINETEENTH CENTURY

Ivan Sergeyevich Turgenev
1818-1883

TURGENEV, the Russian who chose to live nearly half his adult life outside his own country, was nonetheless one of Russia's greatest patriots. "No man," said Ernest Renan at Turgenev's funeral, "has been as much as he the incarnation of a whole race: generations of ancestors, lost in the sleep of centuries, speechless, came through him to life and utterance." Although born into the landed gentry, of a family of enormous wealth, Turgenev understood the "little" people, and, by his simple direct stories, awakened Russia to her responsibilities to them.

The incredible ménage in which Turgenev grew up might well have justified a revolution on its own count: five thousand serfs at the command of a single family, and cruelty accepted as a matter of course. (Turgenev's grandmother, it is said, killed a serf with her own hands.) But Turgenev was not a revolutionary, nor was he a propagandist. He was merely a Russian aristocrat who preferred his native tongue to any other, and came to know his serfs not as properties but as persons. Like all young men of his class he was brought up to speak French, and it was only through close companionship with the old serf who used to take him hunting that he learned to love Russian. Together the two strolled the countryside, chatted with villagers and farmers, and became their friends. It was a far-reaching experience for Turgenev, and *A Sportsman's Sketches*, from which "Yermolaï and the Miller's Wife" comes, was his artist's tribute to a people sometimes gay and charming, oftener tired and sad.

After *Fathers and Sons* had been published (1862), and had been completely misunderstood by both critics and the public, Turgenev left Russia in disgust, and for much of the next twenty years lived in France. We read of him at Flaubert's Sunday afternoons at Croisset; in his own green-shuttered house on Montmartre; or at the home of Pauline Garcia (Mme Viardot), the singer, whom he loved long but hopelessly. He continued to write while abroad, but only about Russia. For all his seeming adaptation to Parisian life, the great towering, white-bearded Turgenev remained eternally Russian.

Yermolaï and the Miller's Wife

BY IVAN TURGENEV

ONE evening I went with the hunts-man Yermolaï "stand-shooting." . . . But perhaps all my readers may not know what "stand-shooting" is. I will tell you.

A quarter of an hour before sunset in springtime you go out into the woods with your gun, but without your dog. You seek out a spot for yourself on the outskirts of the forest, take a look round, examine your caps, and glance at your companion. A quarter of an hour passes; the sun has set, but it is still light in the forest; the sky is clear and transparent; the birds are chattering and twittering; the young grass shines with the brilliance of emerald. . . . You wait. Gradually the recesses of the forest grow dark; the blood-red glow of the evening sky creeps slowly on to the roots and the trunks of the trees, and keeps rising higher and higher, passes from the lower, still almost leafless branches, to the motionless, slumbering treetops. . . . And now even the topmost branches are darkened; the purple sky fades to dark blue. The forest fragrance grows stronger; there is a scent of warmth and damp earth; the fluttering breeze dies away at your side. The birds go to sleep—not all at once—but after their kinds; first the finches are hushed, a few minutes later the warblers, and after them the yellow buntings. In the forest it grows darker and darker. The trees melt together into great masses of blackness; in the dark-blue sky the first stars come timidly out. All the birds are asleep. Only the red-starts and the nuthatches are still chirping drowsily. . . . And now they too are still. The last echoing call of the peewit rings over our heads; the oriole's melancholy cry sounds somewhere in the distance; then the nightingale's first note. Your heart is weary with suspense, when suddenly—but only sportsmen can understand me—suddenly in the deep hush there is a peculiar croaking and whirring sound, the measured sweep of swift wings is heard, and the snipe, gracefully bending its long beak, sails smoothly down behind a dark bush to meet your shot.

That is the meaning of "stand-shooting." And so I had gone out stand-shooting with Yermolaï; but excuse me, reader: I must first introduce you to Yermolaï.

Picture to yourself a tall, gaunt man of forty-five, with a long, thin nose, a narrow forehead, little gray eyes, a bristling head of hair, and

Translated from the Russian by Constance Garnett. From *A Sportsman's Sketches* by Ivan Turgenev. By permission of The Macmillan Company and A. P. Watt & Son of London.

thick sarcastic lips. This man wore, winter and summer alike, a yellow nankeen coat of German cut, but with a sash round the waist; he wore blue pantaloons and a cap of astrakhan, presented to him in a merry hour by a spendthrift land-owner. Two bags were fastened on to his sash, one in front, skillfully tied into two halves, for powder and for shot; the other behind for game: wadding Yermolaï used to produce out of his peculiar, seemingly inexhaustible cap. With the money he gained by the game he sold, he might easily have bought himself a cartridge box and powder flask; but he never once even contemplated such a purchase, and continued to load his gun after his old fashion, exciting the admiration of all beholders by the skill with which he avoided the risks of spilling or mixing his powder and shot. His gun was a single-barreled flintlock, endowed, moreover, with a villainous habit of "kicking." It was due to this that Yermolaï's right cheek was permanently swollen to a larger size than the left. How he ever succeeded in hitting anything with this gun, it would take a shrewd man to discover—but he did. He had too a setter dog, by name Valetka, a most extraordinary creature. Yermolaï never fed him. "Me feed a dog!" he reasoned; "why, a dog's a clever beast; he finds a living for himself." And certainly, though Valetka's extreme thinness was a shock even to an indifferent observer, he still lived and had a long life; and in spite of his pitiable position he was not even once lost, and never showed an inclination to desert his master. Once indeed, in his youth, he had absented himself for two days, on courting bent, but this folly was soon over with him. Valetka's most noticeable peculiarity was his impenetrable indifference to everything in the world. . . . If it were not a dog I was speaking of, I should have called him "disillusioned." He usually sat with his cropped tail curled up under him, scowling and twitching at times, and he never smiled. (It is well known that dogs can smile, and smile very sweetly.) He was exceedingly ugly; and the idle house serfs never lost an opportunity of jeering cruelly at his appearance; but all these jeers, and even blows, Valetka bore with astonishing indifference. He was a source of special delight to the cooks, who would all leave their work at once and give him chase with shouts and abuse, whenever, through a weakness not confined to dogs, he thrust his hungry nose through the half-open door of the kitchen, tempting with its warmth and appetizing smells. He distinguished himself by untiring energy in the chase, and had a good scent; but if he chanced to overtake a slightly wounded hare, he devoured it with relish to the last bone, somewhere in the cool shade under the green bushes, at a respectful distance from Yermolaï, who was abusing him in every known and unknown dialect.

Yermolaï belonged to one of my neighbors, a landowner of the old style. Landowners of the old style don't care for game, and prefer the domestic fowl. Only on extraordinary occasions, such as birthdays, name days, and elections, the cooks of the old-fashioned landowners set to work to prepare some long-beaked birds, and, falling into the state of frenzy peculiar to Russians when they don't quite know what to do, they concoct such marvelous sauces for them that the guests examine the proffered dishes curiously and attentively, but rarely make up their minds to try them. Yermolaï was under orders to provide his master's kitchen with two brace of grouse and partridges once a month. But he might live where and how he pleased. They had given him up, as a man of no use for work of any kind—"bone lazy," as the expression is among us in Orel. Powder and shot, of course, they did not provide him, following precisely the same principle in virtue of which he did not feed his dog. Yermolaï was a very strange kind of man; heedless as a bird, rather fond of talking, awkward and vacant-looking; he was excessively fond of drink, and never could sit still long; in walking he shambled along, and rolled from side to side; and yet he got over fifty miles in the day with his rolling, shambling gait. He exposed himself to the most varied adventures: spent the night in the marshes, in trees, on roofs, or under bridges; more than once he had got shut up in lofts, cellars, or barns; he sometimes lost his gun, his dog, his most indispensable garments; got long and severe thrashings; but he always returned home after a little while, in his clothes, and with his gun and his dog. One could not call him a cheerful man, though one almost always found him in an even frame of mind; he was looked on generally as an eccentric. Yermolaï liked a little chat with a good companion, especially over a glass, but he would not stop long; he would get up and go. "But where the devil are you going? It's dark out-of-doors." "To Tchaplino." "But what's taking you to Tchaplino, ten miles away?" "I am going to stay the night at Sophron's there." "But stay the night here." "No, I can't." And Yermolaï, with his Valetka, would

go off into the dark night, through woods and water courses, and the peasant Sophron very likely did not let him into his place, and even, I am afraid, gave him a blow to teach him "not to disturb honest folks." But none could compare with Yermolaï in skill in deep-water fishing in springtime, in catching crayfish with his hands, in tracking game by scent, in snaring quails, in training hawks, in capturing the nightingales who had the greatest variety of notes. . . . One thing he could not do, train a dog; he had not patience enough. He had a wife too. He went to see her once a week. She lived in a wretched, tumbledown little hut, and led a hand-to-mouth existence, never knowing overnight whether she would have food to eat on the morrow; and in every way her lot was a pitiful one. Yermolaï, who seemed such a careless and easygoing fellow, treated his wife with cruel harshness; in his own house he assumed a stern and menacing manner; and his poor wife did everything she could to please him, trembled when he looked at her, and spent her last farthing to buy him vodka; and when he stretched himself majestically on the stove and fell into a heroic sleep, she obsequiously covered him with a sheepskin. I happened myself more than once to catch an involuntary look in him of a kind of savage ferocity; I did not like the expression of his face when he finished off a wounded bird with his teeth. But Yermolaï never remained more than a day at home, and away from home he was once more the same "Yermolka" (i.e., the shooting cap), as he was called for a hundred miles round, and as he sometimes called himself. The lowest house serf was conscious of being superior to this vagabond—and perhaps this was precisely why they treated him with friendliness; the peasants at first amused themselves by chasing him and driving him like a hare over the open country, but afterwards they left him in God's hands, and when once they recognized him as "queer," they no longer tormented him, and even gave him bread and entered into talk with him. . . . This was the man I took as my huntsman, and with him I went stand-shooting to a great birch wood on the banks of the Ista.

Many Russian rivers, like the Volga, have one bank rugged and precipitous, the other bounded by level meadows; and so it is with the Ista. This small river winds extremely capriciously, coils like a snake, and does not keep a straight course for half a mile together; in some places, from the top of a sharp acclivity, one can see the river for ten miles, with its dikes, its pools and mills, and the gardens on its banks, shut in with willows and thick flower gardens. There are fish in the Ista in endless numbers, especially roaches (the peasants take them in hot weather from under the bushes with their hands); little sandpipers flutter whistling along the stony banks, which are streaked with cold clear streams; wild ducks dive in the middle of the pools, and look round warily; in the coves under the overhanging cliffs herons stand out in the shade. . . . We stood in ambush nearly an hour, killed two brace of wood snipe, and, as we wanted to try our luck again at sunrise (stand-shooting can be done as well in the early morning), we resolved to spend the night at the nearest mill. We came out of the wood, and went down the slope. The dark-blue waters of the river

ran below; the air was thick with the mists of night. We knocked at the gate. The dogs began barking in the yard.

"Who is there?" asked a hoarse and sleepy voice.

"We are sportsmen; let us stay the night." There was no reply. "We will pay."

"I will go and tell the master— Sh! curse the dogs! Go to the devil with you!"

We listened as the workman went into the cottage; he soon came back to the gate. "No," he said; "the master tells me not to let you in."

"Why not?"

"He is afraid; you are sportsmen; you might set the mill on fire; you've firearms with you, to be sure."

"But what nonsense!"

"We had our mill on fire like that last year; some fish dealers stayed the night, and they managed to set it on fire somehow."

"But, my good friend, we can't sleep in the open air!"

"That's your business." He went away, his boots clacking as he walked.

Yermolaï promised him various unpleasant things in the future. "Let us go to the village," he brought out at last, with a sigh. But it was two miles to the village.

"Let us stay the night here," I said, "in the open air—the night is warm; the miller will let us have some straw if we pay for it."

Yermolaï agreed without discussion. We began again to knock.

"Well, what do you want?" the workman's voice was heard again; "I've told you we can't."

We explained to him what we wanted. He went to consult the master of the house, and returned with him. The little side gate creaked. The miller appeared, a tall, fat-faced man with a bull neck, round-bellied and corpulent. He agreed to my proposal. A hundred paces from the mill there was a little outhouse open to the air on all sides. They carried straw and hay there for us; the workman set a samovar down on the grass near the river, and, squatting on his heels, began to blow vigorously into the pipe of it. The embers glowed, and threw a bright light on his young face. The miller ran to wake his wife, and suggested at last that I myself should sleep in the cottage; but I preferred to remain in the open air. The miller's wife brought us milk, eggs, potatoes, and bread. Soon the samovar boiled, and we began drinking tea. A mist had risen from the river; there was no wind; from all round came the cry of the corn-crake, and faint sounds from the mill wheels of drops that dripped from the paddles and of water gurgling through the bars of the lock. We built a small fire on the ground. While Yermolaï was baking the potatoes in the embers, I had time to fall into a doze. I was waked by a discreetly subdued whispering near me. I lifted my head; before the fire, on a tub turned upside down, the miller's wife sat talking to my huntsman. By her dress, her movements, and her manner of speaking, I had already recognized that she had been in domestic service, and was neither peasant nor city-bred; but now for the first time I got a clear view of her features. She looked about thirty; her thin, pale face still showed the traces of remarkable beauty; what particularly charmed me was her eyes, large and mournful in expression. She was leaning her elbows on her knees, and had her face in her hands. Yermolaï

was sitting with his back to me, and thrusting sticks into the fire.

"They've the cattle plague again at Zheltonhiny," the miller's wife was saying; "Father Ivan's two cows are dead—Lord have mercy on them!"

"And how are your pigs doing?" asked Yermolaï, after a brief pause.

"They're alive."

"You ought to make me a present of a sucking pig."

The miller's wife was silent for a while, then she sighed.

"Who is it you're with?" she asked.

"A gentleman from Kostomarovo."

Yermolaï threw a few pine twigs on the fire; they all caught at once, and a thick white smoke came puffing into his face.

"Why didn't your husband let us into the cottage?"

"He's afraid."

"Afraid! the fat old tub! Arina Timofyevna, my darling, bring me a little glass of spirits."

The miller's wife rose and vanished into the darkness. Yermolaï began to sing in an undertone:

When I went to see my sweetheart,
I wore out all my shoes.

Arina returned with a small flask and a glass. Yermolaï got up, crossed himself, and drank it off at a draught. "Good!" was his comment.

The miller's wife sat down again on the tub.

"Well, Arina Timofyevna, are you still ill?"

"Yes."

"What is it?"

"My cough troubles me at night."

"The gentleman's asleep, it seems," observed Yermolaï after a short silence. "Don't go to a doctor, Arina; it will be worse if you do."

"Well, I am not going."

"But come and pay me a visit."

Arina hung down her head dejectedly.

"I will drive my wife out for the occasion," continued Yermolaï. "Upon my word, I will."

"You had better wake the gentleman, Yermolaï Petrovitch; you see, the potatoes are done."

"Oh, let him snore," observed my faithful servant indifferently; "he's tired with walking, so he sleeps sound."

I turned over in the hay. Yermolaï got up and came to me. "The potatoes are ready; will you come and eat them?"

I came out of the outhouse; the miller's wife got up from the tub and was going away. I addressed her.

"Have you kept this mill long?"

"It's two years since I came on Trinity day."

"And where does your husband come from?"

Arina had not caught my question.

"Where's your husband from?" repeated Yermolaï, raising his voice.

"From Byelev. He's a Byelev townsman."

"And are you too from Byelev?"

"No, I'm a serf; I was a serf."

"Whose?"

"Zvyerkov was my master. Now I am free."

"What Zvyerkov?"

"Alexander Selitch."

"Weren't you his wife's lady's maid?"

"How did you know? Yes."

I looked at Arina with redoubled curiosity and sympathy.

"I know your master," I continued.

"Do you?" she replied in a low voice, and her head drooped.

I must tell the reader why I looked with such sympathy at Arina. During my stay at Petersburg I had become quite by chance acquainted with Mr. Zvyerkov. He had a rather influential position, and was reputed a man of sense and education. He had a wife, fat, sentimental, lachrymose, and spiteful—a vulgar and disagreeable creature; he had too a son, the very type of the young swell of today, pampered and stupid. The exterior of Mr. Zvyerkov himself did not prepossess one in his favor; his little mouselike eyes peeped slyly out of a broad, almost square, face; he had a large, prominent nose, with distended nostrils; his close-cropped gray hair stood up like a brush above his scowling brow; his thin lips were forever twitching and smiling mawkishly. Mr. Zvyerkov's favorite position was standing with his legs wide apart and his fat hands in his trousers pockets. Once I happened somehow to be driving alone with Mr. Zvyerkov in a coach out of town. We fell into conversation. As a man of experience and of judgment, Mr. Zvyerkov began to try to set me in "the path of truth."

"Allow me to observe to you," he drawled at last; "all you young people criticize and form judgments on everything at random; you have little knowledge of your own country; Russia, young gentleman, is an unknown land to you; that's where it is! . . . You are forever reading German. For instance, now you say this and that and the other about anything; for instance, about the house serfs. . . . Very fine; I don't dispute it's all very fine; but you don't know them; you don't know the kind of people they are." (Mr. Zvyerkov blew his nose loudly and took a pinch of snuff.) "Allow me to tell you as an illustration one little anecdote; it may perhaps interest you." (Mr. Zvyerkov cleared his throat.) "You know, doubtless, what my wife is; it would be difficult, I should imagine, to find a more kind-hearted woman, you will agree. For her waiting maids, existence is simply a perfect paradise, and no mistake about it. . . . But my wife has made it a rule never to keep married lady's maids. Certainly it would not do; children come—and one thing and the other—and how is a lady's maid to look after her mistress as she ought, to fit in with her ways; she is no longer able to do it; her mind is on other things. One must look at things through human nature. Well, we were driving once through our village, it must be—let me be correct—yes, fifteen years ago. We saw, at the bailiff's, a young girl, his daughter, very pretty indeed; something even—you know—something attractive in her manners. And my wife said to me: 'Kokó'—you understand, of course, that is her pet name for me—'let us take this girl to Petersburg; I like her, Kokó . . .' I said, 'Let us take her, by all means.' The bailiff, of course, was at our feet; he could not have expected such good fortune, you can imagine. . . . Well, the girl, of course, cried violently. Of course, it was hard for her at first; the parental home . . . in fact . . . there was nothing surprising in that. However, she soon got used to us: at first we put her in the maidservants' room; they trained her, of course. And what do you think? The girl made wonderful progress; my wife became simply devoted to her, promoted her at last above the rest to wait on herself . . . observe. . . . And one must do her the justice to say, my wife had never such a maid, absolutely never; attentive, modest, and obedient—simply all that could be desired. But my wife, I must con-fess, spoiled her too much; she dressed her well, fed her from our own table, gave her tea to drink, and so on, as you can imagine! So she waited on my wife like this for ten years. Suddenly, one fine morning, picture to yourself, Arina—her name was Arina—rushes unannounced into my study, and flops down at my feet. That's a thing, I tell you plainly, I can't endure. No human being ought ever to lose sight of their personal dignity. Am I not right? What do you say? 'Your honor, Alexander Selitch, I beseech a favor of you.' 'What favor?' 'Let me be married.' I must confess I was taken aback. 'But you know, you stupid, your mistress has no other lady's maid?' 'I will wait on mistress as before.' 'Nonsense! nonsense! your mistress can't endure married lady's maids.' 'Malanya could take my place.' 'Pray don't argue.' 'I obey your will.' I must confess it was quite a shock. I assure you, I am like that; nothing wounds me so—nothing, I venture to say, wounds me so deeply as ingratitude. I need not tell you—you know what my wife is; an angel upon earth, goodness inexhaustible. One would fancy even the worst of men would be ashamed to hurt her. Well, I got rid of Arina. I thought perhaps she would come to her senses; I was unwilling, do you know, to believe in wicked, black ingratitude in anyone. What do you think? Within six months she thought fit to come to me again with the same request. I felt revolted. But imagine my amazement when, some time later, my wife comes to me in tears, so agitated that I felt positively alarmed. 'What has happened?' 'Arina. . . . You understand . . . I am ashamed to tell it. . . .' 'Impossible! . . . Who is the man?' 'Petrushka, the footman.' My indignation broke out then. I am like that. I don't like half measures! Petrushka was not to blame. We might flog him, but in my opinion he was not to blame. Arina . . . Well, well, well! what more's to be said? I gave orders, of course, that her hair should be cut off, she should be dressed in sackcloth, and sent into the country. My wife was deprived of an excellent lady's maid; but there was no help for it: immorality cannot be tolerated in a household in any case. Better to cut off the infected member at once. There, there! now you can judge the thing for yourself—you know that my wife is . . . yes, yes, yes! indeed! . . . an angel! She had grown attached to Arina, and Arina knew it, and had the face to . . . Eh? no, tell me . . . eh? And what's the use of talking about it? Anyway, there was no help for it. I, indeed— I, in particular, felt hurt, felt wounded for a long time by the ingratitude of this girl. Whatever you say—it's no good to look for feeling, for heart, in these people! You may feed the wolf as you will; he has always a hankering for the woods Education, by all means! But I only wanted to give you an example . . .'

And Mr. Zvyerkov, without finishing his sentence, turned away his head, and, wrapping himself more closely into his cloak, manfully repressed his involuntary emotion.

The reader now probably understands why I looked with sympathetic interest at Arina.

"Have you long been married to the miller?" I asked her at last.

"Two years."

"How was it? Did your master allow it?"

"They bought my freedom."

"Who?"

"Savely Alexyevich."

"Who is that?"

"My husband." (Yermolaï smiled to himself.) "Has my master perhaps spoken to you of me?" added Arina, after a brief silence.

I did not know what reply to make to her question.

"Arina!" cried the miller from a distance. She got up and walked away.

"Is her husband a good fellow?" I asked Yermolaï.

"So-so."

"Have they any children?"

"There was one, but it died."

"How was it? Did the miller take a liking to her? Did he give much to buy her freedom?"

"I don't know. She can read and write; in their business it's of use. I suppose he liked her."

"And have you known her long?"

"Yes. I used to go to her master's. Their house isn't far from here."

"And do you know the footman Petrushka?"

"Piotr Vassilyevich? Of course, I knew him."

"Where is he now?"

"He was sent for a soldier."

We were silent for a while.

"She doesn't seem well?" I asked Yermolaï at last.

"I should think not! Tomorrow, I say, we shall have a good sport. A little sleep now would do us no harm."

A flock of wild ducks swept whizzing over our heads, and we heard them drop down into the river not far from us. It was now quite dark, and it began to be cold; in the thicket sounded the melodious notes of a nightingale. We buried ourselves in the hay and fell asleep.

Leo Nikolayevich Tolstoi

1828-1910

THOUGH THE pattern of Tolstoi's life matched that of many another Russian noble—for the first half, at any rate—the seething undercurrent of spiritual turmoil set him apart. His university years were a gay social whirl; his army career was traditional. He liked to hunt and drink and gamble. Once he turned over a manuscript, *The Cossacks,* to pay off a gambling debt. His ancestral house was bodily removed from the estate, to pay off another. At the age of thirty-four he made a conventional marriage, took his bride to Yasnaya Polyana, in Tula, and settled down to the role of country gentleman. During these years of comparative serenity he wrote *War and Peace* and most of *Anna Karenina.*

But he had already begun to be restless. Below the surface, even in his gayest days, Tolstoi was troubled, as his books of that time testify. Now he began to question the purpose of existence—to weigh the artificialities of his own living against the simple life of the very poor. And shortly before *Anna Karenina* was finished, when he was almost fifty, the convulsive inner struggle broke forth into the open.

What Tolstoi went through in the three or four years of crisis that followed can be gleaned from *Diary of a Madman.* With the vision of death ever before him, he turned to religion and then abruptly away. He shunned visitors, wept, and sat alone. But out of the long agony emerged Tolstoi the evangelist, who for the next thirty years preached the doctrine of Christian living that made him one of the most revered men of his time: love of one's fellow men and the abnegation of all worldly possessions. Tolstoi's wife never subscribed to his teachings, and their life together was embittered by constant quarreling. Of all his children, only Alexandra, the youngest, was sympathetic, and when her father finally left home, she left with him. They set out secretly at night, destination unknown, and the old man died less than a month later, at a railroad station.

The Death of Ivan Ilyich

BY LEO TOLSTOI

I

INSIDE the great building of the law courts, during the interval in the hearing of the Melvinsky case, the members of the judicial council and the public prosecutor were gathered together in the private room of Ivan Yegorovich Shebek, and the conversation turned upon the celebrated Krasovsky case. Fyodor Vassilievich hotly maintained that the case was not in the jurisdiction of the court. Yegor Ivanovich stood up for his own view; but from the first Piotr Ivanovich, who had not entered into the discussion, took no interest in it, but was looking through the newspapers which had just been brought in.

"Gentlemen!" he said, "Ivan Ilyich is dead!"

"You don't say so!"

"Here, read it," he said to Fyodor Vassilievich, handing him the fresh, still damp-smelling paper.

Within a black margin was printed: "Praskovya Fyodorovna Golovin with heartfelt affliction informs friends and relatives of the decease of her beloved husband, member of the Court of Justice, Ivan Ilyich Golovin, who passed away on the 4th of February. The funeral will take place on Thursday at one o'clock."

Ivan Ilyich was a colleague of the gentlemen present, and all liked him. It was some weeks now since he had been taken ill; his illness had been said to be incurable. His post had been kept open for him, but it had been thought that in case of his death Alexyeev might receive his appointment, and either Vinnikov or Shtabel would succeed to Alexyeev's. So that on hearing of Ivan Ilyich's death, the first thought of each of the gentlemen in the room was of the effect this death might have on the transfer or promotion of themselves or their friends.

"Now I am sure of getting Shtabel's place or Vinnikov's," thought Fyodor Vassilievich. "It was promised me long ago, and the promotion means eight hundred rubles' additional income, besides the grants for office expenses."

"Now I shall have to petition for my brother-in-law to be transferred from Kaluga," thought Piotr Ivanovich. "My wife will be very glad. She won't be able to say now that I've never done anything for her family."

"I thought somehow that he'd never get up from his bed again,"

Translated from the Russian by Constance Garnett. By permission of The Modern Library, Inc.

Piotr Ivanovich said aloud. "I'm sorry!"

"But what was it exactly was wrong with him?"

"The doctors could not decide. That's to say, they did decide, but differently. When I saw him last, I thought he would get over it."

"Well, I positively haven't called there ever since the holidays. I've kept meaning to go."

"Had he any property?"

"I think there's something, very small, of his wife's. But something quite trifling."

"Yes, one will have to go and call. They live such a terribly long way off."

"A long way from you, you mean. Everything's a long way from your place."

"There, he can never forgive me for living the other side of the river," said Piotr Ivanovich, smiling at Shavek. And they began to talk of the great distances between different parts of the town, and went back into the court.

Besides the reflections upon the changes and promotions in the service likely to ensue from this death, the very fact of the death of an intimate acquaintance excited in everyone who heard of it, as such a fact always does, a feeling of relief that "It is he that is dead, and not I."

"Only think! he is dead, but here am I all right," each one thought or felt. The more intimate acquaintances, the so-called friends of Ivan Ilyich, could not help thinking too that now they had the exceedingly tiresome social duties to perform of going to the funeral service and paying the widow a visit of condolence.

The most intimately acquainted with their late colleague were Fyodor Vassilievich and Piotr Ivanovich.

Piotr Ivanovich had been a comrade of his at the school of jurisprudence, and considered himself under obligations to Ivan Ilyich.

Telling his wife at dinner of the news of Ivan Ilyich's death and his reflections as to the possibility of getting her brother transferred into their circuit, Piotr Ivanovich, without lying down for his usual nap, put on his frock coat and drove to Ivan Ilyich's.

At the entrance before Ivan Ilyich's flat stood a carriage and two hired flies. Downstairs in the entry near the hatstand there was leaning against the wall a coffin lid with tassels and braiding freshly rubbed up with pipe clay. Two ladies were taking off their cloaks. One of them he knew, the sister of Ivan Ilyich; the other was a lady he did not know. Piotr Ivanovich's colleague, Shvarts, was coming down; and from the top stair, seeing who it was coming in, he stopped and winked at him, as though to say: "Ivan Ilyich has made a mess of it; it's a very different matter with you and me."

Shvarts' face, with his English whiskers and all his thin figure in his frock coat, had, as it always had, an air of elegant solemnity; and this solemnity, always such a contrast to Shvarts' playful character, had a special piquancy here. So thought Piotr Ivanovich.

Piotr Ivanovich let the ladies pass on in front of him, and walked slowly up the stairs after them. Shvarts had not come down, but was waiting at the top. Piotr Ivanovich knew what for; he wanted obviously to settle with him where their game of "screw" was to be that evening. The ladies went up to the widow's room; while Shvarts, with his lips tightly and gravely shut, and amusement in his eyes, with a twitch of his eyebrows motioned Piotr Ivanovich to the right, to the room where the dead man was.

Piotr Ivanovich went in, as people always do on such occasions, in uncertainty as to what he would have to do there. One thing he felt sure of—that crossing himself never comes amiss on such occasions. As to whether it was necessary to bow down while doing so, he did not feel quite sure and so chose a middle course. On entering the room he began crossing himself, and made a slight sort of bow. So far as the movements of his hands and head permitted him, he glanced while doing so about the room. Two young men, one a high-school boy, nephews probably, were going out of the room, crossing themselves. An old lady was standing motionless; and a lady, with her eyebrows queerly lifted, was saying something to her in a whisper. A deacon in a frock coat, resolute and hearty, was reading something aloud with an expression that precluded all possibility of contradiction. A young peasant who used to wait at table, Gerasim, walking with light footsteps in front of Piotr Ivanovich, was sprinkling something on the floor. Seeing this, Piotr Ivanovich was at once aware of the faint odor of the decomposing corpse. On his last visit to Ivan Ilyich, Piotr Ivanovich had seen this peasant in his room; he was performing the duties of a sicknurse, and Ivan Ilyich liked him particularly. Piotr Ivanovich continued crossing himself and bowing in a direction intermediate between the coffin, the deacon, and the holy pictures on the table in the corner. Then when this action of making the sign of the cross with his hand seemed to him to have been

unduly prolonged, he stood still and began to scrutinize the dead man.

The dead man lay, as dead men always do lie, in a peculiarly heavy dead way, his stiffened limbs sunk in the cushions of the coffin, and his head bent back forever on the pillow, and thrust up, as dead men always do, his yellow waxen forehead with bald spots on the sunken temples, and his nose that stood out sharply and, as it were, squeezed on the upper lip. He was much changed, even thinner since Piotr Ivanovich had seen him, but his face—as always with the dead—was more handsome, and, above all, more impressive than it had been when he was alive. On the face was an expression of what had to be done having been done, and rightly done. Besides this, there was too in that expression a reproach or a reminder for the living. This reminder seemed to Piotr Ivanovich uncalled for, or, at least, to have nothing to do with him. He felt something unpleasant; and so Piotr Ivanovich once more crossed himself hurriedly, and, as it struck him, too hurriedly, not quite in accordance with the proprieties, turned and went to the door. Shvarts was waiting for him in the adjoining room, standing with his legs apart and both hands behind his back playing with his top hat. A single glance at the playful, sleek, and elegant figure of Shvarts revived Piotr Ivanovich. He felt that he, Shvarts, was above it, and would not give way to depressing impressions. The mere sight of him said plainly: the incident of the service over the body of Ivan Ilyich cannot possibly constitute a sufficient ground for recognizing the business of the session suspended—in other words, in no way can it hinder us from shuffling and cutting a pack of cards this evening, while the footman sets four unsanctified candles on the table for us; in fact, there is no ground for supposing that this incident could prevent us from spending the evening agreeably. He said as much indeed to Piotr Ivanovich as he came out, proposing that the party should meet at Fyodor Vassilievich's. But apparently it was Piotr Ivanovich's destiny not to play "screw" that evening. Praskovya Fyodorovna, a short, fat woman who, in spite of all efforts in a contrary direction, was steadily broader from her shoulders downwards, all in black, with lace on her head and her eyebrows as queerly arched as those of the lady standing beside the coffin, came out of her own apartments with some other ladies and, conducting them to the dead man's room, said: "The service will take place immediately; come in."

Shvarts, making an indefinite bow, stood still, obviously neither accepting nor declining this invitation. Praskovya Fyodorovna, recognizing Piotr Ivanovich, sighed, went right up to him, took his hand, and said, "I know that you were a true friend of Ivan Ilyich's . . ." and looked at him, expecting from him the suitable action in response to these words. Piotr Ivanovich knew that, just as before he had to cross himself, now what he had to do was to press her hand, to sigh, and to say, "Ah, I was indeed!" And he did so. And as he did so, he felt that the desired result had been attained; that he was touched, and she was touched.

"Come, since it's not begun yet, I have something I want to say to you," said the widow. "Give me your arm."

Piotr Ivanovich gave her his arm, and they moved toward the inner rooms, passing Shvarts, who winked gloomily at Piotr Ivanovich.

"So much for our 'screw'! Don't complain if we find another partner. You can make a fifth when you do get away," said his humorous glance.

Piotr Ivanovich sighed still more deeply and despondently, and Praskovya Fyodorovna pressed his hand gratefully. Going into her drawing room, which was upholstered with pink cretonne and lighted by a dismal-looking lamp, they sat down at the table, she on a sofa and Piotr Ivanovich on a low ottoman with deranged springs which yielded spasmodically under his weight. Praskovya Fyodorovna was about to warn him to sit on another seat, but felt such a recommendation out of keeping with her position, and changed her mind. Sitting down on the ottoman, Piotr Ivanovich remembered how Ivan Ilyich had arranged this drawing room, and had consulted him about this very pink cretonne with green leaves. Seating herself on the sofa, and pushing by the table (the whole drawing room was crowded with furniture and things), the widow caught the lace of her black fichu in the carving of the table. Piotr Ivanovich got up to disentangle it for her; and the ottoman, freed from his weight, began bobbing up spasmodically under him. The widow began unhooking her lace herself, and Piotr Ivanovich again sat down, suppressing the mutinous ottoman springs under him. But the widow could not quite free herself, and Piotr Ivanovich rose again, and again the ottoman became mutinous and popped up with a positive snap. When this was all over, she took out a clean cambric handkerchief and began weeping.

Piotr Ivanovich had been cooled off by the incident with the lace and the struggle with the ottoman springs, and he sat looking sullen. This awkward position was cut short by the entrance of Sokolov, Ivan Ilyich's butler, who came in to announce that the place in the cemetery fixed on by Praskovya Fyodorovna would cost two hundred rubles. She left off weeping and, with the air of a victim, glancing at Piotr Ivanovich, said in French that it was very terrible for her. Piotr Ivanovich made a silent gesture signifying his unhesitating conviction that it must indeed be so.

"Please smoke," she said in a magnanimous, and at the same time, crushed voice, and she began discussing with Sokolov the question of the price of the site for the grave. Piotr Ivanovich, lighting a cigarette, listened to her very circumstantial inquiries as to the various prices of sites and her decision as to the one to be selected. Having settled on the site for the grave, she made arrangements also about the choristers. Sokolov went away.

"I see to everything myself," she said to Piotr Ivanovich, moving on one side the albums that lay on the table; and noticing that the table was in danger from the cigarette ash, she promptly passed an ash tray to Piotr Ivanovich, and said: "I consider it affectation to pretend that my grief prevents me from looking after practical matters. On the contrary, if anything could—not console me . . . but distract me, it is seeing after everything for him." She took out her handkerchief again, as though preparing to weep again; and suddenly, as though struggling with herself, she shook herself, and

began speaking calmly: "But I've business to talk about with you."

Piotr Ivanovich bowed, carefully keeping in check the springs of the ottoman, which had at once begun quivering under him.

"The last few days his sufferings were awful."

"Did he suffer very much?" asked Piotr Ivanovich.

"Oh, awfully! For the last moments, hour indeed, he never left off screaming. For three days and nights in succession he screamed incessantly. It was insufferable. I can't understand how I bore it; one could hear it through three closed doors. Ah, what I suffered!"

"And was he really conscious?" asked Piotr Ivanovich.

"Yes," she whispered, "up to the last minute. He said good-by to us a quarter of an hour before his death, and asked Volodya to be taken away too."

The thought of the sufferings of a man he had known so intimately, at first as a lighthearted boy, a schoolboy, then grown up as a partner at whist, in spite of the unpleasant consciousness of his own and this woman's hypocrisy, suddenly horrified Piotr Ivanovich. He saw again that forehead, the nose that seemed squeezing the lip, and he felt frightened for himself. "Three days and nights of awful suffering and death. Why, that may at once, any minute, come upon me too," he thought, and he felt for an instant terrified. But immediately, he could not himself have said how, there came to his support the customary reflection that this had happened to Ivan Ilyich and not to him, and that to him this must not and could not happen; that in thinking thus he was giving way to depression, which was not the right thing to do, as was evident from Shvarts' expression of face. And making these reflections, Piotr Ivanovich felt reassured, and began with interest inquiring details about Ivan Ilyich's end, as though death were a mischance peculiar to Ivan Ilyich, but not at all incidental to himself.

After various observations about the details of the truly awful physical sufferings endured by Ivan Ilyich (these details Piotr Ivanovich learned only through the effect Ivan Ilyich's agonies had had on the nerves of Praskovya Fyodorovna), the widow apparently thought it time to get to business.

"Ah, Piotr Ivanovich, how hard it is, how awfully, awfully hard!" and she began to cry again.

Piotr Ivanovich sighed, and waited for her to blow her nose. When she had done so, he said, "Indeed it is," and again she began to talk, and brought out what was evidently the business she wished to discuss with him; that business consisted in the inquiry as to how on the occasion of her husband's death she was to obtain a grant from the government. She made a show of asking Piotr Ivanovich's advice about a pension. But he perceived that she knew already to the minutest details, what he did not know himself indeed, everything that could be got out of the government on the ground of this death; but that what she wanted to find out was whether there were not any means of obtaining a little more. Piotr Ivanovich tried to imagine such means; but after pondering a little, and out of politeness abusing the government for its stinginess, he said that he believed that it was impossible to obtain more. Then she sighed and began unmistakably looking about for an excuse for getting rid of her

visitor. He perceived this, put out his cigarette, got up, pressed her hand, and went out into the passage.

In the dining room, where was the bric-à-brac clock that Ivan Ilyich had been so delighted at buying, Piotr Ivanovich met the priest and several people he knew who had come to the service for the dead, and saw too Ivan Ilyich's daughter, a handsome young lady. She was all in black. Her very slender figure looked even slenderer than usual. She had a gloomy, determined, almost wrathful expression. She bowed to Piotr Ivanovich as though he were to blame in some way. Behind the daughter, with the same offended air on his face, stood a rich young man, whom Piotr Ivanovich knew, too, an examining magistrate, the young lady's fiancé, as he had heard. He bowed dejectedly to him, and would have gone on into the dead man's room, when from the staircase there appeared the figure of the son, the high-school boy, extraordinarily like Ivan Ilyich. He was the little Ivan Ilyich over again as Piotr Ivanovich remembered him at school. His eyes were red with crying and had that look often seen in unclean boys of thirteen or fourteen. The boy, seeing Piotr Ivanovich, scowled morosely and bashfully. Piotr Ivanovich nodded to him and went into the dead man's room. The service for the dead began—candles, groans, incense, tears, sobs. Piotr Ivanovich stood frowning, staring at his feet in front of him. He did not once glance at the dead man, and right through to the end did not once give way to depressing influences, and was one of the first to walk out. In the hall there was no one. Gerasim, the young peasant, darted out of the dead man's room, tossed over with his strong hand all the fur cloaks to find Piotr Ivanovich's, and gave it him.

"Well, Gerasim, my boy?" said Piotr Ivanovich, so as to say something. "A sad business, isn't it?"

"It's God's will. We shall come to the same," said Gerasim, showing his white, even, peasant teeth in a smile, and like a man in a rush of extra work, he briskly opened the door, called up the coachman, saw Piotr Ivanovich into the carriage, and darted back to the steps as though bethinking himself of what he had to do next.

Piotr Ivanovich had a special pleasure in the fresh air after the smell of incense, of the corpse, and of carbolic acid.

"Where to?" asked the coachman.

"It's not too late. I'll still go round to Fyodor Vassilievich's."

And Piotr Ivanovich drove there. And he did, in fact, find them just finishing the first rubber, so that he came just at the right time to take a hand.

II

The previous history of Ivan Ilyich was the simplest, the most ordinary, and the most awful.

Ivan Ilyich died at the age of forty-five, a member of the Judicial Council. He was the son of an official, whose career in Petersburg through various ministries and departments had been such as leads people into that position in which, though it is distinctly obvious that they are unfit to perform any kind of real duty, they yet cannot, owing to their long past service and their official rank, be dismissed; and they therefore receive a specially created fictitious post, and by no means fictitious thousands—from six to ten —on which they go on living till extreme old age. Such was the privy councilor, the superfluous member of various superfluous institutions, Ilya Efimovich Golovin.

He had three sons. Ivan Ilyich was the second son. The eldest son's career was exactly like his father's, only in a different department, and he was by now close upon that stage in the service in which the same sinecure would be reached. The third son was the unsuccessful one. He had in various positions always made a mess of things, and was now employed in the railway department. And his father and his brothers, and still more their wives, did not merely dislike meeting him, but avoided, except in extreme necessity, recollecting his existence. His sister had married Baron Greff, a Petersburg official of the same stamp as his father-in-law. Ivan Ilyich was *le phénix de la famille*, as people said. He was not so frigid and precise as the eldest son, nor so wild as the youngest. He was the happy mean between them—a shrewd, lively, pleasant, and well-bred man. He had been educated with his younger brother at the school of jurisprudence. The younger brother had not finished the school course, but was expelled when in the fifth class. Ivan Ilyich completed the course successfully. At school he was just the same as he was later on all his life—an intelligent fellow, highly good-humored and sociable, but strict in doing what he considered to be his duty. His duty he considered whatever was so considered by those persons who were set in authority over him. He was not a toady as a boy, nor later on as a grown-up person; but from his earliest years he was attracted, as a fly to the light, to persons of good standing in the world, assimilated their manners and their views of life, and established friendly relations with them. All the enthusiasms of childhood and youth passed, leaving no great traces in him; he gave way to sensuality and to vanity, and latterly when in the higher classes at school to liberalism, but always keeping within certain limits which were unfailingly marked out for him by his instincts.

At school he had committed actions which had struck him beforehand as great vileness, and gave him a feeling of loathing for himself at the very time he was committing them. But later on, perceiving that such actions were committed also by men of good position, and were not regarded by them as base, he was able, not to regard them as good, but to forget about them completely, and was never mortified by recollections of them.

Leaving the school of jurisprudence in the tenth class, and receiving from his father a sum of money for his outfit, Ivan Ilyich ordered his clothes at Sharmer's, hung on his watch chain a medallion inscribed *Respice finem*, said good-by to the prince who was the principal of his school, had a farewell dinner with his comrades at Donon's, and with all his new fashionable belongings— traveling trunk, linen, suits of clothes, shaving and toilet appurtenances, and traveling rug, all ordered and purchased at the very best shops—set off to take the post of secretary on special commissions for the governor of a province, a post which had been obtained for him by his father.

In the province Ivan Ilyich without loss of time made himself a position as easy and agreeable as his position had been in the school of jurisprudence. He did his work, made his career, and at the same time led a life of well-bred social gaiety. Occasionally he visited various districts on official duty, behaved with dignity both with his superiors and his inferiors; and, with exactitude and an incorruptible honesty of which he could not help feeling proud, performed the duties with which he was intrusted, principally having to do with the dissenters. When engaged in official work he was, in spite of his youth and taste for frivolous amusement, exceedingly reserved, official, and even severe. But in social life he was often amusing and witty, and always good-natured, well bred, and *bon enfant*, as was said of him by his chief and his chief's wife, with whom he was like one of the family.

In the province there was, too, a connection with one of the ladies who obtruded their charms on the stylish young lawyer. There was a dressmaker, too, and there were drinking bouts with smart officers visiting the neighborhood, and visits to a certain outlying street after supper; there was a rather cringing obsequiousness in his behavior, too, with his chief, and even his chief's wife. But all this was accompanied with such a tone of the highest breeding that it could not be called by harsh names; it all came under the rubric of the French saying, *Il faut que la jeunesse se passe*. Everything was done with clean hands, in clean shirts, with French phrases, and, what was of most importance, in the highest society, and consequently with the approval of people of rank.

Such was Ivan Ilyich's career for five years, and then came a change in his official life. New methods of judicial procedure were established; new men were wanted to carry them out. And Ivan Ilyich became such a new man. Ivan Ilyich was offered the post of examining magistrate, and he accepted it in spite of the fact that this post was in another province, and he would have to break off all the ties he had formed and form new ones. Ivan Ilyich's friends met together to see him off, had their photographs taken in a group, presented him with a silver cigarette case, and he set off to his new post.

As an examining magistrate, Ivan Ilyich was as *comme il faut*, as well bred, as adroit in keeping official duties apart from private life, and as successful in gaining universal respect, as he had been as secretary of private commissions. The duties of his new office were in themselves of far greater interest and attractiveness for Ivan Ilyich. In his former post it had been pleasant to pass in his smart uniform from Sharmer's through the crowd of petitioners and officials waiting timorously and envying him, and to march with his easy swagger straight into the governor's private room, there to sit down with him to tea and cigarettes. But the persons directly subject to his authority were few. The only such persons were the district police superintendents and the dissenters, when he was serving on special commissions. And he liked treating such persons affably, almost like comrades; liked to make them feel that he, able to annihilate them, was behaving in this simple, friendly way with them. But such people were then few in number. Now as an examining magistrate Ivan Ilyich felt that everyone—everyone without exception—the most dignified, the most self-satisfied people, all were in his hands, and that he had but to write certain words on a sheet of paper with a printed heading, and this dignified, self-satisfied person

would be brought before him in the capacity of a defendant or a witness; and if he did not care to make him sit down, he would have to stand up before him and answer his questions. Ivan Ilyich never abused this authority of his; on the contrary, he tried to soften the expression of it. But the consciousness of this power and the possibility of softening its effect constituted for him the chief interest and attractiveness of his new position. In the work itself, in the preliminary inquiries, that is, Ivan Ilyich very rapidly acquired the art of setting aside every consideration irrelevant to the official aspect of the case, and of reducing every case, however complex, to that form in which it could in a purely external fashion be put on paper, completely excluding his personal view of the matter and, what was of paramount importance, observing all the necessary formalities. All this work was new. And he was one of the first men who put into practical working the reforms in judicial procedure enacted in 1864.

On settling in a new town in his position as examining magistrate, Ivan Ilyich made new acquaintances, formed new ties, took up a new line, and adopted a rather different attitude. He took up an attitude of somewhat dignified aloofness toward the provincial authorities, while he picked out the best circle among the legal gentlemen and wealthy gentry living in the town, and adopted a tone of slight dissatisfaction with the government, moderate liberalism, and lofty civic virtue. With this, while making no change in the elegance of his get-up, Ivan Ilyich in his new office gave up shaving, and left his beard free to grow as it liked. Ivan Ilyich's existence in the new town proved to be very agreeable; the society which took the line of opposition to the governor was friendly and good; his income was larger, and he found a source of increased enjoyment in whist, at which he began to play at this time; and having a faculty for playing cards good-humoredly, and being rapid and exact in his calculations, he was as a rule on the winning side.

After living two years in the new town, Ivan Ilyich met his future wife. Praskovya Fyodorovna Mihel was the most attractive, clever, and brilliant girl in the set in which Ivan Ilyich moved. Among other amusements and recreations after his labors as a magistrate, Ivan Ilyich started a light, playful flirtation with Praskovya Fyodorovna.

Ivan Ilyich when he was an assistant secretary had danced as a rule; as an examining magistrate he danced only as an exception. He danced now as it were under protest, as though to show "that though I am serving on the new reformed legal code, and am of the fifth class in official rank, still if it comes to a question of dancing, in that line, too, I can do better than others." In this spirit he danced now and then toward the end of the evening with Praskovya Fyodorovna, and it was principally during these dances that he won the heart of Praskovya Fyodorovna. She fell in love with him. Ivan Ilyich had no clearly defined intention of marrying; but when the girl fell in love with him, he put the question to himself: "After all, why not get married?"

The young lady, Praskovya Fyodorovna, was of good family, nice-looking. There was a little bit of property. Ivan Ilyich might have reckoned on a more brilliant match, but this was a good match. Ivan Ilyich had his salary; she, he hoped, would have as much of her own. It was a good family; she was a sweet, pretty, and perfectly *comme il faut* young woman. To say that Ivan Ilyich got married because he fell in love with his wife and found in her sympathy with his views of life would be as untrue as to say that he got married because the people of his world approved of the match. Ivan Ilyich was influenced by both considerations; he was doing what was agreeable to himself in securing such a wife, and at the same time doing what persons of higher standing looked upon as the correct thing.

And Ivan Ilyich got married.

The process itself of getting married and the early period of married life, with the conjugal caresses, the new furniture, the new crockery, the new house linen, all up to the time of his wife's pregnancy, went off very well, so that Ivan Ilyich had already begun to think that so far from marriage breaking up that kind of frivolous, agreeable, lighthearted life, always decorous and always approved by society, which he regarded as the normal life, it would even increase its agreeableness. But at that point, in the early months of his wife's pregnancy, there came in a new element, unexpected, unpleasant, tiresome, and unseemly, which could never have been anticipated, and from which there was no escape.

His wife, without any kind of reason, it seemed to Ivan Ilyich, *de gaieté de cœur*, as he expressed it, began to disturb the agreeableness and decorum of their life. She began without any sort of justification to be jealous, exacting in her demands on his attention, squabbled over everything, and treated him to the coarsest and most unpleasant scenes.

At first Ivan Ilyich hoped to escape from the unpleasantness of this position by taking up the same frivolous and well-bred line that had served him well on other occasions of difficulty. He endeavored to ignore his wife's ill-humor, went on living lightheartedly and agreeably as before, invited friends to play cards, tried to get away himself to the club or to his friends. But his wife began on one occasion with such energy abusing him in such coarse language, and so obstinately persisted in her abuse of him every time he failed in carrying out her demands, obviously having made up her mind firmly to persist till he gave way, that is, stayed at home and was as dull as she was, that Ivan Ilyich took alarm. He perceived that matrimony, at least with his wife, was not invariably conducive to the pleasure and proprieties of life; but, on the contrary, often destructive of them, and that it was therefore essential to erect some barrier to protect himself from these disturbances. And Ivan Ilyich began to look about for such means of protecting himself. His official duties were the only thing that impressed Praskovya Fyodorovna, and Ivan Ilyich began to use his official position and the duties arising from it in his struggle with his wife to fence off his own independent world apart.

With the birth of the baby, the attempts at nursing it, and the various unsuccessful experiments with foods, with the illnesses, real and imaginary, of the infant and its mother, in which Ivan Ilyich was expected to sympathize, though he never had the slightest idea about them, the need for him to fence off a world apart for himself outside his family life became still more imperative. As his wife grew more irritable and exacting, so did Ivan Ilyich more and more transfer the center of gravity of his life to his official work. He became fonder and fonder of official life, and more ambitious than he had been.

Very quickly, not more than a year after his wedding, Ivan Ilyich had become aware that conjugal life, though providing certain comforts, was in reality a very intricate and difficult business toward which one must, if one is to do one's duty, that is, lead the decorous life approved by society, work out for oneself a definite line, just as in the government service.

And such a line Ivan Ilyich did work out for himself in his married life. He expected from his home life only those comforts—of dinner at home, of housekeeper and bed—which it could give him, and, above all, that perfect propriety in external observances required by public opinion. For the rest, he looked for good-humored pleasantness, and if he found it he was very thankful. If he met with antagonism and querulousness, he promptly retreated into the separate world he had shut off for himself in his official life and there he found solace.

Ivan Ilyich was prized as a good official, and three years later he was made assistant public prosecutor. The new duties of this position, their dignity, the possibility of bringing anyone to trial and putting anyone in prison, the publicity of the speeches and the success Ivan Ilyich had in that part of his work—all this made his official work still more attractive to him.

Children were born to him. His wife became steadily more querulous and ill-tempered, but the line Ivan Ilyich had taken up for himself in home life put him almost out of reach of her grumbling.

After seven years of service in the same town, Ivan Ilyich was transferred to another province with the post of public prosecutor. They moved, money was short, and his wife did not like the place they had moved to. The salary was indeed a little higher than before, but their expenses were larger. Besides, a couple of the children died, and home life consequently became even less agreeable for Ivan Ilyich.

For every mischance that occurred in their new place of residence, Praskovya Fyodorovna blamed her husband. The greater number of subjects of conversation between husband and wife, especially the education of the children, led to questions which were associated with previous quarrels, and quarrels were ready to break out at every instant. There remained only those rare periods of being in love which did indeed come upon them, but never lasted long. These were the islands at which they put in for a time, but they soon set off again upon the ocean of concealed hostility that was made manifest in their aloofness from one another. This aloofness might have distressed Ivan Ilyich if he had believed that this ought not to be so, but by now he regarded this position as perfectly normal, and it was indeed the goal toward which he worked in his home life. His aim was to make himself more and more free from the unpleasant aspects of domestic life and to render them harmless and decorous. And he attained this aim by spending less and less time with his family; and when he was forced to be at home, he endeavored to secure his tranquillity by the presence of outsiders. The great thing for Ivan Ilyich was having his office. In the official world all the interest of life was concentrated for him. And this interest absorbed him. The sense of his own power, the consciousness of being able to ruin anyone he wanted to ruin, even the external dignity of his office, when he made his entry into the court or met subordinate officials, his success in the eyes of his superiors and his subordinates, and, above all, his masterly handling of cases, of which he was conscious—all this delighted him and, together with chats with his colleagues, dining out, and whist, filled his life. So that, on the whole, Ivan Ilyich's life still went on in the way he thought it should go—agreeably and decorously.

So he lived for another seven years. His eldest daughter was already sixteen, another child had died, and there was left only one other, a boy at the high school, a subject of dissension. Ivan Ilyich wanted to send him to the school of jurisprudence, while Praskovya Fyodorovna to spite him sent him to the high school. The daughter had been educated at home, and had turned out well; the boy too did fairly well at his lessons.

III

Such was Ivan Ilyich's life for seventeen years after his marriage. He had been by now a long while prosecutor, and had refused several appointments offered him, looking out for a more desirable post, when there occurred an unexpected incident which utterly destroyed his peace of mind. Ivan Ilyich had been expecting to be appointed presiding judge in a university town, but a certain Goppe somehow stole a march on him and secured the appointment. Ivan Ilyich took offense, began upbraiding him, and quarreled with him and with his own superiors. A coolness was felt toward him, and on the next appointment that was made he was again passed over.

This was in the year 1880. That year was the most painful one in Ivan Ilyich's life. During that year it became evident on the one hand that his pay was insufficient for his expenses; on the other hand, that he had been forgotten by everyone, and that what seemed to him the most monstrous, the cruelest injustice appeared to other people as a quite commonplace fact. Even his father felt no obligation to assist him. He felt that everyone had deserted him, and that everyone regarded his position with an income of three thousand five hundred rubles as a quite normal and even fortunate one. He alone, with a sense of the injustice done him, and the everlasting nagging of his wife and the debts he had begun to accumulate, living beyond his means, knew that his position was far from being normal.

The summer of that year, to cut down his expenses, he took a holiday and went with his wife to spend the summer in the country at her brother's.

In the country, with no official duties to occupy him, Ivan Ilyich was for the first time a prey not to simple boredom, but to intolerable depression, and he made up his mind that things could not go on like that, and that it was absolutely necessary to take some decisive steps.

After a sleepless night spent by Ivan Ilyich walking up and down the terrace, he determined to go to Petersburg to take active steps and to get transferred to some other department, so as to revenge himself on them, the people, that is, who had not known how to appreciate him.

Next day, in spite of all the efforts of his wife and his mother-in-law to dissuade him, he set off to Petersburg.

He went with a single object before him—to obtain a post with an income of five thousand. He was ready now to be satisfied with a post in any department, of any tendency, with any kind of work. He must only have a post—a post with five thousand, in the executive department, the banks, the railways, the Empress Marya's institutions, even in the customs duties—what was essential was five thousand, and essential it was, too, to get out of the department in which they had failed to appreciate his value.

And, behold, this quest of Ivan Ilyich's was crowned with wonderful, unexpected success. At Kursk there got into the same first-class carriage F. S. Ilyin, an acquaintance, who told him of a telegram just received by the governor of Kursk, announcing a change about to take place in the ministry—Piotr Ivanovich was to be superseded by Ivan Semyonovich.

The proposed change, apart from its significance for Russia, had special significance for Ivan Ilyich from the fact that by bringing to the front a new person, Piotr Petrovich, and obviously, therefore, his friend Zahar Ivanovich, it was in the highest degree propitious to Ivan Ilyich's own plans. Zahar Ivanovich was a friend and schoolfellow of Ivan Ilyich's.

At Moscow the news was confirmed. On arriving at Petersburg, Ivan Ilyich looked up Zahar Ivano-

vich, and received a positive promise
of an appointment in his former department—that of justice.

A week later he telegraphed to
his wife: "Zahar Miller's place. At
first report I receive appointment."

Thanks to these changes, Ivan
Ilyich unexpectedly obtained, in the
same department as before, an appointment which placed him two
stages higher than his former colleagues, and gave him an income of
five thousand, together with the official allowance of three thousand five
hundred for traveling expenses. All
his ill-humor with his former enemies
and the whole department was forgotten, and Ivan Ilyich was completely happy.

Ivan Ilyich went back to the
country more lighthearted and good-
tempered than he had been for a
very long while. Praskovya Fyodorovna was in better spirits, too, and
peace was patched up between
them. Ivan Ilyich described what
respect everyone had shown him in
Petersburg; how all those who had
been his enemies had been put to
shame, and were cringing now before him; how envious they were of
his appointment, and still more of
the high favor in which he stood in
Petersburg.

Praskovya Fyodorovna listened to
this, and pretended to believe it,
and did not contradict him in anything, but confined herself to making plans for her new arrangements
in the town to which they would be
moving. And Ivan Ilyich saw with
delight that these plans were his
plans; that they were agreed; and
that his life after this disturbing
hitch in its progress was about to
regain its true, normal character of
lighthearted agreeableness and propriety.

Ivan Ilyich had come back to the
country for a short stay only. He
had to enter upon the duties of his
new office on the 10th of September; and besides, he needed some
time to settle in a new place, to
move all his belongings from the
other province, to purchase and
order many things in addition; in
short, to arrange things as settled in
his own mind and almost exactly as
settled in the heart, too, of Praskovya Fyodorovna.

And now when everything was so
successfully arranged and when he
and his wife were agreed in their
aim, and were, besides, so little together, they got on with one another
as they had not got on together
since the early years of their married life. Ivan Ilyich had thought of
taking his family away with him at
once; but his sister and his brother-
in-law, who had suddenly become
extremely cordial and intimate with
him and his family, were so pressing
in urging them to stay that he set
off alone.

Ivan Ilyich started off; and the
lighthearted temper produced by
his success, and his good understanding with his wife, one thing
backing up another, did not desert
him all the time. He found a charming set of apartments, the very thing
both husband and wife had dreamed
of. Spacious, lofty reception rooms
in the old style, a comfortable, digni-
fied-looking study for him, rooms for
his wife and daughter, a schoolroom
for his son, everything as though
planned on purpose for them. Ivan
Ilyich himself looked after the furnishing of them, chose the wall-
papers, bought furniture, by pref-
erence antique furniture, which had
a peculiar *comme il faut* style to his
mind, and it all grew up and grew
up, and really attained the ideal he
had set before himself. When he

had half finished arranging the house, his arrangement surpassed his own expectations. He saw the *comme il faut* character, elegant and free from vulgarity, that the whole would have when it was all ready. As he fell asleep he pictured to himself the reception room as it would be. Looking at the drawing room, not yet finished, he could see the hearth, the screen, the *étagère,* and the little chairs dotted here and there, the plates and dishes on the wall, and the bronzes as they would be when they were all put in their places. He was delighted with the thought of how he would impress Praskovya and Lizanka, who had taste too in this line. They would never expect anything like it. He was particularly successful in coming across and buying cheap old pieces of furniture, which gave a peculiarly aristocratic air to the whole. In his letters he purposely disparaged everything so as to surprise them. All this so absorbed him that the duties of his new office, though he was so fond of his official work, interested him less than he had expected. During sittings of the court he had moments of inattention; he pondered the question which sort of cornices to have on the window blinds, straight or fluted. He was so interested in this business that he often set to work with his own hands, moved a piece of furniture, or hung up curtains himself. One day he went up a ladder to show a workman, who did not understand, how he wanted some hangings draped, made a false step, and slipped; but, like a strong and nimble person, he clung on, and only knocked his side against the corner of a frame. The bruised place ached, but it soon passed off. Ivan Ilyich felt all this time particularly good-humored and well. He wrote: "I feel fifteen years younger." He thought his house furnishing would be finished in September, but it dragged on to the middle of October. But then the effect was charming; not only he said so, but everyone who saw it told him so, too.

In reality, it was all just what is commonly seen in the houses of people who are not exactly wealthy but want to look like wealthy people, and so succeed only in being like one another—hangings, dark wood, flowers, rugs, and bronzes, everything dark and highly polished, everything that all people of a certain class have so as to be like all people of a certain class. And in his case it was all so like that it made no impression at all; but it all seemed to him somehow special. When he met his family at the railway station and brought them to his newly furnished rooms, all lighted up in readiness, and a footman in a white tie opened the door into an entry decorated with flowers, and then they walked into the drawing room and the study, uttering cries of delight, he was very happy, conducted them everywhere, eagerly drinking in their praises, and beaming with satisfaction. The same evening, while they talked about various things at tea, Praskovya Fyodorovna inquired about his fall, and he laughed and showed them how he had gone flying, and how he had frightened the upholsterer.

"It's all well I'm something of an athlete. Another man might have been killed, and I got nothing worse than a blow here; when it's touched it hurts, but it's going off already; nothing but a bruise."

And they began to live in their new abode, which, as is always the case, when they had got thoroughly settled in they found to be short of just one room, and with their new income, which, as always, was only a little—some five hundred rubles —too little, and everything went very well. Things went particularly well at first, before everything was quite finally arranged, and there was still something to do to the place— something to buy, something to order, something to move, something to make to fit. Though there were indeed several disputes between husband and wife, both were so well satisfied, and there was so much to do, that it all went off without serious quarrels. When there was nothing left to arrange, it became a little dull, and something seemed to be lacking, but by then they were making acquaintances and forming habits, and life was filled up again.

Ivan Ilyich, after spending the morning in the court, returned home to dinner, and at first he was generally in a good humor, although this was apt to be upset a little, and precisely on account of the new abode. Every spot on the tablecloth, on the hangings, the string of a window blind broken, irritated him. He had devoted so much trouble to the arrangement of the rooms that any disturbance of their order distressed him. But, on the whole, the life of Ivan Ilyich ran its course as, according to his conviction, life ought to do—easily, agreeably, and decorously. He got up at nine, drank his coffee, read the newspaper, then put on his official uniform, and went to the court. There the routine of the daily work was already mapped out for him, and he stepped into it at once. People with petitions, inquiries in the office, the office itself, the sittings—public and preliminary. In all this the great thing necessary was to exclude everything with the sap of life in it, which always disturbs the regular course of official business, not to admit any sort of relations with people except the official relations; the motive of all intercourse had to be simply the official motive and the intercourse itself to be only official. A man would come, for instance, anxious for certain information. Ivan Ilyich, not being the functionary on duty, would have nothing whatever to do with such a man. But if this man's relation to him as a member of the court is such as can be formulated on official stamped paper—within the limits of such a relation Ivan Ilyich would do everything, positively everything, he could, and in doing so would observe the semblance of human friendly relations, that is, the courtesies of social life. But where the official relation ended, there everything else stopped, too. This art of keeping the official aspect of things apart from his real life, Ivan Ilyich possessed in the highest degree; and through long practice and natural aptitude, he had brought it to such a pitch of perfection that he even permitted himself at times, like a skilled specialist as it were in jest, to let the human and official relations mingle. He allowed himself this liberty just because he felt he had the power at any moment if he wished it to take up the purely official line again and to drop the human relation. This thing was not simply easy, agreeable, and decorous; in Ivan Ilyich's hands it attained a positively artistic character. In the intervals of business he smoked, drank tea, chatted a little about politics, a little about public affairs, a little about cards, but most of all about appointments in the service. And tired, but feeling like some artist who has skillfully played his part in the performance, one of the first violins in the orchestra, he returned home. At home his daughter and her mother had been paying calls somewhere, or else someone had been calling on them; the son had been at school, had been preparing his lessons with his teachers, and duly learning correctly what was taught at the high school. Everything was as it should be. After dinner, if there were no visitors, Ivan Ilyich sometimes read some book of which people were talking, and in the evening sat down to work, that is, read official papers, compared them with the laws, sorted depositions, and put them under the laws. This he found neither tiresome nor entertaining. It was tiresome when he might have been playing "screw"; but if there were no "screw" going on, it was anyway better than sitting alone or with his wife. Ivan Ilyich's pleasures were little dinners, to which he invited ladies and gentlemen of good social position, and such methods of passing the time with them as were usual with such persons, so that his drawing room might be like all other drawing rooms.

Once they even gave a party—a dance. And Ivan Ilyich enjoyed it, and everything was very successful, except that it led to a violent quarrel with his wife over the tarts and sweetmeats. Praskovya Fyodorovna had her own plan; while Ivan Ilyich insisted on getting everything from an expensive pastry cook, and ordered a great many tarts, and the quarrel was because these tarts were left over and the pastry cook's bill came to forty-five rubles. The quarrel was a violent and unpleasant one, so much so that Praskovya Fyodorovna called him, "Fool, imbecile." And he clutched at his head, and in his anger made some allusion to a divorce. But the party itself was enjoyable. There were all the best people, and Ivan Ilyich danced with Princess Trufonov, the sister of the one so well known in connection with the charitable association called, "Bear My Burden." His official pleasures lay in the gratification of his pride; his social pleasures lay in the gratification of his vanity. But Ivan Ilyich's most real pleasure was the pleasure of playing "screw," the Russian equivalent for bridge. He admitted to himself that, after all, after whatever unpleasant incidents there had been in his life, the pleasure which burned like a candle before all others was sitting with good players, and not noisy partners, at "screw"; and, of course, a four-hand game (playing with five was never a success, though one pretends to like it particularly), and with good cards, to play a shrewd, serious game, then supper and a glass of wine. And after "screw," especially after winning some small stakes (winning large sums was unpleasant), Ivan Ilyich went to bed in a particularly happy frame of mind.

So they lived. They moved in the very best circle, and were visited by people of consequence and young people.

In their views of their circle of acquaintances, the husband, the wife, and the daughter were in complete accord; and without any expressed agreement on the subject, they all acted alike in dropping and shaking off various friends and relations, shabby persons who swooped down upon them in their drawing room with Japanese plates on the walls, and pressed their civilities on them. Soon these shabby persons ceased fluttering about them, and none but the very best society was seen at the Golovins'. Young men began to pay attention to Lizanka; and Petrishtchev, the son of Dmitry Ivanovich Petrishtchev, and the sole heir of his fortune, an examining magistrate, began to be so attentive to Lizanka that Ivan Ilyich had raised the question with his wife whether it would not be as well to arrange a sleigh drive for them, or to get up some theatricals. So they lived. And everything went on in this way without change, and everything was very nice.

IV

All were in good health. One could not use the word ill-health in connection with the symptoms Ivan Ilyich sometimes complained of, namely, a queer taste in his mouth and a sort of uncomfortable feeling on the left side of the stomach.

But it came to pass that this uncomfortable feeling kept increasing, and became not exactly a pain, but a continual sense of weight in his side, and irritable temper. This irritable temper, continually growing and growing, began at last to mar the agreeable easiness and decorum that had reigned in the Golovin household. Quarrels between the husband and wife became more and more frequent, and soon all the easiness and amenity of life had fallen away, and mere propriety was maintained with difficulty. Scenes became again more frequent. Again there were only islands in the sea of contention—and but few of these— at which the husband and wife could meet without an outbreak. And Praskovya Fyodorovna said now, not without grounds, that her husband had a trying temper. With her characteristic exaggeration, she said

he had always had this awful temper, and she had needed all her sweetness to put up with it for twenty years. It was true that it was he now who began the quarrels. His gusts of temper always broke out just before dinner, and often just as he was beginning to eat, at the soup. He would notice that some piece of the crockery had been chipped, or that the food was not nice, or that his son put his elbow on the table, or his daughter's hair was not arranged as he liked it. And whatever it was, he laid the blame of it on Praskovya Fyodorovna. Praskovya Fyodorovna had at first retorted in the same strain, and said all sorts of horrid things to him; but on two occasions, just at the beginning of dinner, he had flown into such a frenzy that she perceived that it was due to physical derangement, and was brought on by taking food, and she controlled herself; she did not reply, but simply made haste to get dinner over. Praskovya Fyodorovna took great credit to herself for this exercise of self-control. Making up her mind that her husband had a fearful temper, and made her life miserable, she began to feel sorry for herself. And the more she felt for herself, the more she hated her husband. She began to wish he were dead; yet could not wish it because then there would be no income. And this exasperated her against him even more. She considered herself dreadfully unfortunate, precisely even his death could not save her, and she felt irritated and concealed it, and this hidden irritation on her side increased his irritability.

After one violent scene, in which Ivan Ilyich had been particularly unjust, and after which he had said in explanation that he certainly was irritable, but that it was due to illness, she said that if he were ill he ought to take steps, and insisted on his going to see a celebrated doctor.

He went. Everything was as he had expected; everything was as it always is. The waiting and the assumption of dignity, that professional dignity he knew so well, exactly as he assumed it himself in court, and the sounding and listening and questions that called for answers that were foregone conclusions and obviously superfluous, and the significant air that seemed to insinuate—you only leave it all to us, and we will arrange everything, for us it is certain and incontestable how to arrange everything, everything in one way for every man of every sort. It was all exactly as in his court of justice. Exactly the same air as he put on in dealing with a man brought up for judgment, the doctor put on for him.

The doctor said: This and that proves that you have such-and-such a thing wrong inside you; but if that is not confirmed by analysis of this and that, then we must assume this and that, then—and so on. To Ivan Ilyich there was only one question of consequence. Was his condition dangerous or not? But the doctor ignored that irrelevant inquiry. From the doctor's point of view this was a side issue, not the subject under consideration; the only real question was the balance of probabilities between a loose kidney, chronic catarrh, and appendicitis. It was not a question of the life of Ivan Ilyich, but the question between the loose kidney and the intestinal appendix. And this question, as it seemed to Ivan Ilyich, the doctor solved in a brilliant manner in favor of the appendix, with the reservation that analysis of the water might give a fresh clue, and

that then the aspect of the case would be altered. All this was point for point identical with what Ivan Ilyich had himself done in brilliant fashion a thousand times over in dealing with some man on his trial. Just as brilliantly the doctor made his summing up, and triumphantly, gaily even, glanced over his spectacles at the prisoner in the dock. From the doctor's summing up Ivan Ilyich deduced the conclusion—that things looked bad, and that he, the doctor, and most likely everyone else, did not care, but that things looked bad for him. And this conclusion impressed Ivan Ilyich morbidly, arousing in him a great feeling of pity for himself, of great anger against this doctor who could be unconcerned about a matter of such importance.

But he said nothing of that. He got up, and, laying the fee on the table, he said, with a sigh, "We sick people probably often ask inconvenient questions. Tell me, is this generally a dangerous illness or not?"

The doctor glanced severely at him with one eye through his spectacles, as though to say: "Prisoner at the bar, if you will not keep within the limits of the questions allowed you, I shall be compelled to take measures for your removal from the precincts of the court." "I have told you what I thought necessary and suitable already," said the doctor; "the analysis will show anything further." And the doctor bowed him out.

Ivan Ilyich went out slowly and dejectedly, got into his sleigh, and drove home. All the way home he was incessantly going over all the doctor had said, trying to translate all these complicated, obscure, scientific phrases into simple language, and to read in them an answer to the question, It is bad—is it very bad, or nothing much as yet? And it seemed to him that the upshot of all the doctor had said was that it was very bad. Everything seemed dismal to Ivan Ilyich in the streets. The sleigh drivers were dismal, the houses were dismal, the people passing, and the shops were dismal. This ache, this dull gnawing ache, that never ceased for a second, seemed, when connected with the doctor's obscure utterances, to have gained a new, more serious significance. With a new sense of misery Ivan Ilyich kept watch on it now.

He reached home and began to tell his wife about it. His wife listened; but in the middle of his account his daughter came in with her hat on, ready to go out with her mother. Reluctantly she half sat down to listen to these tedious details, but she could not stand it for long, and her mother did not hear his story to the end.

"Well, I'm very glad," said his wife; "now you must be sure and take the medicine regularly. Give me the prescription; I'll send Gerasim to the chemist's!" And she went to get ready to go out.

He had not taken breath while she was in the room, and he heaved a deep sigh when she was gone.

"Well," he said, "maybe it really is nothing as yet."

He began to take the medicine, to carry out the doctor's directions, which were changed after the analysis of the water. But it was just at this point that some confusion arose, either in the analysis or in what ought to have followed from it. The doctor himself, of course, could not be blamed for it, but it turned out that things had not gone as the doctor had told him. Either he had forgotten or told a lie, or was hiding something from him.

But Ivan Ilyich still went on just as exactly carrying out the doctor's directions, and in doing so he found comfort at first.

From the time of his visit to the doctor Ivan Ilyich's principal occupation became the exact observance of the doctor's prescriptions as regards hygiene and medicine and the careful observation of his ailment in all the functions of his organism. Ivan Ilyich's principal interest came to be people's ailments and people's health. When anything was said in his presence about sick people, about deaths and recoveries, especially in the case of an illness resembling his own, he listened, trying to conceal his excitement, asked questions, and applied what he heard to his own trouble.

The ache did not grow less; but Ivan Ilyich made great efforts to force himself to believe that he was better. And he succeeded in deceiving himself so long as nothing happened to disturb him. But as soon as he had a mischance, some unpleasant words with his wife, a failure in his official work, an unlucky hand at "screw," he was at once acutely sensible of his illness. In former days he had borne with such mishaps, hoping soon to retrieve the mistake, to make a struggle, to reach success later, to have a lucky hand. But now he was cast down by every mischance and reduced to despair. He would say to himself: "Here I'm only just beginning to get better, and the medicine has begun to take effect, and now this mischance or disappointment." And he was furious against the mischance or the people who were causing him the disappointment and killing him, and he felt that this fury was killing him, but could not check it. One would have thought that it should have been clear to him that this exasperation against circumstances and people was aggravating his disease, and that therefore he ought not to pay attention to the unpleasant incidents. But his reasoning took quite the opposite direction. He said that he needed peace, and was on the watch for everything that disturbed his peace, and at the slightest disturbance of it he flew into a rage. What made his position worse was that he read medical books and consulted doctors. He got worse so gradually that he might have deceived himself, comparing one day with another, the difference was so slight. But when he consulted the doctors, then it seemed to him that he was getting worse, and very rapidly so indeed. And in spite of this, he was continually consulting the doctors.

That month he called on another celebrated doctor. The second celebrity said almost the same as the first, but put his questions differently; and the interview with this celebrity only redoubled the doubts and terrors of Ivan Ilyich. A friend of a friend of his, a very good doctor, diagnosed the disease quite differently; and in spite of the fact that he guaranteed recovery, by his questions and his suppositions he confused Ivan Ilyich even more and strengthened his suspicions. A homeopath gave yet another diagnosis of the complaint, and prescribed medicine, which Ivan Ilyich took secretly for a week; but after a week of the homeopathic medicine he felt no relief, and losing faith both in the other doctor's treatment and in this, he fell into even deeper depression. One day a lady of his acquaintance talked to him of the healing wrought by the holy pictures. Ivan Ilyich caught himself listening attentively and believing in the reality of the fact alleged. This incident alarmed him. "Can I have degenerated to such a point of intellectual feebleness?" he said to himself. "Nonsense! it's all rubbish. I must not give way to nervous fears, but, fixing on one doctor, adhere strictly to his treatment. That's what I will do. Now it's settled. I won't think about it, but till next summer I will stick to the treatment, and then I shall see. Now I'll put a stop to this wavering!" It was easy to say this, but impossible to carry it out. The pain in his side was always dragging at him, seeming to grow more acute and ever more incessant; it seemed to him that the taste in his mouth was queerer, and there was a loathsome smell even from his breath, and his appetite and strength kept dwindling. There was no deceiving himself; something terrible, new, and so important that nothing more important had ever been in Ivan Ilyich's life, was taking place in him, and he alone knew of it. All about him did not or would not understand, and believed that everything in the world was going on as before. This was what tortured Ivan Ilyich more than anything. Those of his own household, most of all his wife and daughter, who were absorbed in a perfect whirl of visits, did not, he saw, comprehend it at all, and were annoyed that he was so depressed and exacting, as though he were to blame for it. Though they tried indeed to disguise it, he saw he was a nuisance to them; but that his wife had taken up a definite line of her own in regard to his illness, and stuck to it regardless of what he might say or do. This line was expressed thus: "You know," she would say to acquaintances, "Ivan Ilyich cannot, like all other simple-hearted folks, keep to the treatment prescribed him. One day he'll take his drops and eat what he's ordered, and go to bed in good time; the next day, if I don't see to it, he'll suddenly forget to take his medicine, eat sturgeon (which is forbidden by the doctors), yes, and sit up at 'screw' till past midnight."

"Why, when did I do that?" Ivan Ilyich asked in vexation one day at Piotr Ivanovich's.

"Why, yesterday, with Shebek."

"It makes no difference. I couldn't sleep for pain."

"Well, it doesn't matter what you do it for, only you'll never get well like that, and you make us wretched."

Praskovya Fyodorovna's external attitude to her husband's illness, openly expressed to others and to himself, was that Ivan Ilyich was to blame in the matter of his illness, and that the whole illness was another injury he was doing to his wife. Ivan Ilyich felt that the expression of this dropped from her unconsciously, but that made it no easier for him.

In his official life, too, Ivan Ilyich noticed, or fancied he noticed, a strange attitude to him. At one time it seemed to him that people were looking inquisitively at him, as a man who would shortly have to vacate his position; at another time his friends would suddenly begin chaffing him in a friendly way over his nervous fears, as though that awful and horrible, unheard-of thing that was going on within him, incessantly gnawing at him and irresistibly dragging him away somewhere, were the most agreeable subject for joking. Shvarts especially, with his jocoseness, his liveliness, and his *comme il faut* tone, exasper-

ated Ivan Ilyich by reminding him of himself ten years ago.

Friends came sometimes to play cards. They sat down to the card table; they shuffled and dealt the new cards. Diamonds were led and followed by diamonds, the seven. His partner said, "Can't trump," and played the two of diamonds. What then? Why, delightful, capital, it should have been—he had a trump hand. And suddenly Ivan Ilyich feels the gnawing ache, that taste in his mouth, and it strikes him as something grotesque that with that he could be glad of a trump hand.

He looks at Mihail Mihailovich, his partner, how he taps on the table with his red hand, and affably and indulgently abstains from snatching up the trick, and pushes the cards toward Ivan Ilyich so as to give him the pleasure of taking them up, without any trouble, without even stretching out his hand. "What, does he suppose that I'm so weak that I can't stretch out my hand?" thinks Ivan Ilyich, and he forgets the trumps, and trumps his partner's cards, and plays his trump hand without making three tricks; and what's the most awful thing of all is that he sees how upset Mihail Mihailovich is about it, while he doesn't care a bit, and it's awful for him to think why he doesn't care.

They all see that he's in pain, and say to him, "We can stop if you're tired. You go and lie down." Lie down? No, he's not in the least tired; they will play the rubber. All are gloomy and silent. Ivan Ilyich feels that it is he who has brought this gloom upon them, and he cannot disperse it. They have supper, and the party breaks up, and Ivan Ilyich is left alone with the consciousness that his life is poisoned for him and poisons the life of others, and that this poison is not losing its force, but is continually penetrating more and more deeply into his whole existence.

And with the consciousness of this, and with the physical pain in addition, and the terror in addition to that, he must lie in his bed, often not able to sleep for pain the greater part of the night; and in the morning he must get up again, dress, go to the law court, speak, write, or, if he does not go out, stay at home for all the four-and-twenty hours of the day and night, of which each one is a torture. And he had to live thus on the edge of the precipice alone, without one man who would understand and feel for him.

V

In this way one month, then a second, passed by. Just before the New Year his brother-in-law arrived in the town on a visit to them. Ivan Ilyich was at the court when he arrived. Praskovya Fyodorovna had gone out shopping. Coming home and going into his study, he found there his brother-in-law, a healthy, florid man, engaged in unpacking his trunk. He raised his head, hearing Ivan Ilyich's step, and for a second stared at him without a word. That stare told Ivan Ilyich everything. His brother-in-law opened his mouth to utter an "Oh!" of surprise, but checked himself. That confirmed it all.

"What! have I changed?"

"Yes, there is a change."

And all Ivan Ilyich's efforts to draw him into talking of his appearance his brother-in-law met with obstinate silence. Praskovya Fyodorovna came in; the brother-in-law went to see her. Ivan Ilyich locked his door and began gazing at himself in the looking glass, first full face, then in profile. He took up his photograph, taken with his wife, and compared the portrait with what he saw in the looking glass. The change was immense. Then he bared his arm to the elbow, looked at it, pulled the sleeve down again, sat down on an ottoman, and felt blacker than night.

"I mustn't, I mustn't," he said to himself, jumped up, went to the table, opened some official paper, tried to read it, but could not. He opened the door, went into the drawing room. The door into the drawing room was closed. He went up to it on tiptoe and listened.

"No, you're exaggerating," Praskovya Fyodorovna was saying.

"Exaggerating? You can't see it. Why, he's a dead man. Look at his eyes—there's no light in them. But what's wrong with him?"

"No one can tell. Nikolaev" (that was another doctor) "said something, but I don't know. Leshtchetitsky" (this was the celebrated doctor) "said the opposite."

Ivan Ilyich walked away, went to his own room, lay down, and fell to musing. "A kidney—a loose kidney." He remembered all the doctors had told him, how it had detached, and how it was loose; and by an effort of imagination he tried to catch that kidney and to stop it, to strengthen it. So little was needed, he fancied. "No, I'll go again to Piotr Ivanovich" (this was the friend who had for a friend a doctor). He rang, ordered the horse to be put in, and got ready to go out.

"Where are you off to, Jean?" asked his wife with a peculiarly melancholy and exceptionally kind expression.

This exceptionally kind expression exasperated him. He looked darkly at her.

"I want to see Piotr Ivanovich."

He went to the friend who had for a friend a doctor. And with him to the doctor's. He found him in, and had a long conversation with him.

Reviewing the anatomical and physiological details of what, according to the doctor's view, was taking place within him, he understood it all. It was just one thing—a little thing wrong with the intestinal appendix. It might all come right. Only strengthen one sluggish organ, and decrease the undue activity of another, an absorption would take place, and all would be set right. He was a little late for dinner. He ate his dinner, talked cheerfully, but it was a long while before he could go to his own room to work. At last he went to his study, and at once sat down to work. He read his legal documents and did his work, but the consciousness never left him of having a matter of importance very near to his heart which he had put off, but would look into later. When he had finished his work, he remembered that the matter near his heart was thinking about the intestinal appendix. But he did not give himself up to it; he went into the drawing room to tea. There were visitors; and there was talking, playing on the piano, and singing; there was the young examining magistrate, the desirable match for the daughter. Ivan Ilyich spent the evening, as Praskovya Fyodorovna observed, in better spirits than any of them; but he never forgot for an instant that he had an important matter of the intestinal appendix put off for consideration later. At eleven o'clock he said good night and went to his own room. He had slept alone since his illness in a little room adjoining his study. He went in, undressed, and took up a novel of Zola, but did not read it; he fell to thinking. And in his imagination the desired recovery of the intestinal appendix had taken place. There had been absorption, rejection, re-establishment of the regular action.

"Why, it's all simply that," he said to himself. "One only wants to assist nature." He remembered the medicine, got up, took it, lay down on his back, watching for the medicine to act beneficially and overcome the pain. "It's only to take it regularly and avoid injurious influences; why, already I feel rather better, much better." He began to feel his side; it was not painful to the touch. "Yes, I don't feel it—really, much better already." He put out the candle and lay on his side. "The appendix is getting better, absorption." Suddenly he felt the familiar, old, dull, gnawing ache, persistent, quiet, in earnest. In his mouth the same familiar loathsome taste. His heart sank, and his brain felt dim, misty. "My God, my God!" he said, "again, again, and it will never cease." And suddenly the whole thing rose before him in quite a different aspect.

"Intestinal appendix! kidney!" he said to himself. "It's not a question of the appendix, not a question of the kidney, but of life and . . . death. Yes, life has been, and now it's going, going away, and I cannot stop it. Yes. Why deceive myself? Isn't it obvious to everyone, except me, that I'm dying, and it's only a question of weeks, of days—at once, perhaps. There was light, and now there is darkness. I was here, and now I am going! Where?" A cold chill ran over him, his breath stopped. He heard nothing but the throbbing of his heart.

"I shall be no more, then what will there be? There'll be nothing. Where then shall I be when I'm no more? Can this be dying? No; I don't want to!" He jumped up, tried to light the candle; and fumbling with trembling hands, he dropped the candle and the candlestick on the floor and fell back again on the pillow. "Why trouble? It doesn't matter," he said to himself, staring with open eyes into the darkness. "Death. Yes, death. And they —all of them—don't understand, and don't want to understand, and feel no pity. They are playing." (He caught through the closed doors the faraway cadence of a voice and the accompaniment.) "They don't care, but they will die, too. Fools! Me sooner and them later; but it will be the same for them. And they are merry. The beasts!" Anger stifled him. And he was agonizingly, insufferably miserable. "It cannot be that all men always have been doomed to this awful horror!" He raised himself.

"There is something wrong in it; I must be calm, I must think it all over from the beginning." And then he began to consider. "Yes, the beginning of my illness. I knocked my side, and I was just the same, that day and the days after it; it ached a little, then more, then doctors, then depression, misery, and again doctors; and I've gone on getting closer and closer to the abyss. Strength growing less. Nearer and nearer. And here I am, wasting away, no light in my eyes. I think of how to cure the appendix, but this is death. Can it be death?" Again a horror came over him; gasping for breath, he bent over, began feeling for the matches, and knocked his elbow against the bedside table. It was in his way and hurt him; he felt furious with it, in his anger knocked against it more violently and upset it. And in despair, breathless, he fell back on his spine, waiting for death to come that instant.

The visitors were leaving at that time. Praskovya Fyodorovna was seeing them out. She heard something fall, and came in.

"What is it?"

"Nothing. I dropped something by accident."

She went out, brought a candle. He was lying, breathing hard and fast, like a man who has run a mile, and staring with fixed eyes at her.

"What is it, Jean?"

"Nothing, I say. I dropped something." Why speak? She won't understand, he thought.

She certainly did not understand. She picked up the candle, lighted it for him, and went out hastily. She had to say good-by to a departing guest. When she came back, he was lying in the same position on his back, looking upwards.

"How are you—worse?"

"Yes."

She shook her head, sat down.

"Do you know what, Jean? I wonder if we hadn't better send for Leshtchetitsky to see you here?"

This meant calling in the celebrated doctor, regardless of expense. He smiled malignantly, and said no. She sat a moment longer, went up to him, and kissed him on the forehead.

He hated her with all the force of his soul when she was kissing him, and had to make an effort not to push her away.

"Good night. Please God, you'll sleep."

"Yes."

VI

Ivan Ilyich saw that he was dying, and was in continual despair.

At the bottom of his heart Ivan Ilyich knew that he was dying; but so far from growing used to this idea, he simply did not grasp it—he was utterly unable to grasp it.

The example of the syllogism that he had learned in Kiseveter's logic— Caius is a man, men are mortal, therefore Caius is mortal—had seemed to him all his life correct only as regards Caius, but not at all as regards himself. In that case it was a question of Caius, a man, an abstract man, and it was perfectly true, but he was not Caius, and was not an abstract man; he had always been a creature quite, quite different from all others; he had been little Vanya with a mamma and papa, and Mitya and Volodya, with playthings and a coachman and a nurse; afterwards with Katenka, with all the joys and griefs and ecstasies of childhood, boyhood, and youth. What did Caius know of the smell of the leathern ball Vanya had been so fond of? Had Caius kissed his mother's hand like that? Caius had not heard the silk rustle of his mother's skirts. He had not made a riot at school over the pudding. Had Caius been in love like that? Could Caius preside over the sittings of the court?

And Caius certainly was mortal, and it was right for him to die; but for me, little Vanya, Ivan Ilyich, with all my feelings and ideas—for me it's a different matter. And it cannot be that I ought to die. That would be too awful.

That was his feeling.

"If I had to die like Caius, I should have known it was so, some inner voice would have told me so. But there was nothing of the sort in me. And I and all my friends, we felt that it was not at all the same as with Caius. And now here

it is!" he said to himself. "It can't be! It can't be, but it is! How is it? How's one to understand it?" And he could not conceive it, and tried to drive away this idea as false, incorrect, and morbid, and to supplant it by other, correct, healthy ideas. But this idea, not as an idea merely, but as it were an actual fact, came back again and stood confronting him.

And to replace this thought he called up other thoughts, one after another, in the hope of finding support in them. He tried to get back into former trains of thought, which in old days had screened off the thought of death. But, strange to say, all that had in old days covered up, obliterated, the sense of death could not now produce the same effect. Latterly, Ivan Ilyich spent the greater part of his time in these efforts to restore his old trains of thought which had shut off death. At one time he would say to himself, "I'll put myself into my official work; why, I used to live in it." And he would go to the law courts, banishing every doubt. He would enter into conversation with his colleagues, and would sit carelessly, as his old habit was, scanning the crowd below dreamily, and with both his wasted hands he would lean on the arms of the oak armchair just as he always did; and, bending over to a colleague, pass the papers to him and whisper to him, then suddenly dropping his eyes and sitting up straight, he would pronounce the familiar words that opened the proceedings. But suddenly in the middle, the pain in his side, utterly regardless of the stage he had reached in his conduct of the case, began its work. It riveted Ivan Ilyich's attention. He drove away the thought of it, but it still did its work, and then It came and stood confronting him and looked at him, and he felt turned to stone, and the light died away in his eyes, and he began to ask himself again, "Can it be that It is the only truth?" And his colleagues and his subordinates saw with surprise and distress that he, the brilliant, subtle judge, was losing the thread of his speech, was making blunders. He shook himself, tried to regain his self-control, and got somehow to the end of the sitting, and went home with the painful sense that his judicial labors could not as of old hide from him what he wanted to hide; that he could not by means of his official work escape from It. And the worst of it was that It drew him to itself not for him to do anything in particular, but simply for him to look at It straight in the face, to look at It and, doing nothing, suffer unspeakably.

And to save himself from this, Ivan Ilyich sought amusements, other screens, and these screens he found, and for a little while they did seem to save him, but soon again they were not so much broken down as let the light through, as though It pierced through everything, and there was nothing that could shut It off.

Sometimes during those days he would go into the drawing room he had furnished, that drawing room where he had fallen, for which—how bitterly ludicrous it was for him to think of it!—for the decoration of which he had sacrificed his life, for he knew that it was that bruise that had started his illness. He went in and saw that the polished table had been scratched by something. He looked for the cause, and found it in the bronze clasps of the album, which had been twisted on one side.

He took up the album, a costly one, which he had himself arranged with loving care, and was vexed at the carelessness of his daughter and her friends. Here a page was torn, here the photographs had been shifted out of their places. He carefully put it to rights again and bent the clasp back.

Then the idea occurred to him to move all this *établissement* of the albums to another corner where the flowers stood. He called the footman; or his daughter or his wife came to help him. They did not agree with him, contradicted him; he argued, got angry. But all that was very well, since he did not think of It; It was not in sight.

But then his wife would say, as he moved something himself, "Do let the servants do it, you'll hurt yourself again," and all at once It peeped through the screen; he caught a glimpse of It. He caught a glimpse of It, but still he hoped It would hide itself. Involuntarily though, he kept watch on his side; there it is just the same still, aching still, and now he cannot forget it, and It is staring openly at him from behind the flowers. What's the use of it all?

"And it's the fact that here, at that curtain, as if it had been storming a fort, I lost my life. Is it possible? How awful and how silly! It cannot be! It cannot be, and it is."

He went into his own room, lay down, and was again alone with It. Face to face with It, and nothing to be done with it. Nothing but to look at It and shiver.

VII

How it came to pass during the third month of Ivan Ilyich's illness, it would be impossible to say, for it happened little by little, imper-

ceptibly, but it had come to pass that
his wife and his daughter and his
son and their servants and their acquaintances, and the doctors, and,
most of all, he himself—all were
aware that all interest in him for
other people consisted now in the
question how soon he would leave
his place empty, free the living
from the constraint of his presence,
and be set free himself from his
sufferings.

He slept less and less; they gave
him opium, and began to inject
morphine. But this did not relieve
him. The dull pain he experienced
in the half-asleep condition at first
only relieved him as a change, but
then it became as bad, or even more
agonizing, than the open pain. He
had special things to eat prepared
for him according to the doctors'
prescriptions; but these dishes became more and more distasteful,
more and more revolting to him.

Special arrangements, too, had to
be made for his other physical needs,
and this was a continual misery to
him. Misery from the uncleanliness,
the unseemliness, and the stench,
from the feeling of another person
having to assist in it.

But just from this most unpleasant side of his illness there came
comfort to Ivan Ilyich. There always
came into his room on these occasions to clear up for him the peasant
who waited on table, Gerasim.

Gerasim was a clean, fresh, young
peasant, who had grown stout and
hearty on the good fare in town.
Always cheerful and bright. At first
the sight of this lad, always cleanly
dressed in the Russian style, engaged in this revolting task, em-
barrassed Ivan Ilyich.

One day, getting up from the
night stool, too weak to replace his
clothes, he dropped on to a soft low
chair and looked with horror at his
bare, powerless thighs, with the
muscles so sharply standing out on
them.

Then there came in with light,
strong steps Gerasim, in his thick
boots, diffusing a pleasant smell
of tar from his boots, and bringing
in the freshness of the winter air.
Wearing a clean hempen apron, and
a clean cotton shirt, with his sleeves
tucked up on his strong, bare young
arms, without looking at Ivan Ilyich,
obviously trying to check the radiant
happiness in his face so as not to
hurt the sick man, he went up to the
night stool.

"Gerasim," said Ivan Ilyich faintly.

Gerasim started, clearly afraid
that he had done something amiss,
and with a rapid movement turned
toward the sick man his fresh, good-
natured, simple young face, just beginning to be downy with the first
growth of beard.

"Yes, your honor."

"I'm afraid this is very disagreeable for you. You must excuse me.
I can't help it."

"Why, upon my word, sir!" And
Gerasim's eyes beamed, and he
showed his white young teeth in a
smile. "What's a little trouble? It's
a case of illness with you, sir."

And with his deft, strong arms he
performed his habitual task, and
went out, stepping lightly. And five
minutes later, treading just as lightly,
he came back.

Ivan Ilyich was still sitting in the
same way in the armchair.

"Gerasim," he said, when the latter had replaced the night stool all
sweet and clean, "please help me;
come here." Gerasim went up to
him. "Lift me up. It's difficult for
me alone, and I've sent Dmitry
away."

Gerasim went up to him; as

lightly as he stepped he put his strong arms round him, deftly and gently lifted and supported him, with the other hand pulled up his trousers, and would have set him down again. But Ivan Ilyich asked him to carry him to the sofa. Gerasim, without effort, carefully not squeezing him, led him, almost carrying him, to the sofa, and settled him there.

"Thank you; how neatly and well . . . you do everything."

Gerasim smiled again, and would have gone away. But Ivan Ilyich felt his presence such a comfort that he was reluctant to let him go.

"Oh, move that chair near me, please. No, that one, under my legs. I feel easier when my legs are higher."

Gerasim picked up the chair and, without letting it knock, set it gently down on the ground just at the right place, and lifted Ivan Ilyich's legs on to it. It seemed to Ivan Ilyich that he was easier just at the moment when Gerasim lifted his legs higher.

"I'm better when my legs are higher," said Ivan Ilyich. "Put that cushion under me."

Gerasim did so. Again he lifted his legs to put the cushion under them. Again it seemed to Ivan Ilyich that he was easier at that moment when Gerasim held his legs raised. When he laid them down again, he felt worse.

"Gerasim," he said to him, "are you busy just now?"

"Not at all, sir," said Gerasim, who had learned among the town-bred servants how to speak to gentlefolks.

"What have you left to do?"

"Why, what have I to do? I've done everything, there's only the wood to chop for tomorrow."

"Then hold my legs up like that— can you?"

"To be sure, I can." Gerasim lifted the legs up. And it seemed to Ivan Ilyich that in that position he did not feel the pain at all.

"But how about the wood?"

"Don't you trouble about that, sir. We shall have time enough."

Ivan Ilyich made Gerasim sit and hold his legs, and began to talk to him. And, strange to say, he fancied he felt better while Gerasim had hold of his legs.

From that time forward Ivan Ilyich would sometimes call Gerasim, and get him to hold his legs on his shoulders, and he liked talking with him. Gerasim did this easily, readily, simply, and with a good nature that touched Ivan Ilyich. Health, strength, and heartiness in all other people were offensive to Ivan Ilyich; but the strength and heartiness of Gerasim did not mortify him, but soothed him.

Ivan Ilyich's great misery was due to the deception that for some reason or other everyone kept up with him —that he was simply ill, and not dying, and that he need only keep quiet and follow the doctor's orders, and then some great change for the better would be the result. He knew that whatever they might do, there would be no result except more agonizing sufferings and death. And he was made miserable by this lie, made miserable at their refusing to acknowledge what they all knew and he knew, by their persisting in lying over him about his awful position, and in forcing him too to take part in this lie. Lying, lying, this lying carried on over him on the eve of his death, and destined to bring that terrible, solemn act of his death down to the level of all their visits, curtains, sturgeons for dinner . . . was a horrible agony for Ivan Ilyich. And, strange to say, many times when they had been going through the regular performance over him, he had been within a hair's-breadth of screaming at them: "Cease your lying! You know, and I know, that I'm dying; so do, at least, give over lying!" But he had never had the spirit to do this. The terrible, awful act of his dying was, he saw, by all those about him, brought down to the level of a casual, unpleasant, and to some extent indecorous incident (somewhat as they would behave with a person who should enter a drawing room smelling unpleasant). It was brought down to the level by that very decorum to which he had been enslaved all his life. He saw that no one felt for him, because no one would even grasp his position. Gerasim was the only person who recognized the position, and felt sorry for him. And that was why Ivan Ilyich was at ease only with Gerasim. He felt comforted when Gerasim sometimes supported his legs for whole nights at a stretch, and would not go away to bed, saying, "Don't you worry yourself, Ivan Ilyich, I'll get sleep enough yet," or when suddenly dropping into the familiar peasant forms of speech, he added: "If thou weren't sick, but as 'tis, 'twould be strange if I didn't wait on thee." Gerasim alone did not lie; everything showed clearly that he alone understood what it meant, and saw no necessity to disguise it, and simply felt sorry for his sick, wasting master. He even said this once straight out, when Ivan Ilyich was sending him away.

"We shall all die. So what's a little trouble?" he said, meaning by this to express that he did not complain of the trouble just because he was taking this trouble for a dying man, and he hoped that for him too someone would be willing to take the same trouble when his time came.

Apart from this deception, or in consequence of it, what made the greatest misery for Ivan Ilyich was that no one felt for him as he would have liked them to feel for him. At certain moments, after prolonged suffering, Ivan Ilyich, ashamed as he would have been to own it, longed more than anything for someone to feel sorry for him, as for a sick child. He longed to be petted, kissed, and wept over, as children are petted and comforted. He knew that he was an important member of the law courts, that he had a beard turning gray, and that therefore it was impossible. But still he longed for it. And in his relations with Gerasim there was something approaching to that. And that was why being with Gerasim was a comfort to him. Ivan Ilyich longs to weep, longs to be petted and wept over, and then there comes in a colleague, Shebek; and instead of weeping and being petted, Ivan Ilyich puts on his serious, severe, earnest face, and from mere inertia gives his views on the effect of the last decision in the Court of Appeal, and obstinately insists upon them. This falsity around him and within him did more than anything to poison Ivan Ilyich's last days.

VIII

It was morning. All that made it morning for Ivan Ilyich was that Gerasim had gone away, and Piotr the footman had come in; he had put out the candles, opened one of the curtains, and began surreptitiously setting the room to rights. Whether it were morning or evening, Friday or Sunday, it all made no difference; it was always just the same thing. Gnawing, agonizing pain never ceasing for an instant; the hopeless sense of life always ebbing away, but still not yet gone; always swooping down on him that fearful, hated death, which was the only reality, and always the same falsity. What were days, or weeks, or hours of the day to him?

"Will you have tea, sir?"

"He wants things done in their regular order. In the morning the family should have tea," he thought, and only said—

"No."

"Would you care to move onto the sofa?"

"He wants to make the room tidy, and I'm in his way. I'm uncleanness, disorder," he thought, and only said—

"No, leave me alone."

The servant still moved busily about his work. Ivan Ilyich stretched out his hand. Piotr went up to offer his services.

"What can I get you?"

"My watch."

Piotr got out the watch, which lay just under his hand, and gave it to him.

"Half-past eight. Are they up?"

"Not yet, sir. Vladimir Ivanovich" (that was his son) "has gone to the high school, and Praskovya Fyodorovna gave orders that she was to be waked if you asked for her. Shall I send word?"

"No, no need. Should I try some tea?" he thought. "Yes, tea . . . bring it."

Piotr was on his way out. Ivan Ilyich felt frightened of being left alone. How keep him? Oh, the medicine. "Piotr, give me my medicine. Oh, well, maybe medicine may still be some good." He took the spoon, drank it. "No, it does no good. It's all rubbish, deception," he decided, as soon as he tasted the familiar, mawkish, hopeless taste. "No, I can't believe it now. But the pain, why this pain; if it would only cease for a minute." And he groaned. Piotr turned round. "No, go on. Bring the tea."

Piotr went away. Ivan Ilyich, left alone, moaned, not so much from the pain, awful as it was, as from misery. Always the same thing again and again, all these endless days and nights. If it would only be quicker. Quicker to what? Death, darkness. No, no. Anything better than death!

When Piotr came in with the tea on a tray, Ivan Ilyich stared for some time absent-mindedly at him, not grasping who he was and what he wanted. Piotr was disconcerted by this stare. And when he showed he was disconcerted, Ivan Ilyich came to himself.

"Oh, yes," he said, "tea, good, set it down. Only help me to wash and put on a clean shirt."

And Ivan Ilyich began his washing. He washed his hands slowly, and then his face, cleaned his teeth, combed his hair, and looked in the looking glass. He felt frightened at what he saw, especially at the way his hair clung limply to his pale forehead. When his shirt was being changed, he knew he would be still more terrified if he glanced at his body, and he avoided looking at himself. But at last it was all over. He put on his dressing gown, covered himself with a rug, and sat in the armchair to drink his tea. For one moment he felt refreshed; but as soon as he began to drink the tea, again there was the same taste, the same pain. He forced himself to finish it, and lay down, stretched out his legs. He lay down and dismissed Piotr.

Always the same. A gleam of hope flashes for a moment, then again the sea of despair roars about him again, and always pain, always pain, always heartache, and always the same thing. Alone it is awfully dreary; he longs to call someone, but he knows beforehand that with others present it will be worse. "Morphine again—only to forget again. I'll tell him, the doctor, that he must think of something else. It can't go on; it can't go on like this."

One hour, two hours pass like this. Then there is a ring at the front door. The doctor, perhaps. Yes, it is the doctor, fresh, hearty, fat, and cheerful, wearing that expression that seems to say, "You there are in a panic about something, but we'll soon set things right for you." The doctor is aware that this expression is hardly fitting here, but he has put on a frock coat to pay a round of calls.

In a hearty, reassuring manner the doctor rubs his hands.

"I'm cold. It's a sharp frost. Just let me warm myself," he says with an expression as though it's only a matter of waiting a little till he's warm, and as soon as he's warm he'll set everything to rights.

"Well, now, how are you?"

Ivan Ilyich feels that the doctor would like to say, "How's the little trouble?" but that he feels that he can't talk like that, and says, "How did you pass the night?"

Ivan Ilyich looks at the doctor with an expression that asks, "Is it possible you're never ashamed of lying?"

But the doctor does not care to understand this look.

And Ivan Ilyich says, "It's always just as awful. The pain never leaves me, never ceases. If only there were something!"

"Ah, you're all like that, all sick people say that. Come, now I do believe I'm thawed; even Praskovya Fyodorovna, who's so particular, could find no fault with my temperature. Well, now I can say good morning." And the doctor shakes hands.

And dropping his former levity, the doctor, with a serious face, proceeds to examine the patient, feeling his pulse, to take his temperature, and then the tappings and soundings begin.

Ivan Ilyich knows positively and indubitably that it's all nonsense and empty deception; but when the doctor, kneeling down, stretches over him, putting his ear first higher, then lower, and goes through various gymnastic evolutions over him with a serious face, Ivan Ilyich is affected by this, as he used sometimes to be affected by the speeches of the lawyers in court, though he was perfectly well aware that they were telling lies all the while and why they were telling lies.

The doctor, kneeling on the sofa, was still sounding him, when there was the rustle of Praskovya Fyodorovna's silk dress in the doorway, and she was heard scolding Piotr for not having let her know that the doctor had come.

She comes in, kisses her husband, and at once begins to explain that she has been up a long while, and that it was only through a misunderstanding that she was not there when the doctor came.

Ivan Ilyich looks at her, scans her all over, and sets down against her her whiteness and plumpness, and the cleanness of her hands and neck, and the glossiness of her hair, and the gleam full of life in her eyes. With all the force of his soul he hates her. And when she touches him it makes him suffer from the thrill of hatred he feels for her.

Her attitude to him and his illness is still the same. Just as the doctor had taken up a certain line with the patient which he was not now able to drop, so she too had taken up a line with him—that he was not doing something he ought to do, and was himself to blame, and she was lovingly reproaching him for his neglect, and she could not now get out of this attitude.

"Why, you know, he won't listen to me; he doesn't take his medicine at the right times. And what's worse still, he insists on lying in a position that surely must be bad for him —with his legs in the air."

She described how he made Gerasim hold his legs up.

The doctor smiled with kindly condescension that said, "Oh, well, it can't be helped, these sick people do take up such foolish fancies; but we must forgive them."

When the examination was over, the doctor looked at his watch, and then Praskovya Fyodorovna informed Ivan Ilyich that it must, of course, be as he liked, but she had sent today for a celebrated doctor, and that he would examine him, and have a consultation with Mihail Danilovich (that was the name of their regular doctor).

"Don't oppose it now, please. This I'm doing entirely for my own sake," she said ironically, meaning it to be understood that she was doing it all for his sake, and was only saying this to give him no right to refuse her request. He lay silent, knitting his brows. He felt that he was hemmed in by such a tangle of

falsity that it was hard to disentangle anything from it.

Everything she did for him was entirely for her own sake, and she told him she was doing for her own sake what she actually was doing for her own sake as something so incredible that he would take it as meaning the opposite.

At half-past eleven the celebrated doctor came. Again came the sounding, and then grave conversation in his presence and in the other room about the kidney and the appendix, and questions and answers, with such an air of significance that again, instead of the real question of life and death, which was now the only one that confronted him, the question that came uppermost was of the kidney and the appendix, which were doing something not as they ought to do, and were for that reason being attacked by Mihail Danilovich and the celebrated doctor, and forced to mend their ways.

The celebrated doctor took leave of him with a serious, but not a hopeless face. And to the timid question that Ivan Ilyich addressed to him while he lifted his eyes, shining with terror and hope, up toward him, Was there a chance of recovery? he answered that he could not answer for it, but that there was a chance. The look of hope with which Ivan Ilyich watched the doctor out was so piteous that, seeing it, Praskovya Fyodorovna positively burst into tears, as she went out of the door to hand the celebrated doctor his fee in the next room.

The gleam of hope kindled by the doctor's assurance did not last long. Again the same room, the same pictures, the curtains, the wallpaper, the medicine bottles, and ever the same, his aching suffering body. And Ivan Ilyich began to moan; they gave him injections, and he sank into oblivion. When he waked up it was getting dark; they brought him his dinner. He forced himself to eat some broth; and again everything the same, and again the coming night.

After dinner at seven o'clock, Praskovya Fyodorovna came into his room, dressed as though to go to a soiree, with her full bosom laced in tight, and traces of powder on her face. She had in the morning mentioned to him that they were going to the theater. Sarah Bernhardt was visiting the town, and they had a box, which he had insisted on their taking. By now he had forgotten about it, and her smart attire was an offense to him. But he concealed this feeling when he recollected that he had himself insisted on their taking a box and going, because it was an aesthetic pleasure, beneficial and instructive for the children.

Praskovya Fyodorovna came in satisfied with herself, but yet with something of a guilty air. She sat down, asked how he was, as he saw, simply for the sake of asking, and not for the sake of learning anything, knowing indeed that there was nothing to learn, and began telling him how absolutely necessary it was; how she would not have gone for anything, but the box had been taken, and Ellen, their daughter, and Petrishtchev (the examining lawyer, the daughter's suitor) were going, and that it was out of the question to let them go alone. But that she would have liked much better to stay with him. If only he would be sure to follow the doctor's prescription while she was away.

"Oh, and Fyodor Dmitryevich" (the suitor) "would like to come in. May he? And Liza?"

"Yes, let them come in."

The daughter came in, in full dress, her fresh young body bare, while his body made him suffer so. But she made a show of it; she was strong, healthy, obviously in love, and impatient of the illness, suffering, and death that hindered her happiness.

Fyodor Dmitryevich came in too in evening dress, his hair curled à la Capoul, with his long, sinewy neck tightly fenced round by a white collar, with his vast expanse of white chest and strong thighs displayed in narrow black trousers, with one white glove in his hand and a crush opera hat.

Behind him crept in unnoticed the little high-school boy in his new uniform, poor fellow, in gloves, and with that awful blue ring under his eyes that Ivan Ilyich knew the meaning of.

He always felt sorry for his son. And pitiable indeed was his scared face of sympathetic suffering. Except Gerasim, Ivan Ilyich fancied that Volodya was the only one that understood and was sorry.

They all sat down; again they asked how he was. A silence followed. Liza asked her mother about the opera glass. An altercation ensued between the mother and daughter as to who had taken it, and where it had been put. It turned into an unpleasant squabble.

Fyodor Dmitryevich asked Ivan Ilyich whether he had seen Sarah Bernhardt? Ivan Ilyich could not at first catch the question that was asked him, but then he said, "No, have you seen her before?"

"Yes, in *Adrienne Lecouvreur*."

Praskovya Fyodorovna observed that she was particularly good in that part. The daughter made some reply. A conversation sprang up about the art and naturalness of her acting, that conversation that is continually repeated and always the same.

In the middle of the conversation Fyodor Dmitryevich glanced at Ivan Ilyich and relapsed into silence. The others looked at him and became mute, too. Ivan Ilyich was staring with glittering eyes straight before him, obviously furious with them. This had to be set right, but it could not anyhow be set right. This silence had somehow to be broken. No one would venture on breaking it, and all began to feel alarmed that the decorous deception was somehow breaking down, and the facts would be exposed to all. Liza was the first to pluck up courage. She broke the silence. She tried to cover up what they were all feeling, but inadvertently she gave it utterance.

"If we are going, though, it's time to start," she said, glancing at her watch, a gift from her father; and with a scarcely perceptible meaning smile to the young man, referring to something only known to themselves, she got up with a rustle of her skirts.

They all got up, said good-by, and went away. When they were gone, Ivan Ilyich fancied he was easier; there was no falsity—that had gone away with them, but the pain remained. That continual pain, that continual terror, made nothing harder, nothing easier. It was always worse.

Again came minute after minute, hour after hour, still the same and still no end, and ever more terrible the inevitable end.

"Yes, send Gerasim," he said in answer to Piotr's question.

IX

Late at night his wife came back. She came in on tiptoe, but he heard her, opened his eyes, and made haste to close them again. She wanted to send away Gerasim and sit up with him herself instead. He opened his eyes and said, "No, go away."

"Are you in great pain?"

"Always the same."

"Take some opium."

He agreed, and drank it. She went away.

Till three o'clock he slept a miserable sleep. It seemed to him that he and his pain were being thrust somewhere into a narrow, deep, black sack, and they kept pushing him further and further in, and still could not thrust him to the bottom. And this operation was awful to him, and was accompanied with agony. And he was afraid, and yet wanted to fall into it, and struggled and yet tried to get into it. And all of a sudden he slipped, fell, and woke up. Gerasim, still the same, is sitting at the foot of the bed, half dozing peacefully, patient. And he is lying with his wasted legs clad in stockings, raised on Gerasim's shoulders, the same candle burning in the alcove, and the same interminable pain.

"Go away, Gerasim," he whispered.

"It's all right, sir. I'll stay a bit longer."

"No, go away."

He took his legs down, lay sideways on his arm, and he felt very sorry for himself. He only waited till Gerasim had gone away into the next room; he could restrain himself no longer, and cried like a child. He cried at his own helplessness, at his awful loneliness, at the cruelty of people, at the cruelty of God, at the absence of God.

"Why has Thou done all this? What brought me to this? Why, why torture me so horribly?"

He did not expect an answer, and wept indeed that there was and could be no answer. The pain grew more acute again, but he did not stir, did not call.

He said to himself, "Come, more then; come, strike me! But what for? What have I done to Thee? What for?"

Then he was still, ceased weeping, held his breath, and was all attention; he listened, as it were, not to a voice uttering sounds, but to the voice of his soul, to the current of thoughts that rose up within him.

"What is it you want?" was the first clear idea able to be put into words that he grasped.

"What? Not to suffer, to live," he answered.

And again he was utterly plunged into attention so intense that even the pain did not distract him.

"To live? Live how?" the voice of his soul was asking.

"Why, live as I used to live before—happily and pleasantly."

"As you used to live before—happily and pleasantly?" queried the voice. And he began going over in his imagination the best moments of his pleasant life. But strange to say, all these best moments of his pleasant life seemed now not at all what they had seemed then. All—except the first memories of childhood—there, in his childhood there had been something really pleasant in which one could have lived if it had come back. But the creature who had this pleasant experience was no more; it was like a memory of someone else.

As soon as he reached the begin-ning of what had resulted in him as he was now, Ivan Ilyich, all that had seemed joys to him then now melted away before his eyes and were transformed into something trivial, and often disgusting.

And the further he went from childhood, the nearer to the actual present, the more worthless and un-certain were the joys. It began with life at the school of jurisprudence. Then there had still been some-thing genuinely good; then there had been gaiety; then there had been friendship; then there had been hopes. But in the higher classes these good moments were already becoming rarer. Later on, during the first period of his official life, at the governor's, good moments appeared; but it was all mixed, and less and less of it was good. And further on even less was good, and the further he went the less good there was.

His marriage . . . as gratuitous as the disillusion of it and the smell of his wife's breath and the sen-suality, the hypocrisy! And that deadly official life, and anxiety about money, and so for one year, and two, and ten, and twenty, and always the same thing. And the further he went, the more deadly it became. "As though I had been going steadily downhill, imagining that I was going uphill. So it was in fact. In public opinion I was going up-hill, and steadily as I got up it life was ebbing away from me. . . . And now the work's done, there's only to die.

"But what is this? What for? It cannot be! It cannot be that life has been so senseless, so loathsome? And if it really was so loathsome and senseless, then why die, and die in agony? There's something wrong.

"Can it be I have not lived as one

ought?" suddenly came into his head. "But how not so, when I've done everything as it should be done?" he said, and at once dismissed this only solution of all the enigma of life and death as something utterly out of the question. "What do you want now? To live? Live how? Live as you live at the courts when the usher booms out: 'The judge is coming!'" . . . "The judge is coming, the judge is coming," he repeated to himself. "Here he is, the judge! But I'm not to blame!" he shrieked in fury. "What's it for?" And he left off crying and, turning with his face to the wall, fell to pondering always on the same question, "What for, why all this horror?"

But however much he pondered, he could not find an answer. And whenever the idea struck him, as it often did, that it all came of his never having lived as he ought, he thought of all the correctness of his life and dismissed the strange idea.

X

Another fortnight had passed. Ivan Ilyich could not now get up from the sofa. He did not like lying in bed, and lay on the sofa. And lying almost all the time facing the wall, in loneliness he suffered all the inexplicable agonies, and in loneliness pondered always that inexplicable question, "What is it? Can it be true that it's death?" And an inner voice answered, "Yes, it is true." "Why these agonies?" and a voice answered, "For no reason." Beyond and besides this there was nothing.

From the very beginning of his illness, ever since Ivan Ilyich first went to the doctor's, his life had been split up into two contradictory moods, which were continually alternating—one was despair and the anticipation of an uncomprehended and awful death; the other was hope and an absorbed watching over the actual condition of his body. First there was nothing confronting him but a kidney or intestine which had temporarily declined to perform their duties, then there was nothing but unknown awful death, which there was no escaping.

These two moods had alternated from the very beginning of the illness; but the further the illness progressed, the more doubtful and fantastic became the conception of the kidney, and the more real the sense of approaching death.

He had but to reflect on what he had been three months before and what he was now, to reflect how steadily he had been going downhill, for every possibility of hope to be shattered.

Of late, in the loneliness in which he found himself, lying with his face to the back of the sofa, a loneliness in the middle of a populous town and of his numerous acquaintances and his family, a loneliness than which none more complete could be found anywhere—not at the bottom of the sea, not deep down in the earth—of late in this fearful loneliness Ivan Ilyich had lived only in imagination in the past. One by one the pictures of his past rose up before him. It always began from what was nearest in time and went back to the most remote, to childhood, and rested there. If Ivan Ilyich thought of the stewed prunes that had been offered him for dinner that day, his mind went back to the damp, wrinkled French plum of his childhood, of its peculiar taste and the flow of saliva when the stone was sucked; and along with this memory of a taste there rose up a whole series of memories of that period—his nurse, his brother, his playthings. "I mustn't . . . it's too painful," Ivan Ilyich said to himself, and he brought himself back to the present. The button on the back of the sofa and the creases in the morocco. "Morocco's dear, and doesn't wear well; there was a quarrel over it. But the morocco was different, and different too the quarrel when we tore Father's portfolio and were punished, and Mamma bought us the tarts." And again his mind rested on his childhood, and again it was painful, and he tried to drive it away and think of something else.

And again at that point, together with that chain of associations, quite another chain of memories came into his heart, of how this illness had grown up and become more acute. It was the same there, the further back the more life there had been. There had been both more that was good in life and more of life itself. And the two began to melt into one. "Just as the pain goes on getting worse and worse, so has my whole life gone on getting worse and worse," he thought. One light spot was there at the back, at the beginning of life, and then it kept getting blacker and blacker, and going faster and faster. "In inverse ratio to the square of the distance from death," thought Ivan Ilyich. And the image of a stone falling downwards with increasing velocity sank into his soul. Life, a series of increasing sufferings, falls more and more swiftly to the end, the most fearful sufferings. "I am falling." He shuddered, shifted himself, would have resisted, but he knew beforehand that he could not resist; and again, with eyes weary with gazing at it,

but unable not to gaze at what was before him, he stared at the back of the sofa and waited, waited expecting that fearful fall and shock and dissolution. "Resistance is impossible," he said to himself. "But if one could at least comprehend what it's for? Even that's impossible. It could be explained if one were to say that I hadn't lived as I ought. But that can't be alleged," he said to himself, thinking of all the regularity, correctness, and propriety of his life. "That really can't be admitted," he said to himself, his lips smiling ironically as though someone could see his smile and be deceived by it. "No explanation! Agony, death . . . What for?"

XI

So passed a fortnight. During that fortnight an event occurred that had been desired by Ivan Ilyich and his wife. Petrishtchev made a formal proposal. This took place in the evening. Next day Praskovya Fyodorovna went in to her husband, resolving in her mind how to inform him of Fyodor Dmitryevich's proposal, but that night there had been a change for the worse in Ivan Ilyich. Praskovya Fyodorovna found him on the same sofa, but in a different position. He was lying on his face, groaning, and staring straight before him with a fixed gaze.

She began talking of remedies. He turned his stare on her. She did not finish what she had begun saying; such hatred of her in particular was expressed in that stare.

"For Christ's sake, let me die in peace," he said.

She would have gone away, but at that moment the daughter came in and went up to say good morning to him. He looked at his daughter just as at his wife, and to her inquiries how he was, he told her dryly that they would soon all be rid of him. Both were silent, sat a little while, and went out.

"How are we to blame?" said Liza to her mother. "As though we had done it! I'm sorry for Papa, but why punish us?"

At the usual hour the doctor came. Ivan Ilyich answered, "Yes, no," never taking his exasperated stare from him, and toward the end he said, "Why, you know that you can do nothing, so let me be."

"We can relieve your suffering," said the doctor.

"Even that you can't do; let me be."

The doctor went into the drawing room and told Praskovya Fyodorovna that it was very serious, and that the only resource left them was opium to relieve his sufferings, which must be terrible. The doctor said his physical sufferings were terrible, and that was true; but even more terrible than his physical sufferings were his mental sufferings, and in that lay his chief misery.

His moral sufferings were due to the fact that during that night, as he looked at the sleepy, good-natured, broad-cheeked face of Gerasim, the thought had suddenly come into his head, "What if in reality all my life, my conscious life, has been not the right thing?" The thought struck him that what he had regarded before as an utter impossibility, that he had spent his life not as he ought, might be the truth. It struck him that those scarcely detected impulses of struggle within him against what was considered good by persons of higher position, scarcely detected impulses which he had dismissed, that they might be the real thing, and everything else might be not the right thing. And

his official work, and his ordering of his daily life and of his family, and these social and official interests— all that might be not the right thing. He tried to defend it all to himself. And suddenly he felt all the, weakness of what he was defending. And it was useless to defend it.

"But if it's so," he said to himself, "and I am leaving life with the consciousness that I have lost all that was given me, and there's no correcting it, then what?" He lay on his back and began going over his whole life entirely anew. When he saw the footman in the morning, then his wife, then his daughter, then the doctor, every movement they made, every word they uttered, confirmed for him the terrible truth that had been revealed to him in the night. In them he saw himself, saw all in which he had lived, and saw distinctly that it was all not the right thing; it was a horrible, vast deception that concealed both life and death. This consciousness intensified his physical agonies, multiplied them tenfold. He groaned and tossed from side to side and pulled at the covering over him. It seemed to him that it was stifling him and weighing him down. And for that he hated them.

They gave him a big dose of opium; he sank into unconsciousness; but at dinnertime the same thing began again. He drove them all away, and tossed from side to side.

His wife came to him and said, "Jean, darling, do this for my sake" (for my sake?). "It can't do harm, and it often does good. Why, it's nothing. And often in health people——"

He opened his eyes wide.

"What? Take the sacrament? What for? No. Besides . . ."

She began to cry.

"Yes, my dear. I'll send for our priest, he's so nice."

"All right, very well," he said.

When the priest came and confessed him he was softened, felt as it were a relief from his doubts, and consequently from his sufferings, and there came a moment of hope. He began once more thinking of the intestinal appendix and the possibility of curing it. He took the sacrament with tears in his eyes.

When they laid him down again after the sacrament for a minute, he felt comfortable, and again the hope of life sprang up. He began to think about the operation, which had been suggested to him. "To live, I want to live," he said to himself. His wife came in to congratulate him; she uttered the customary words and added—

"It's quite true, isn't it, that you're better?"

Without looking at her, he said, "Yes."

Her dress, her figure, the expression of her face, the tone of her voice—all told him the same: "Not the right thing. All that in which you lived and are living is lying, deceit, hiding life and death away from you." And as soon as he had formed that thought, hatred sprang up in him, and with that hatred agonizing physical sufferings, and with these sufferings the sense of inevitable, approaching ruin. Something new was happening; there were screwing and shooting pains, and a tightness in his breathing.

The expression of his face as he uttered that "Yes" was terrible. After uttering that "Yes," looking her straight in the face, he turned on his face, with a rapidity extraordinary in his weakness, and shrieked—

"Go away, go away, let me be!"

XII

From that moment there began the scream that never ceased for three days, and was so awful that through two closed doors one could not hear it without horror. At the moment when he answered his wife he grasped that he had fallen, that there was no return, that the end had come, quite the end, while doubt was still as unsolved, still remained doubt.

"Oo! Oo—o! Oo!" he screamed in varying intonations. He had begun screaming, "I don't want to!" and so had gone on screaming on the same vowel sound—oo!

All those three days, during which time did not exist for him, he was struggling in that black sack into which he was being thrust by an unseen, resistless force. He struggled as the man condemned to death struggles in the hands of the executioner, knowing that he cannot save himself. And every moment he felt that in spite of all his efforts to struggle against it, he was getting nearer and nearer to what terrified him. He felt that his agony was due both to his being thrust into this black hole and still more to his not being able to get right into it. What hindered him from getting into it was the claim that his life had been good. That justification of his life held him fast and would not let him get forward, and it caused him more agony than all.

All at once some force struck him in the chest, in the side, and stifled his breathing more than ever; he rolled forward into the hole, and there at the end there was some sort of light. It had happened with him, as it had sometimes happened to him in a railway carriage, when he had thought he was going forward while he was going back, and all of a sudden recognized his real direction.

"Yes, it has all been not the right thing," he said to himself, "but that's no matter." He could, he could do the right thing. "What is the right thing?" he asked himself, and suddenly he became quiet.

This was at the end of the third day, two hours before his death. At that very moment the schoolboy had stealthily crept into his father's room and gone up to his bedside. The dying man was screaming and waving his arms. His hand fell on the schoolboy's head. The boy snatched it, pressed it to his lips, and burst into tears.

At that very moment Ivan Ilyich had rolled into the hole, and caught sight of the light, and it was revealed to him that his life had not been what it ought to have been, but that that could still be set right. He asked himself, "What is the right thing?"— and became quiet, listening. Then he felt someone was kissing his hand. He opened his eyes and glanced at his son. He felt sorry for him. His wife went up to him. He glanced at her. She was gazing at him with open mouth, the tears unwiped streaming over her nose and cheeks, a look of despair on her face. He felt sorry for her.

"Yes, I'm making them miserable," he thought. "They're sorry, but it will be better for them when I die." He would have said this, but had not the strength to utter it. "Besides, why speak, I must act," he thought. With a glance to his wife he pointed to his son and said—

"Take away . . . sorry for him . . . And you too . . ." He tried to say "forgive," but said "forgo" . . . and too weak to correct himself, shook his hand, knowing that He would understand Whose understanding mattered.

And all at once it became clear to him that what had tortured him and would not leave him was suddenly dropping away all at once on both sides and on ten sides and on all sides. He was sorry for them, must act so that they might not suffer. Set them free and be free himself of those agonies. "How right and how simple!" he thought. "And the pain?" he asked himself. "Where's it gone? Eh, where are you, pain?"

He began to watch for it.

"Yes, here it is. Well, what of it, let the pain be.

"And death. Where is it?"

He looked for his old accustomed terror of death, and did not find it. "Where is it? What death?" There was no terror, because death was not either.

In the place of death there was light.

"So this is it!" he suddenly exclaimed aloud.

"What joy!"

To him all this passed in a single instant, and the meaning of that instant suffered no change after. For those present his agony lasted another two hours. There was a rattle in his throat, a twitching in his wasted body. Then the rattle and the gasping came at longer and longer intervals.

"It is over!" someone said over him.

He caught those words and repeated them in his soul.

"Death is over," he said to himself. "It's no more."

He drew in a breath, stopped midway in the breath, stretched, and died.

Anton Pavlovich Chekhov

1860-1904

CHEKHOV once said that melancholy is to the Russian writer what the potato is to a French chef: it can be dished out in a hundred different ways. Certainly, as he prepared it, melancholy made his reputation in western Europe. In Russia, however, he was best known and loved as a humorist.

Son of an ex-serf who kept a general store in Taganrog, on the Sea of Azov, Chekhov was born into a lively and clever family. The three Chekhov brothers were all artists: two of them began writing comic stories during their university years, and the third drew cartoons. "Schiller Shakespearovich Goethe" was Anton's signature when writing to his brothers. Though he was graduated from the medical school of the University of Moscow, he practiced very little as a doctor. For Chekhov was essentially a writer—as someone said, though medicine was his wife, literature was his mistress. When he had attained enough success to enable him to write as he chose, he abandoned the comic papers and settled down to the serious work by which we know him best. He wrote about lazy, good-humored, kindly peasants living in dirt and ignorance. To Chekhov, those who suffered and succumbed were noble, while those who endured and triumphed over misery were unfeeling and brutal. It was this note of melancholy—Chekhov's "gray mood"—that delighted the aesthetes of the late nineteenth century, tired as they were of the wholesomeness of the Victorians. "A Day in the Country" contributes to this mood.

Chekhov's great love was the theater. Most of his plays—*The Seagull, Uncle Vanya, The Cherry Orchard, The Three Sisters*—were produced by Stanislavsky at the Moscow Art Theater, and in 1901 he married the actress Olga Knipper, who played leading parts in them. Three years later, he died of tuberculosis in Germany. His coffin was sent home in a green freight car marked FOR OYSTERS.

A Day in the Country

BY ANTON CHEKHOV

BETWEEN eight and nine o'clock in the morning.

A dark leaden-colored mass is creeping over the sky toward the sun. Red zigzags of lightning gleam here and there across it. There is a sound of faraway rumbling. A warm wind frolics over the grass, bends the trees, and stirs up the dust. In a minute there will be a spurt of May rain and a real storm will begin.

Fyokla, a little beggar girl of six, is running through the village, looking for Terenty the cobbler. The white-haired, barefoot child is pale. Her eyes are wide-open, her lips are trembling.

"Uncle, where is Terenty?" she asks everyone she meets. No one answers. They are all preoccupied with the approaching storm and take refuge in their huts. At last she meets Silanty Silich, the sacristan, Terenty's bosom friend. He is coming along, staggering from the wind.

"Uncle, where is Terenty?"

"At the kitchen gardens," answers Silanty.

The beggar girl runs behind the huts to the kitchen gardens and there finds Terenty; the tall old man with a thin, pockmarked face, very long legs, and bare feet, dressed in a woman's tattered jacket, is standing near the vegetable plots, looking with drowsy, drunken eyes at the dark storm cloud. On his long crane-like legs he sways in the wind like a starling cote.

"Uncle Terenty!" the white-headed beggar girl addresses him. "Uncle, darling!"

Terenty bends down to Fyokla, and his grim, drunken face is overspread with a smile, such as come into people's faces when they look at something little, foolish, and absurd, but warmly loved.

"Ah! servant of God, Fyokla," he says, lisping tenderly, "where have you come from?"

"Uncle Terenty," says Fyokla, with a sob, tugging at the lapel of the cobbler's coat. "Brother Danilka has had an accident! Come along!"

"What sort of accident? Ough, what thunder! Holy, holy, holy . . . What sort of accident?"

"In the count's copse Danilka stuck his hand into a hole in a tree, and he can't get it out. Come along, Uncle, do be kind and pull his hand out!"

"How was it he put his hand in? What for?"

"He wanted to get a cuckoo's egg out of the hole for me."

54

"The day has hardly begun and already you are in trouble . . ." Terenty shook his head and spat deliberately. "Well, what am I to do with you now? I must come . . . I must, may the wolf gobble you up, you naughty children! Come, little orphan!"

Terenty comes out of the kitchen garden and, lifting high his long legs, begins striding down the village street. He walks quickly without stopping or looking from side to side, as though he were shoved from behind or afraid of pursuit. Fyokla can hardly keep up with him.

They come out of the village and turn along the dusty road toward the count's copse that lies dark blue in the distance. It is about a mile and a half away. The clouds have by now covered the sun, and soon afterwards there is not a speck of blue left in the sky. It grows dark.

"Holy, holy, holy . . ." whispers Fyokla, hurrying after Terenty. The first raindrops, big and heavy, lie, dark dots on the duty road. A big drop falls on Fyokla's cheek and glides like a tear down her chin.

"The rain has begun," mutters the cobbler, kicking up the dust with his bare, bony feet. "That's fine, Fyokla, old girl. The grass and the trees are fed by the rain, as we are by bread. And as for the thunder, don't you be frightened, little orphan. Why should it kill a little thing like you?"

As soon as the rain begins, the wind drops. The only sound is the patter of rain dropping like fine shot on the young rye and the parched road.

"We shall get soaked, Fyokla," mutters Terenty. "There won't be a dry spot left on us. . . . Ho-ho, my girl! It's run down my neck! But don't be frightened, silly. . . . The grass will be dry again, the earth will be dry again, and we shall be dry again. There is the same sun for us all."

A flash of lightning, some fourteen feet long, gleams above their heads. There is a loud peal of thunder, and it seems to Fyokla that something big, heavy, and round is rolling over the sky and tearing it open, exactly over her head.

"Holy, holy, holy . . ." says Terenty, crossing himself. "Don't be afraid, little orphan! It is not from spite that it thunders."

Terenty's and Fyokla's feet are covered with lumps of heavy, wet clay. It is slippery and difficult to walk, but Terenty strides on more and more rapidly. The weak little beggar girl is breathless and ready to drop.

But at last they go into the count's copse. The washed trees, stirred by a gust of wind, drop a perfect waterfall upon them. Terenty stumbles over stumps and begins to slacken his pace.

"Whereabouts is Danilka?" he asks. "Lead me to him."

Fyokla leads him into a thicket, and, after going a quarter of a mile, points to Danilka. Her brother, a little fellow of eight, with hair as red as ocher and a pale, sickly face, stands leaning against a tree, and, with his head on one side, looking sideways at the sky. In one hand he holds his shabby old cap, the other is hidden in an old lime tree. The boy is gazing at the stormy sky, and apparently not thinking of his trouble. Hearing footsteps and seeing the cobbler he gives a sickly smile and says:

"A terrible lot of thunder, Terenty. . . . I've never heard so much thunder in all my life."

"And where is your hand?"

"In the hole. . . . Pull it out, please, Terenty!"

The wood had broken at the edge of the hole and jammed Danilka's hand; he could push it farther in, but could not pull it out. Terenty snaps off the broken piece, and the boy's hand, red and crushed, is released.

"It's terrible how it's thundering," the boy says again rubbing his hand. "What makes it thunder, Terenty?"

"One cloud runs against the other," answers the cobbler. The party come out of the copse, and walk along the edge of it toward the darkened road. The thunder gradually abates, and its rumbling is heard far away beyond the village.

"The ducks flew by here the other day, Terenty," says Danilka, still rubbing his hand. "They must be nesting in the Gniliya Zaimishtcha marshes. . . . Fyokla, would you like me to show you a nightingale's nest?"

"Don't touch it, you might disturb them," says Terenty, wringing the water out of his cap. "The nightingale is a singing bird, without sin. He has had a voice given him in his throat, to praise God and gladden the heart of man. It's a sin to disturb him."

"What about the sparrow?"

"The sparrow doesn't matter, he's a bad, spiteful bird. He is like a pickpocket in his ways. He doesn't like man to be happy. When Christ was crucified it was the sparrow brought nails to the Jews, and called 'alive! alive!'"

A bright patch of blue appears in the sky.

"Look!" says Terenty. "An ant heap burst open by the rain! They've been flooded, the rogues!"

They bend over the ant heap. The downpour has damaged it; the insects are scurrying to and fro in the mud, agitated, and busily trying to carry away their drowned companions.

"You needn't be in such a taking, you won't die of it!" says Terenty, grinning. "As soon as the sun warms you, you'll come to your senses again. . . . It's a lesson to you, you stupids. You won't settle on low ground another time."

They go on.

"And here are some bees," cries Danilka, pointing to the branch of a young oak tree.

The drenched and chilled bees are huddled together on the branch. There are so many of them that neither bark nor leaf can be seen. Many of them are settled on one another.

"That's a swarm of bees," Terenty informs them. "They were flying looking for a home, and when the rain came down upon them they settled. If a swarm is flying, you need only sprinkle water on them to make them settle. Now if, say, you wanted to take the swarm, you would bend the branch with them into a sack and shake it, and they all fall in."

Little Fyokla suddenly frowns and rubs her neck vigorously. Her brother looks at her neck, and sees a big swelling on it.

"Hey-hey!" laughs the cobbler. "Do you know where you got that from, Fyokla, old girl? There are Spanish flies on some tree in the wood. The rain has trickled off them, and a drop has fallen on your neck—that's what has made the swelling."

The sun appears from behind the clouds and floods the wood, the fields, and the three friends with its warm light. The dark menacing cloud has gone far away and taken the storm with it. The air is warm and fragrant. There is a scent of bird-cherry, meadowsweet, and lilies-of-the-valley.

"That herb is given when your nose bleeds," says Terenty, pointing to a woolly-looking flower. "It does good."

They hear a whistle and a rumble, but not such a rumble as the storm clouds carried away. A goods train races by before the eyes of Terenty, Danilka, and Fyokla. The engine, panting and puffing out black smoke, drags more than twenty vans after it. Its power is tremendous. The children are interested to know how an engine, not alive and without the help of horses, can move and drag such weights, and Terenty undertakes to explain it to them:

"It's all the steam's doing, children. . . . The steam does the work. . . . You see, it shoves under that thing near the wheels, and it . . . you see . . . it works . . ."

They cross the railway line, and, going down from the embankment, walk toward the river. They walk not with any object, but just at random, and talk all the way . . . Danilka asks questions, Terenty answers them.

Terenty answers all his questions, and there is no secret in nature which baffles him. He knows everything. Thus, for example, he knows the names of all the wild flowers, animals, and stones. He knows what herbs cure diseases, he has no difficulty in telling the age of a horse or a cow. Looking at the sunset, at the moon, or the birds, he can tell what sort of weather it will be next day. And indeed, it is not only Terenty who is so wise. Silanty Silich, the innkeeper, the market gardener, the shepherd, and all the villagers, gen-erally speaking, know as much as he does. These people have learned not from books, but in the fields, in the wood, on the riverbank. Their teachers have been the birds themselves, when they sang to them, the sun when it left a glow of crimson behind it at setting, the very trees, and wild herbs.

Danilka looks at Terenty and greedily drinks in every word. In spring, before one is weary of the warmth and the monotonous green of the fields, when everything is fresh and full of fragrance, who would not want to hear about the golden May beetles, about the cranes, about the gurgling streams, and the corn mounting into ear?

The two of them, the cobbler and the orphan, walk about the fields, talk unceasingly, and are not weary. They could wander about the world endlessly. They walk, and in their talk of the beauty of the earth do not notice the frail little beggar girl tripping after them. She is breathless and moves with a lagging step. There are tears in her eyes; she would be glad to stop these inexhaustible wanderers, but to whom and where can she go? She has no home or people of her own; whether she likes it or not, she must walk and listen to their talk.

Toward midday, all three sit down on the riverbank. Danilka takes out of his bag a piece of bread, soaked and reduced to a mash, and they begin to eat. Terenty says a prayer when he has eaten the bread, then stretches himself on the sandy bank and falls asleep. While he is asleep, the boy gazes at the water, pondering. He has many different things to think of. He has just seen the storm, the bees, the ants, the train. Now, before his eyes, fishes are whisking about. Some are two inches long and more, others. are no bigger than one's nail. A viper, with its head held high, is swimming from one bank to the other.

Only toward the evening our wanderers return to the village. The children go for the night to a deserted barn, where the corn of the commune used to be kept, while Terenty, leaving them, goes to the tavern. The children lie huddled together on the straw, dozing.

The boy does not sleep. He gazes into the darkness, and it seems to him that he is seeing all that he has seen in the day: the storm clouds, the bright sunshine, the birds, the fish, lanky Terenty. The number of his impressions, together with ex-haustion and hunger, are too much for him; he is as hot as though he were on fire, and tosses from side to side. He longs to tell someone all that is haunting him now in the darkness and agitating his soul, but there is no one to tell. Fyokla is too little and could not understand.

"I'll tell Terenty tomorrow," thinks the boy.

The children fall asleep, thinking of the homeless cobbler, and, in the night Terenty comes to them, makes the sign of the cross over them, and puts bread under their heads. And no one sees his love. It is seen only by the moon which floats in the sky and peeps caressingly through the holes in the wall of the deserted barn.

Honoré de Balzac
1799-1850

SOMERSET MAUGHAM says: "I suppose Balzac is the greatest novelist who ever lived." Certainly, he left behind him one of the great literary monuments of all time. At the age of thirty he started writing *La Comédie humaine,* worked almost without stop for twenty years, and died at fifty, worn out from overwork. In those twenty years he had little opportunity for life or family or love, hardly enough for friends.

Balzac wrote sixteen hours daily, sometimes not leaving his room for three days at a time, eating very little, and drinking cup after cup of black coffee. His routine was a dinner of sorts at five in the afternoon, sleep until midnight, then work all night and most of the next day. It is said that the manifold intricacies of the novels and stories that make up the many volumes of *The Human Comedy* were all in his head at the same time. He knew all the details of the lives of every one of his two thousand or more characters, the condition of the country and province from which each came, the nature of the trade or profession each belonged to, and the political changes that were going on in their world. He was in their consciousness, in their clothes, business, palaces, even in their beds. "After Shakespeare, he is our great magazine of documents on human nature," said Taine.

Never satisfied with his finished manuscripts, Balzac went over the proofs time and time again, changing the order of stories, rewriting, spending a fortune on printers' bills for revised proofs.

"A Passion in the Desert" was written in Balzac's first year of work on *La Comédie humaine* and is a part of *Tales from the Military Life.*

A Passion in the Desert

BY HONORÉ DE BALZAC

"The whole show is dreadful," she cried, coming out of the menagerie of M. Martin. She had just been looking at that daring speculator "working with his hyena"—to speak in the style of the program.

"By what means," she continued, "can he have tamed these animals to such a point as to be certain of their affection for——."

"What seems to you a problem," said I, interrupting, "is really quite natural."

"Oh!" she cried, letting an incredulous smile wander over her lips.

"You think that beasts are wholly without passions?" I asked her. "Quite the reverse; we can communicate to them all the vices arising in our own state of civilization."

She looked at me with an air of astonishment.

"Nevertheless," I continued, "the first time I saw M. Martin, I admit, like you, I did give vent to an exclamation of surprise. I found myself next to an old soldier with the right leg amputated, who had come in with me. His face had struck me. He had one of those intrepid heads, stamped with the seal of warfare, and on which the battles of Napoleon are written. Besides, he had that

frank good-humored expression which always impresses me favorably. He was without doubt one of those troopers who are surprised at nothing, who find matter for laughter in the contortions of a dying comrade, who bury or plunder him quite lightheartedly, who stand intrepidly in the way of bullets; in fact, one of those men who waste no time in deliberation, and would not hesitate to make friends with the devil himself. After looking very attentively at the proprietor of the menagerie getting out of his box, my companion pursed up his lips with an air of mockery and contempt, with that peculiar and expressive twist which superior people assume to show they are not taken in. Then when I was expatiating on the courage of M. Martin, he smiled, shook his head knowingly, and said, 'Well known.'

"How 'well known'? I said. 'If you would only explain to me the mystery I should be vastly obliged.'

"After a few minutes, during which we made acquaintance, we went to dine at the first restaurateur's whose shop caught our eye. At dessert a bottle of champagne completely refreshed and brightened up the memories of this odd old soldier. He told me his story, and I said he had every reason to exclaim, 'Well known.' "

When she got home, she teased me to that extent and made so many promises that I consented to communicate to her the old soldier's confidences. Next day she received the following episode of an epic which one might call "The Frenchman in Egypt."

During the expedition in Upper Egypt under General Desaix, a Provençal soldier fell into the hands of the Mangrabins, and was taken by these Arabs into the deserts beyond the falls of the Nile.

In order to place a sufficient distance between themselves and the French army, the Mangrabins made forced marches, and only rested during the night. They camped round a well overshadowed by palm trees under which they had previously concealed a store of provisions. Not surmising that the notion of flight would occur to their prisoner, they contented themselves with binding his hands, and after eating a few dates, and giving provender to their horses, went to sleep.

When the brave Provençal saw that his enemies were no longer watching him, he made use of his teeth to steal a scimitar, fixed the blade between his knees, and cut the cords which prevented using his hands; in a moment he was free. He at once seized a rifle and dagger, then taking the precaution to provide himself with a sack of dried dates, oats, and powder and shot, and to fasten a scimitar to his waist he leaped onto a horse, and spurred on vigorously in the direction where he thought to find the French army. So impatient was he to see a bivouac again that he pressed on the already tired courser at such speed that its flanks were lacerated with his spurs, and at last the poor animal died, leaving the Frenchman alone in the desert. After walking some time in the sand with all the courage of an escaped convict, the soldier was obliged to stop, as the day had already ended. In spite of the beauty of an Oriental sky at night, he felt he had not strength enough to go on. Fortunately he had been able to find a small hill, on the summit of which a few palm trees shot up into the air; it was their verdure seen from afar which had brought hope and consolation to his heart. His fatigue was so great that he lay down upon a rock of granite, capriciously cut out like a camp bed, there he fell asleep without taking any precaution to defend himself while he slept. He had made the sacrifice of his life. His last thought was one of regret. He repented having left the Mangrabins, whose nomad life seemed to smile on him now that he was afar from them and without help. He was awakened by the sun, whose pitiless rays fell with all their force on the granite and produced an intolerable heat—for he had had the stupidity to place himself inversely to the shadow thrown by the verdant majestic heads of the palm trees. He looked at the solitary trees and shuddered —they reminded him of the graceful shafts crowned with foliage which characterize the Saracen columns in the cathedral of Arles.

But when, after counting the palm trees, he cast his eye around him, the most horrible despair was infused into his soul. Before him stretched an ocean without limit. The dark sand of the desert spread farther than sight could reach in every direction, and glittered like steel struck with a bright light. It might have been a sea of looking glass, or lakes melted together in a mirror. A fiery vapor carried up in streaks made a perpetual whirlwind over the quivering land. The sky was lit with an Oriental splendor of insupportable purity, leaving naught for the imagination to desire. Heaven and earth were on fire.

The silence was awful in its wild and terrible majesty. Infinity, immensity, closed in upon the soul from every side. Not a cloud in the sky, not a breath in the air, not a flaw on the bosom of the sand, ever moving in diminutive waves; the horizon ended as at sea on a clear day, with one line of light, definite as the cut of a sword.

The Provençal threw his arms around the trunk of one of the palm trees, as though it were the body of a friend, and then in the shelter of the thin straight shadow that the palm cast upon the granite, he wept. Then sitting down he remained as he was, contemplating with profound sadness the implacable scene, which was all he had to look upon. He cried aloud, to measure the solitude. His voice, lost in the hollows of the hill, sounded faintly, and aroused no echo—the echo was in his own heart. The Provençal was twenty-two years old; he loaded his carbine.

"There'll be time enough," he said to himself, laying on the ground the weapon which alone could bring him deliverance.

Looking by turns at the black expanse and the blue expanse, the soldier dreamed of France—he smelled with delight the gutters of Paris—he remembered the towns through which he had passed, the faces of his fellow soldiers, the most minute details of his life. His southern fancy soon showed him the

stones of his beloved Provence, in the play of the heat which waved over the spread sheet of the desert. Fearing the danger of this cruel mirage, he went down the opposite side of the hill to that by which he had come up the day before. The remains of a rug showed that this place of refuge had at one time been inhabited; at a short distance he saw some palm trees full of dates. Then the instinct which binds us to life awoke again in his heart. He hoped to live long enough to await the passing of some Arabs, or perhaps he might hear the sound of cannon; for at this time Bonaparte was traversing Egypt.

This thought gave him new life. The palm tree seemed to bend with the weight of the ripe fruit. He shook some of it down. When he tasted this unhoped-for manna, he felt sure that the palms had been cultivated by a former inhabitant—the savory, fresh meat of the dates was proof of the care of his predecessor. He passed suddenly from dark despair to an almost insane joy. He went up again to the top of the hill, and spent the rest of the day in cutting down one of the sterile palm trees, which the night before had served him for shelter. A vague memory made him think of the animals of the desert; and in case they might come to drink at the spring, visible from the base of the rocks but lost farther down, he resolved to guard himself from their visits by placing a barrier at the entrance of his hermitage.

In spite of his diligence, and the strength which the fear of being devoured asleep gave him, he was unable to cut the palm in pieces, though he succeeded in cutting it down. At eventide the king of the desert fell; the sound of its fall resounded far and wide, like a sign in the solitude; the soldier shuddered as though he had heard some voice predicting woe.

But like an heir who does not long bewail a deceased parent, he tore off from this beautiful tree the tall broad green leaves which are its poetic adornment, and used them to mend the mat on which he was to sleep.

Fatigued by the heat and his work, he fell asleep under the red curtains of his wet cave.

In the middle of the night his sleep was troubled by an extraordinary noise; he sat up, and the deep silence around him allowed him to distinguish the alternative accents of a respiration whose savage energy could not belong to a human creature.

A profound terror, increased still further by the darkness, the silence, and his waking images, froze his heart within him. He almost felt his hair stand on end, when by straining his eyes to their utmost he perceived through the shadows two faint yellow lights. At first he attributed these lights to the reflection of his own pupils, but soon the vivid brilliance of the night aided him gradually to distinguish the objects around him in the cave, and he beheld a huge animal lying but two steps from him. Was it a lion, a tiger, or a crocodile?

The Provençal was not educated enough to know under what species his enemy ought to be classed; but his fright was all the greater, as his ignorance led him to imagine all terrors at once; he endured a cruel torture, noting every variation of the breathing close to him without daring to make the slightest movement. An odor, pungent like that of a fox, but more penetrating, profounder—

so to speak—filled the cave, and when the Provençal became sensible of this, his terror reached its height, for he could not longer doubt the proximity of a terrible companion, whose royal dwelling served him for shelter.

Presently the reflection of the moon, descending on the horizon, lit up the den, rendering gradually visible and resplendent the spotted skin of a panther.

This lion of Egypt slept, curled up like a big dog, the peaceful possessor of a sumptuous niche at the gate of a hotel; its eyes opened for a moment and closed again; its face was turned toward the man. A thousand confused thoughts passed through the Frenchman's mind; first he thought of killing it with a bullet from his gun, but he saw there was not enough distance between them for him to take proper aim—the shot would miss the mark. And if it were to wake!—the thought made his limbs rigid. He listened to his own heart beating in the midst of the silence, and cursed the too violent pulsations which the flow of blood brought on, fearing to disturb that sleep which allowed him time to think of some means of escape.

Twice he placed his hand on his scimitar, intending to cut off the head of his enemy; but the difficulty of cutting stiff, short hair compelled him to abandon this daring project. To miss would be to die for *certain,* he thought; he preferred the chances of fair fight, and made up his mind to wait till morning; the morning did not leave him long to wait.

He could now examine the panther at ease; its muzzle was smeared with blood.

"She's had a good dinner," he thought, without troubling himself as to whether her feast might have been on human flesh. "She won't be hungry when she gets up."

It was a female. The fur on her belly and flanks was glistening white; many small marks like velvet formed beautiful bracelets round her feet; her sinuous tail was also white, ending with black rings; the over-part of her dress, yellow like un-burnished gold, very lissome and soft, had the characteristic blotches in the form of rosettes which distinguish the panther from every other feline species.

This tranquil and formidable hostess snored in an attitude as graceful as that of a cat lying on a cushion. Her bloodstained paws, nervous and well armed, were stretched out before her face, which rested upon them, and from which radiated her straight, slender whiskers, like threads of silver.

If she had been like that in a cage, the Provençal would doubtless have admired the grace of the animal, and the vigorous contrasts of vivid color which gave her robe an imperial splendor; but just then his sight was troubled by her sinister appearance.

The presence of the panther, even asleep, could not fail to produce the effect which the magnetic eyes of the serpent are said to have on the nightingale.

For a moment the courage of the soldier began to fail before this danger, though no doubt it would have risen at the mouth of a cannon charged with shell. Nevertheless, a bold thought brought daylight in his soul and sealed up the source of the cold sweat which sprang forth on his brow. Like men driven to bay who defy death and offer their body to the smiter, so he, seeing in this

merely a tragic episode, resolved to play his part with honor to the last.

"The day before yesterday the Arabs would have killed me per-haps," he said; so considering him-self as good as dead already, he waited bravely, with excited curi-osity, his enemy's awakening.

When the sun appeared, the panther suddenly opened her eyes; then she put out her paws with energy, as if to stretch them and get rid of cramp. At last she yawned, showing the formidable apparatus of her teeth and pointed tongue, rough as a file.

"A regular *petite maîtresse*," thought the Frenchman, seeing her roll herself about so softly and coquettishly. She licked off the blood which stained her paws and muzzle, and scratched her head with re-iterated gestures full of prettiness. "All right, make a little toilet," the Frenchman said to himself, begin-ning to recover his gaiety with his courage; "we'll say good morning to each other presently," and he seized the small, short dagger which he had taken from the Mangrabins. At this moment the panther turned her head toward the man and looked at him fixedly without moving.

The rigidity of her metallic eyes and their insupportable luster made him shudder, especially when the animal walked toward him. But he looked at her caressingly, staring into her eyes in order to magnetize her, and let her come quite close to him; then with a movement both gentle and amorous, as though he were caressing the most beautiful of women, he passed his hand over her whole body, from the head to the tail, scratching the flexible vertebrae which divided the panther's yellow back. The animal waved her tail voluptuously, and her eyes grew gentle; and when for the third time the Frenchman accomplished this interesting flattery, she gave forth one of those purrings by which our cats express their pleasure; but this murmur issued from a throat so powerful and so deep that it resounded through the cave like the last vibrations of an organ in a church. The man, understanding the importance of his caresses, redoubled them in such a way as to surprise and stupefy his imperious courtesan. When he felt sure of having extinguished the ferocity of his capricious companion, whose hunger had so fortunately been satisfied the day before, he got up to go out of the cave; the panther let him go out, but when he had reached the summit of the hill she sprang with the lightness of a sparrow hopping from twig to twig, and rubbed herself against his legs, putting up her back after the manner of all the race of cats. Then regarding her guest with eyes whose glare had softened a little, she gave vent to that wild cry which naturalists compare to the grating of a saw.

"She is exacting," said the Frenchman, smilingly.

He was bold enough to play with her ears; he caressed her belly and scratched her head as hard as he could.

When he saw that he was successful, he tickled her skull with the point of his dagger, watching for the right moment to kill her, but the hardness of her bones made him tremble for his success.

The sultana of the desert showed herself gracious to her slave; she lifted her head, stretched out her neck, and manifested her delight by the tranquillity of her attitude. It suddenly occurred to the soldier that to kill this savage princess with one blow he must poignard her in the throat.

He raised the blade, when the panther, satisfied no doubt, laid herself gracefully at his feet, and cast up at him glances in which, in spite of their natural fierceness, was mingled confusedly a kind of good will. The poor Provençal ate his dates, leaning against one of the palm trees, and casting his eyes alternately on the desert in quest of some liberator and on his terrible companion to watch her uncertain clemency.

The panther looked at the place where the date stones fell, and every time that he threw one down her eyes expressed an incredible mistrust.

She examined the man with an almost commercial prudence. However, this examination was favorable to him, for when he had finished his meager meal she licked his boots with her powerful rough tongue, brushing off with marvellous skill the dust gathered in the creases.

"Ah, but when she's really hungry!" thought the Frenchman. In spite of the shudder this thought caused him, the soldier began to measure curiously the proportions of the panther, certainly one of the most splendid specimens of its race. She was three feet high and four feet long without counting her tail; this powerful weapon, rounded like a cudgel, was nearly three feet long. The head, large as that of a lioness, was distinguished by a rare expression of refinement. The cold cruelty of a tiger was dominant, it was true, but there was also a vague resemblance to the face of a sensual woman. Indeed, the face of this solitary queen had something of the gaiety of a drunken Nero: she had satiated herself with blood, and she wanted to play.

The soldier tried if he might walk up and down, and the panther left him free, contenting herself with following him with her eyes, less like a faithful dog than a big Angora cat, observing everything and every movement of her master.

When he looked around, he saw, by the spring, the remains of his horse; the panther had dragged the carcass all that way; about two thirds of it had been devoured already. The sight reassured him.

It was easy to explain the panther's absence, and the respect she had had for him while he slept. The first piece of good luck emboldened him to tempt the future, and he conceived the wild hope of continuing on good terms with the panther during the entire day, neglecting no means of taming her, and remaining in her good graces.

He returned to her, and had the unspeakable joy of seeing her wag her tail with an almost imperceptible movement at his approach. He sat down then, without fear, by her side, and they began to play together; he took her paws and muzzle, pulled her ears, rolled her over on her back, stroked her warm, delicate flanks. She let him do whatever he liked, and when he began to stroke the hair on her feet she drew her claws in carefully.

The man, keeping the dagger in one hand, thought to plunge it into the belly of the too-confiding panther, but he was afraid that he would be immediately strangled in her last conclusive struggle; besides, he felt in his heart a sort of remorse which bid him respect a creature that had done him no harm. He seemed to have found a friend, in a boundless desert; half unconsciously

he thought of his first sweetheart, whom he had nicknamed "Mignonne" by way of contrast, because she was so atrociously jealous that all the time of their love he was in fear of the knife with which she had always threatened him.

This memory of his early days suggested to him the idea of making the young panther answer to this name, now that he began to admire with less terror her swiftness, suppleness, and softness. Toward the end of the day he had familiarized himself with his perilous position; he now almost liked the painfulness of it. At last his companion had got into the habit of looking up at him whenever he cried in a falsetto voice, "Mignonne."

At the setting of the sun Mignonne gave, several times running, a profound melancholy cry. "She's been well brought up," said the lighthearted soldier; "she says her prayers." But this mental joke only occurred to him when he noticed what a pacific attitude his companion remained in. "Come, *ma petite blonde*, I'll let you go to bed first," he said to her, counting on the activity of his own legs to run away as quickly as possible, directly she was asleep, and seek another shelter for the night.

The soldier waited with impatience the hour of his flight, and when it had arrived he walked vigorously in the direction of the Nile; but hardly had he made a quarter of a league in the sand when he heard the panther bounding after him, crying with that sawlike cry more dreadful even than the sound of her leaping.

"Ah!" he said, "then she's taken a fancy to me; she has never met anyone before, and it is really quite flattering to have her first love."

That instant the man fell into one of those movable quicksands so terrible to travelers and from which it is impossible to save oneself. Feeling himself caught, he gave a shriek of alarm; the panther seized him with her teeth by the collar, and, springing vigorously backward, drew him as if by magic out of the whirling sand.

"Ah, Mignonne!" cried the soldier, caressing her enthusiastically; "we're bound together for life and death—but no jokes, mind!" and he retraced his steps.

From that time the desert seemed inhabited. It contained a being to whom the man could talk, and whose ferocity was rendered gentle by him, though he could not explain to himself the reason for their strange friendship. Great as was the soldier's desire to stay upon guard, he slept.

On awakening he could not find Mignonne; he mounted the hill, and in the distance saw her springing toward him after the habit of these animals, who cannot run on account of the extreme flexibility of the vertebral column. Mignonne arrived, her jaws covered with blood; she received the wonted caress of her companion, showing with much purring how happy it made her. Her eyes, full of languor, turned still more gently than the day before toward the Provençal who talked to her as one would to a tame animal.

"Ah! Mademoiselle, you are a nice girl, aren't you? Just look at that! So we like to be made much of, don't we? Aren't you ashamed of yourself? So you have been eating some Arab or other, have you? That doesn't matter. They're animals just the same as you are; but don't you take to eating Frenchmen, or I shan't like you any longer."

She played like a dog with its master, letting herself be rolled over, knocked about, and stroked, alternately; sometimes she herself would provoke the soldier, putting up her paw with a soliciting gesture.

Some days passed in this manner. This companionship permitted the Provençal to appreciate the sublime beauty of the desert; now that he had a living thing to think about, alternations of fear and quiet, and plenty to eat, his mind became filled with contrast and his life began to be diversified.

Solitude revealed to him all her secrets, and enveloped him in her delights. He discovered in the rising and setting of the sun sights unknown to the world. He knew what it was to tremble when he heard over his head the hiss of a bird's wing, so rarely did they pass, or when he saw the clouds, changing and many-colored travelers, melt one into another. He studied in the night time the effect of the moon upon the ocean of sand, where the simoom made waves swift of movement and rapid in their change. He lived the life of the Eastern day, marveling at its wonderful pomp; then, after having reveled in the sight of a hurricane over the plain where the whirling sands made red, dry mists and death-bearing clouds, he would welcome the night with joy, for then fell the healthful freshness of the stars, and he listened to imaginary music in the skies. Then solitude taught him to unroll the treasures of dreams. He passed whole hours in remembering mere nothings, and comparing his present life with his past.

At last he grew passionately fond of the panther; for some sort of affection was a necessity.

Whether it was that his will powerfully projected had modified the character of his companion, or whether, because she found abundant food in her predatory excursions in the desert, she respected the man's life, he began to fear for it no longer, seeing her so well tamed.

He devoted the greater part of his time to sleep, but he was obliged to watch like a spider in its web that the moment of his deliverance might not escape him, if anyone should pass the line marked by the horizon. He had sacrificed his shirt to make a flag with, which he hung at the top of a palm tree, whose foliage he had torn off. Taught by necessity, he found the means of keeping it spread out, by fastening it with little sticks; for the wind might not be blowing at the moment when the passing traveler was looking through the desert.

It was during the long hours, when he had abandoned hope, that he amused himself with the panther. He had come to learn the different inflections of her voice, the expressions of her eyes; he had studied the capricious patterns of all the rosettes which marked the gold of her robe. Mignonne was not even angry when he took hold of the tuft at the end of her tail to count her rings, those graceful ornaments which glittered in the sun like jewelry. It gave him pleasure to contemplate the supple, fine outlines of her form, the whiteness of her belly, the graceful pose of her head. But it was especially when she was playing that he felt most pleasure in looking at her; the agility and youthful lightness of her movements were a continual surprise to him; he wondered at the supple way in which she jumped and climbed, washed herself and arranged her fur, crouched down and prepared to spring. However rapid her spring might be, however slippery the stone she was on, she would always stop short at the word "Mignonne."

One day, in a bright midday sun, an enormous bird coursed through the air. The man left his panther to look at this new guest; but after waiting a moment the deserted sultana growled deeply.

"My goodness! I do believe she's jealous," he cried, seeing her eyes become hard again; "the soul of Virginie has passed into her body; that's certain."

The eagle disappeared into the air, while the soldier admired the curved contour of the panther.

But there was such youth and grace in her form! she was beautiful as a woman! the blond fur of her robe mingled well with the delicate tints of faint white which marked her flanks.

The profuse light cast down by the sun made this living gold, these russet markings, to burn in a way to give them an indefinable attraction.

The man and the panther looked at one another with a look full of meaning; the coquette quivered when she felt her friend stroke her head; her eyes flashed like lightning—then she shut them tightly.

"She has a soul," he said, looking at the stillness of this queen of the sands, golden like them, white like them, solitary and burning like them.

"Well," she said, "I have read your plea in favor of beasts; but how did two so well adapted to understand each other end?"

"Ah, well! you see, they ended as all great passions do end—by a misunderstanding. For some reason *one* suspects the other of treason; they don't come to an explanation through pride, and quarrel and part from sheer obstinacy."

"Yet sometimes at the best moments a single word or a look is enough—but anyhow go on with your story."

"It's horribly difficult, but you will understand, after what the old villain told me over his champagne.

"He said—'I don't know if I hurt her, but she turned round, as if enraged, and with her sharp teeth caught hold of my leg—gently, I daresay; but I, thinking she would devour me, plunged my dagger into her throat. She rolled over, giving a cry that froze my heart; and I saw her dying, still looking at me without anger. I would have given all the world—my cross even, which I had not then—to have brought her to life again. It was as though I had murdered a real person; and the soldiers who had seen my flag, and were come to my assistance, found me in tears.'

" 'Well sir,' he said, after a moment of silence, 'since then I have been in war in Germany, in Spain, in Russia, in France; I've certainly carried my carcass about a good deal, but never have I seen anything like the desert. Ah! yes, it is very beautiful!'

" 'What did you feel there?' I asked him.

" 'Oh! that can't be described, young man. Besides, I am not always regretting my palm trees and my panther. I should have to be very melancholy for that. In the desert, you see, there is everything, and nothing.'

" 'Yes, but explain——'

" 'Well,' he said, with an impatient gesture, 'it is God without mankind.' "

Gustave Flaubert

1821-1880

LIKE BALZAC, Flaubert dedicated his life to writing. Unlike Balzac, however, in his twenty-seven years of diligent work Flaubert produced only five novels, three short stories, and two plays. "His life," said Henry James, "was that of a pearl diver, breathless in the thick element while he groped for the priceless word. . . . He passed it in reconstructing sentences, exterminating repetitions, calculating and comparing cadences. . . . The horror that haunted all his years was the horror of the cliché, the stereotyped, the things usually said. . . ." His reward was to become the most powerful artistic influence on his own and the following generation of writers. He was "the novelists' novelist."

Flaubert lived with his mother at Croisset, near Rouen, in a fine old house overlooking the Seine. It was a quiet, hard-working, sequestered existence, interrupted only when his friends came out from Paris of a Sunday afternoon to visit him. These were the great writers of a great day—George Sand, seventeen years older than he but his closest friend, Zola, Daudet, the Goncourts, Turgenev, and Maupassant, his disciple. Flaubert never married, though for several years he carried on a somewhat intellectual affair with Louise Colet, the poet, whose salon Barbey d'Aurevilly described as an "academic oyster bed." When Flaubert embarked upon *Madame Bovary*, the liaison ended, with Emma Bovary supplanting Louise.

He was an enormous man, with a head of flaming-red hair and a general appearance of robust strength. But he was never well. In later years he was almost continuously ill, the war of 1870 took further toll of his health, and he aged long before his time. "A Simple Heart," one of the *Trois Contes*, was written in these last desolate years. His mother had died, and he was ill and alone.

A Simple Heart

BY GUSTAVE FLAUBERT

I

MADAME AUBAIN's servant Félicité was the envy of the ladies of Pont-l'Évêque for half a century.

She received four pounds a year. For that she was cook and general servant, and did the sewing, washing, and ironing; she could bridle a horse, fatten poultry, and churn butter—and she remained faithful to her mistress, unamiable as the latter was.

Mme Aubain had married a gay bachelor without money who died at the beginning of 1809, leaving her with two small children and a quantity of debts. She then sold all her property except the farms of Toucques and Geffosses, which brought in two hundred pounds a year at most, and left her house in Saint-Melaine for a less expensive one that had belonged to her family and was situated behind the market.

This house had a slate roof and stood between an alley and a lane that went down to the river. There was an unevenness in the levels of the rooms which made you stumble. A narrow hall divided the kitchen from the "parlor" where Mme Aubain spent her day, sitting in a wicker easy chair by the window.

Against the panels, which were painted white, was a row of eight mahogany chairs. On an old piano under the barometer a heap of wooden and cardboard boxes rose like a pyramid. A stuffed armchair stood on either side of the Louis Quinze chimney piece, which was in yellow marble with a clock in the middle of it modeled like a temple of Vesta. The whole room was a little musty, as the floor was lower than the garden.

The first floor began with "Madame's" room: very large, with a pale-flowered wallpaper and a portrait of "Monsieur" as a dandy of the period. It led to a smaller room, where there were two children's cots without mattresses. Next came the drawing room, which was always shut up and full of furniture covered with sheets. Then there was a corridor leading to a study. The shelves of a large bookcase were respectably lined with books and papers, and its three wings surrounded a broad writing table in dark wood. The two panels at the end of the room were covered with pen drawings, water-color landscapes, and engravings by Audran, all relics of better days and vanished splendor. Félicité's room on the top floor got its light from a dormer window, which looked over the meadows.

She rose at daybreak to be in time for Mass, and worked till evening without stopping. Then, when dinner was over, the plates and dishes in order, and the door shut fast, she thrust the log under the ashes and went to sleep in front of the hearth with her rosary in her hand. Félicité was the stubbornest of all bargainers; and as for cleanness, the polish on her saucepans was the despair of other servants. Thrifty in all things, she ate slowly, gathering off the table in her fingers the crumbs of her loaf—a twelve-pound loaf expressly baked for her, which lasted for three weeks.

At all times of year she wore a print handkerchief fastened with a pin behind, a bonnet that covered her hair, gray stockings, a red skirt, and a bibbed apron—such as hospital nurses wear—over her jacket.

Her face was thin and her voice sharp. At twenty-five she looked like forty. From fifty onwards she seemed of no particular age; and with her silence, straight figure, and precise movements she was like a woman made of wood, and going by clockwork.

II

She had had her love story like another.

Her father, a mason, had been killed by falling off some scaffolding. Then her mother died, her sisters scattered, and a farmer took her in and employed her, while she was still quite little, to herd the cows at pasture. She shivered in rags and would lie flat on the ground to drink water from the ponds; she was beaten for nothing, and finally turned out for the theft of a shilling which she did not steal. She went to another farm, where she became dairymaid; and as she was liked by her employers her companions were jealous of her.

One evening in August (she was then eighteen) they took her to the assembly at Colleville. She was dazed and stupefied in an instant by the noise of the fiddlers, the lights in the trees, the gay medley of dresses, the lace, the gold crosses, and the throng of people jigging all together. While she kept shyly apart a young man with a well-to-do air, who was leaning on the shaft of a cart and smoking his pipe, came up to ask her to dance. He treated her to cider, coffee, and cake, and bought her a silk handkerchief; and then, imagining she had guessed his meaning, offered to see her home. At the edge of a field of oats he pushed her roughly down. She was frightened and began to cry out; and he went off.

One evening later she was on the Beaumont road. A big hay wagon was moving slowly along; she wanted to get in front of it, and as she brushed past the wheels she recognized Theodore. He greeted her quite calmly, saying she must excuse it all because it was "the fault of the drink." She could not think of any answer and wanted to run away.

He began at once to talk about the harvest and the worthies of the commune, for his father had left Colleville for the farm at Les Écots, so that now he and she were neighbors. "Ah!" she said. He added that they thought of settling him in life. Well, he was in no hurry; he was waiting for a wife to his fancy. She dropped her head; and then he asked her if she thought of marrying. She answered with a smile that it was meant to make fun of her.

"But I am not, I swear!"—and he passed his left hand round her waist.

She walked in the support of his embrace; their steps grew slower. The wind was soft, the stars glittered, the huge wagonload of hay swayed in front of them, and dust rose from the dragging steps of the four horses. Then, without a word of command, they turned to the right. He clasped her once more in his arms, and she disappeared into the shadow.

The week after Theodore secured some assignations with her.

They met at the end of farmyards, behind a wall, or under a solitary tree. She was not innocent as young ladies are—she had learned knowledge from the animals—but her reason and the instinct of her honor would not let her fall. Her resistance exasperated Theodore's passion; so much so that to satisfy it—or perhaps quite artlessly—he made her an offer of marriage. She was in doubt whether to trust him, but he swore great oaths of fidelity.

Soon he confessed to something troublesome; the year before his parents had bought him a substitute for the army, but any day he might be taken again, and the idea of serving was a terror to him. Félicité took this cowardice of his as a sign of affection, and it redoubled hers. She stole away at night to see him, and when she reached their meeting place Theodore racked her with his anxieties and urgings.

At last he declared that he would go himself to the prefecture for information, and would tell her the result on the following Sunday, between eleven and midnight.

When the moment came she sped toward her lover. Instead of him she found one of his friends.

He told her that she would not see Theodore any more. To ensure himself against conscription he had married an old woman, Madame Lehoussais, of Toucques, who was very rich.

There was an uncontrollable burst of grief. She threw herself on the ground, screamed, called to the God of mercy, and moaned by herself in the fields till daylight came. Then she came back to the farm and announced that she was going to leave; and at the end of the month she received her wages, tied all her small belongings with a handkerchief, and went to Pont-l'Évêque.

In front of the inn there she made inquiries of a woman in a widow's cap, who, as it happened, was just looking for a cook. The girl did not know much, but her willingness seemed so great and her demands so small that Mme Aubain ended by saying:

"Very well, then, I will take you."

A quarter of an hour afterwards Félicité was installed in her house.

She lived there at first in a tremble, as it were, at "the style of the house" and the memory of "Monsieur" floating over it all. Paul and Virginie, the first aged seven and the other hardly four, seemed to her beings of a precious substance; she carried them on her back like a horse; it was a sorrow to her that Mme Aubain would not let her kiss them every minute. And yet she was happy there. Her grief had melted in the pleasantness of things all round.

Every Thursday regular visitors came in for a game of boston, and Félicité got the cards and footwarmers ready beforehand. They arrived punctually at eight and left before the stroke of eleven.

On Monday mornings the dealer who lodged in the covered passage spread out all his old iron on the ground. Then a hum of voices began to fill the town, mingled with the neighing of horses, bleating of lambs, grunting of pigs, and the sharp rattle of carts along the street. About noon, when the market was at its height, you might see a tall, hook-nosed old countryman with his cap pushed back making his appearance at the door. It was Robelin, the farmer of Geffosses. A little later came Liébard, the farmer from Toucques—short, red, and corpulent —in a gray jacket and gaiters shod with spurs.

Both had poultry or cheese to offer their landlord. Félicité was invariably a match for their cunning and they went away filled with respect for her.

At vague intervals Mme Aubain had a visit from the Marquis de Gremanville, one of her uncles, who had ruined himself by debauchery and now lived at Falaise on his last remaining morsel of land. He invariably came at the luncheon hour, with a dreadful poodle whose paws left all the furniture in a mess. In spite of efforts to show his breeding, which he carried to the point of raising his hat every time he mentioned "my late father," habit was too strong for him; he poured himself out glass after glass and fired off improper remarks. Félicité edged him politely out of the house—"You have had enough, Monsieur de Gremanville! Another time!"—and she shut the door on him.

She opened it with pleasure to M. Bourais, who had been a lawyer. His boldness, his white stock, frilled shirt, and roomy brown coat, his way of rounding the arm as he took snuff —his whole person, in fact, created that disturbance of mind which overtakes us at the sight of extraordinary men.

As he looked after the property of "Madame" he remained shut up with her for hours in "Monsieur's" study, though all the time he was afraid of compromising himself. He respected the magistracy immensely, and had some pretensions to Latin.

To combine instruction and amusement he gave the children a geography book made up of a series of prints. They represented scenes in different parts of the world: cannibals with feathers on their heads, a monkey carrying off a young lady, Bedouins in the desert, the harpooning of a whale, and so on. Paul explained these engravings to Félicité; and that, in fact, was the whole of her literary education. The children's education was undertaken by Guyot, a poor creature employed at the town hall, who was famous for his beautiful hand and sharpened his penknife on his boots.

When the weather was bright the household set off early for a day at Geffosses Farm.

Its courtyard is on a slope, with the farmhouse in the middle, and the sea looks like a gray streak in the distance.

Félicité brought slices of cold meat out of her basket, and they breakfasted in a room adjoining the dairy. It was the only surviving fragment of a country house which was now no more. The wallpaper hung in tatters, and quivered in the drafts. Mme Aubain sat with bowed head, overcome by her memories; the children became afraid to speak. "Why don't you play, then?" she would say, and off they went.

Paul climbed into the barn, caught birds, played at ducks and drakes over the pond, or hammered with his stick on the big casks which boomed like drums. Virginie fed the rabbits or dashed off to pick cornflowers, her quick legs showing their embroidered little drawers.

One autumn evening they went home by the fields. The moon was in its first quarter, lighting part of the sky; and mist floated like a scarf over the windings of the Toucques. Cattle, lying out in the middle of the grass, looked quietly at the four people as they passed. In the third meadow some of them got up and made a half circle in front of the walkers. "There's nothing to be afraid of," said Félicité, as she stroked the nearest on the back with a kind of crooning song; he wheeled round and others did the same. But when they crossed the next pasture there was a formidable bellow. It was a bull, hidden by the mist. Mme Aubain was about to run. "No! no! don't go so fast!" They mended their pace, however, and heard a loud breathing behind them which came nearer. His hoofs thudded on the meadow grass like hammers; why, he was galloping now! Félicité turned round, and tore up clods of earth with both hands and threw them in his eyes. He lowered his muzzle, waved his horns, and quivered with fury, bellowing terribly. Mme Aubain, now at the end of the pasture with her two little ones, was looking wildly for a place to get over the high bank. Félicité was retreating, still with her face to the bull, keeping up a shower of clods which blinded him, and crying all the time, "Be quick! be quick!"

Mme Aubain went down into the ditch, pushed Virginie first and then Paul, fell several times as she tried to climb the bank, and managed it at last by dint of courage.

The bull had driven Félicité to bay against a rail fence; his slaver was streaming into her face; another second, and he would have gored her. She had just time to slip between two of the rails and the big animal stopped short in amazement.

This adventure was talked of at Pont-l'Évêque for many a year. Félicité did not pride herself on it in the least, not having the barest suspicion that she had done anything heroic.

Virginie was the sole object of her thoughts, for the child developed a nervous complaint as a result of her fright, and M. Poupart, the doctor, advised seabathing at Trouville. It was not a frequented place then. Mme Aubain collected information, consulted Bourais, and made preparations as though for a long journey.

Her luggage started a day in advance, in Liébard's cart. The next day he brought round two horses, one of which had a lady's saddle with a velvet back to it, while a cloak was rolled up to make a kind of seat on the crupper of the other. Mme Aubain rode on that, behind the farmer. Félicité took charge of Virginie, and Paul mounted M. Lechaptois' donkey, lent on condition that great care was taken of it.

The road was so bad that its five miles took two hours. The horses sank in the mud up to their pasterns, and their haunches jerked abruptly in the effort to get out; or else they stumbled in the ruts, and at other moments had to jump. In some places Liébard's mare came suddenly to a halt. He waited patiently until she went on again, talking about the people who had properties along the road, and adding moral reflections to their history. So it was that as they were in the middle of Toucques, and passed under some windows bowered with nasturtiums, he shrugged his shoulders and said:

"There's a Mme Lehoussais lives there; instead of taking a young man she . . ." Félicité did not hear the rest; the horses were trotting and the donkey galloping. They all turned down a bypath; a gate swung open and two boys appeared; and the party dismounted in front of a manure heap at the very threshold of the farmhouse door.

When Mme Liébard saw her mistress she gave lavish signs of joy. She served her a luncheon with a sirloin of beef, tripe, black pudding, a fricassee of chicken, sparkling cider, a fruit tart, and brandied plums; seasoning it all with compliments to Madame, who seemed in better health; Mademoiselle, who was "splendid" now; and Monsieur Paul, who had "filled out" wonderfully. Nor did she forget their deceased grandparents, whom the Liébards had known, as they had been in the service of the family for several generations. The farm, like them, had the stamp of antiquity. The beams on the ceiling were worm-eaten, the walls blackened with smoke, and the windowpanes gray with dust. There was an oak dresser laden with every sort of useful article—jugs, plates, pewter bowls, wolftraps, and sheep shears; and a huge syringe made the children laugh. There was not a tree in the three courtyards without mushrooms growing at the bottom of it or a tuft of mistletoe on its boughs. Several of them had been thrown down by the wind. They had taken root again at the middle; and all were bending under their wealth of apples. The thatched roofs, like brown velvet and of varying thickness, withstood the heaviest squalls. The cart shed, however, was falling into ruin. Mme Aubain said she would see about it, and ordered the animals to be saddled again.

It was another half-hour before they reached Trouville. The little caravan dismounted to pass Écores —it was an overhanging cliff with boats below it—and three minutes later they were at the end of the quay and entered the courtyard of the Golden Lamb, kept by good Mme David.

From the first days of their stay Virginie began to feel less weak, thanks to the change of air and the effect of the sea baths. These, for want of a bathing dress, she took in her chemise; and her nurse dressed her afterwards in a coastguard's cabin which was used by the bathers.

In the afternoons they took the donkey and went off beyond the Black Rocks, in the direction of Hennequeville. The path climbed at first through ground with dells in it like the green sward of a park, and then reached a plateau where grass fields and arable lay side by side. Hollies rose stiffly out of the briary tangle at the edge of the road; and here and there a great withered tree made zigzags in the blue air with its branches.

They nearly always rested in a meadow, with Deauville on their left, Havre on their right, and the open sea in front. It glittered in the sunshine, smooth as a mirror and so quiet that its murmur was scarcely to be heard; sparrows chirped in hiding and the immense sky arched over it all. Mme Aubain sat doing her needlework; Virginie plaited rushes by her side; Félicité pulled up lavender, and Paul was bored and anxious to start home.

Other days they crossed the Toucques in a boat and looked for shells. When the tide went out sea urchins, starfish, and jellyfish were left exposed; and the children ran in pursuit of the foam flakes which scudded in the wind. The sleepy waves broke on the sand and unrolled all along the beach; it stretched away out of sight, bounded on the land side by the dunes which parted it from the Marsh, a wide meadow shaped like an arena. As they came home that way, Trouville, on the hill slope in the background, grew bigger at every step, and its miscellaneous throng of houses seemed to break into a gay disorder.

On days when it was too hot they did not leave their room. From the dazzling brilliance outside light fell in streaks between the laths of the blinds. There were no sounds in the village; and on the pavement below not a soul. This silence round them deepened the quietness of things. In the distance, where men were calking, there was a tap of hammers as they plugged the hulls, and a sluggish breeze wafted up the smell of tar.

The chief amusement was the return of the fishing boats. They began to tack as soon as they had passed the buoys. The sails came down on two of the three masts; and they drew on with the foresail swelling like a balloon, glided through the splash of the waves, and when they had reached the middle of the harbor suddenly dropped anchor. Then the boats drew up against the quay. The sailors threw quivering fish over the side; a row of carts was waiting, and women in cotton bonnets darted out to take the baskets and give their men a kiss.

One of them came up to Félicité one day, and she entered the lodgings a little later in a state of delight. She had found a sister again—and then Nastasie Barette, "wife of Le-roux," appeared, holding an infant at her breast and another child with her right hand, while on her left was a little cabin boy with his hands on his hips and a cap over his ear.

After a quarter of an hour Mme Aubain sent them off; but they were always to be found hanging about the kitchen, or encountered in the course of a walk. The husband never appeared.

Félicité was seized with affection for them. She bought them a blanket, some shirts, and a stove; it was clear that they were making a good thing out of her. Mme Aubain was annoyed by this weakness of hers, and she did not like the liberties taken by the nephew, who said "thee" and "thou" to Paul. So as Virginie was coughing and the fine weather gone, she returned to Pont-l'Évêque.

There M. Bourais enlightened her on the choice of a boys' school. The one at Caen was reputed to be the best, and Paul was sent to it. He said his good-bys bravely, content enough at going to live in a house where he would have companions.

Mme Aubain resigned herself to her son's absence as a thing that had to be. Virginie thought about it less and less. Félicité missed the noise he made. But she found an occupation to distract her; from Christmas onward she took the little girl to catechism every day.

III

After making a genuflexion at the door she walked up between the double row of chairs under the lofty nave, opened Mme Aubain's pew, sat down, and began to look about her. The choir stalls were filled with the boys on the right and the girls on the left, and the curé stood by the lectern. On a painted window in the apse the Holy Ghost looked down upon the Virgin. Another window showed her on her knees before the child Jesus, and a group carved in wood behind the altar shrine represented St. Michael overthrowing the dragon.

The priest began with a sketch of sacred history. The Garden, the Flood, the Tower of Babel, cities in flames, dying nations, and overturned idols passed like a dream before her eyes; and the dizzying vision left her with reverence for the Most High and fear of His wrath. Then she wept at the story of the Passion. Why had they crucified Him, when He loved the children, fed the multitudes, healed the blind, and had willed, in His meekness, to be born among the poor, on the dung heap of a stable? The sowings, harvests, wine presses, all the familiar things the Gospel speaks of, were a part of her life. They had been made holy by God's passing; and she loved the lambs more tenderly for her love of the Lamb, and the doves because of the Holy Ghost.

She found it hard to imagine Him in person, for He was not merely a bird, but a flame as well, and a breath at other times. It may be His light, she thought, which flits at night about the edge of the marshes, His breathing which drives on the clouds, His voice which gives harmony to the bells; and she would sit rapt in adoration, enjoying the cool walls and the quiet of the church.

Of doctrines she understood nothing—did not even try to understand. The curé discoursed, the children repeated their lesson, and finally she went to sleep, waking up with a start when their wooden shoes clattered on the flagstones as they went away.

It was thus that Félicité, whose religious education had been neglected in her youth, learned the catechism by dint of hearing it; and from that time she copied all Virginie's observances, fasting as she did and confessing with her. On Corpus Christi Day they made a festal altar together.

The first communion loomed distractingly ahead. She fussed over the shoes, the rosary, the book and gloves; and how she trembled as she helped Virginie's mother to dress her!

All through the Mass she was racked with anxiety. She could not see one side of the choir because of M. Bourais; but straight in front of her was the flock of maidens, with white crowns above their hanging veils, making the impression of a field of snow; and she knew her dear child at a distance by her dainty neck and thoughtful air. The bell tinkled. The heads bowed, and there was silence. As the organ pealed, singers and congregation took up the *Agnus Dei*; then the procession of the boys began, and after them the girls rose. Step by step, with their hands joined in prayer, they went toward the lighted altar, knelt on the first step, received the sacrament in turn, and came back in the same order to their places. When Virginie's turn came Félicité leaned forward to see her; and with the imaginativeness of deep and tender feeling it seemed to her that she actually was the child; Virginie's face became hers, she was dressed in her clothes, it was her heart beating in her breast. As the moment came to open her mouth she closed her eyes and nearly fainted.

She appeared early in the sacristy

next morning for monsieur the curé to give her the communion. She took it with devotion, but it did not give her the same exquisite delight.

Mme Aubain wanted to make her daughter into an accomplished person; and as Guyot could not teach her music or English she decided to place her in the Ursuline Convent at Honfleur as a boarder. The child made no objection. Félicité sighed and thought that Madame lacked feeling. Then she reflected that her mistress might be right; matters of this kind were beyond her.

So one day an old spring van drew up at the door, and out of it stepped a nun to fetch the young lady. Félicité hoisted the luggage on to the top, admonished the driver, and put six pots of preserves, a dozen pears, and a bunch of violets under the seat.

At the last moment Virginie broke into a fit of sobbing; she threw her arms round her mother, who kissed her on the forehead, saying over and over, "Come, be brave! be brave!" The step was raised, and the carriage drove off.

Then Mme Aubain's strength gave way; and in the evening all her friends—the Lormeau family, Mme Lechaptois, the Rochefeuille ladies, M. de Houppeville, and Bourais—came in to console her.

To be without her daughter was very painful for her at first. But she heard from Virginie three times a week, wrote to her on the other days, walked in the garden, and so filled up the empty hours.

From sheer habit Félicité went into Virginie's room in the mornings and gazed at the walls. It was boredom to her not to have to comb the child's hair now, lace up her boots, tuck her into bed—and not to see her charming face perpetually and

hold her hand when they went out together. In this idle condition she tried making lace. But her fingers were too heavy and broke the threads; she could not attend to anything, she had lost her sleep, and was, in her own words, "destroyed."

To "divert herself" she asked leave to have visits from her nephew Victor.

He arrived on Sundays after Mass, rosy-cheeked, bare-chested, with the scent of the country he had walked through still about him. She laid her table promptly and they had lunch, sitting opposite each other. She ate as little as possible herself to save expense, but stuffed him with food so generously that at last he went to sleep. At the first stroke of vespers she woke him up, brushed his trousers, fastened his tie, and went to church, leaning on his arm with maternal pride.

Victor was always instructed by his parents to get something out of her—a packet of moist sugar, it might be, a cake of soap, spirits, or even money at times. He brought his things for her to mend and she took over the task, only too glad to have a reason for making him come back.

In August his father took him off on a coasting voyage. It was holiday time, and she was consoled by the arrival of the children. Paul, however, was getting selfish, and Virginie was too old to be called "thou" any longer; this put a constraint and barrier between them.

Victor went to Morlaix, Dunkirk, and Brighton in succession and made Félicité a present on his return from each voyage. It was a box made of shells the first time, a coffee cup the next, and on the third occasion a large gingerbread man. Victor was growing handsome. He was well made, had a hint of a mustache, good honest eyes, and a small leather hat pushed backwards like a pilot's. He entertained her by telling stories embroidered with nautical terms.

On a Monday, July 14, 1819 (she never forgot the date), he told her that he had signed on for the big voyage and next night but one he would take the Honfleur boat and join his schooner, which was to weigh anchor from Havre before long. Perhaps he would be gone two years.

The prospect of this long absence threw Félicité into deep distress; one more good-by she must have, and on the Wednesday evening, when Madame's dinner was finished, she put on her clogs and made short work of the twelve miles between Pont-l'Évêque and Honfleur.

When she arrived in front of the Calvary she took the turn to the right instead of the left, got lost in the timber yards, and retraced her steps; some people to whom she spoke advised her to be quick. She went all round the harbor basin, full of ships, and knocked against hawsers; then the ground fell away, lights flashed across each other, and she thought her wits had left her, for she saw horses up in the sky.

Others were neighing by the quayside, frightened at the sea. They were lifted by a tackle and deposited in a boat, where passengers jostled each other among cider casks, cheese baskets, and sacks of grain; fowls could be heard clucking, the captain swore; and a cabin boy stood leaning over the bows, indifferent to it all. Félicité, who had not recognized him, called "Victor!" and he raised his head; all at once, as she was darting forwards, the gangway was drawn back.

The Honfleur packet, women singing as they hauled it, passed out of harbor. Its framework creaked and the heavy waves whipped its bows. The canvas had swung round, no one could be seen on board now; and on the moon-silvered sea the boat made a black speck which paled gradually, dipped, and vanished.

As Félicité passed by the Calvary she had a wish to commend to God what she cherished most, and she stood there praying a long time with her face bathed in tears and her eyes toward the clouds. The town was asleep, coast guards were walking to and fro; and water poured without cessation through the hole in the sluice, with the noise of a torrent. The clocks struck two.

The convent parlor would not be open before day. If Félicité were late Madame would most certainly be annoyed; and in spite of her desire to kiss the other child she turned home. The maids at the inn were waking up as she came in to Pont-l'Évêque.

So the poor slip of a boy was going to toss for months and months at sea! She had not been frightened by his previous voyages. From England or Brittany you came back safe enough; but America, the colonies, the islands—these were lost in a dim region at the other end of the world.

Félicité's thoughts from that moment ran entirely on her nephew. On sunny days she was harassed by the idea of thirst; when there was a storm she was afraid of the lightning on his account. As she listened to the wind growling in the chimney or carrying off the slates she pictured him lashed by that same tempest, at the top of a shattered mast, with his body thrown backwards under a sheet of foam; or else (with a reminiscence of the illustrated geography) he was being eaten by savages, captured in a wood by monkeys, or dying on a desert shore. And never did she mention her anxieties.

Mme Aubain had anxieties of her own, about her daughter. The good sisters found her an affectionate but delicate child. The slightest emotion unnerved her. She had to give up the piano.

Her mother stipulated for regular letters from the convent. She lost patience one morning when the postman did not come, and walked to and fro in the parlor from her armchair to the window. It was really amazing; not a word for four days!

To console Mme Aubain by her own example Félicité remarked:

"As for me, Madame, it's six months since I heard . . ."

"From whom, pray?"

"Why . . . from my nephew," the servant answered gently.

"Oh! your nephew!" And Mme Aubain resumed her walk with a shrug of the shoulders, as much as to say: "I was not thinking of him! And what is more, it's absurd! A scamp of a cabin boy—what does he matter? . . . whereas my daughter . . . why, just think!"

Félicité, though she had been brought up on harshness, felt indignant with Madame—and then forgot. It seemed the simplest thing in the world to her to lose one's head over the little girl. For her the two children were equally important; a bond in her heart made them one, and their destinies must be the same.

She heard from the chemist that Victor's ship had arrived at Havana. He had read this piece of news in a gazette.

Cigars—they made her imagine Havana as a place where no one does anything but smoke, and there was Victor moving among the Negroes in a cloud of tobacco. Could you, she wondered, "in case you needed," return by land? What was the distance from Pont-l'Évêque? She questioned M. Bourais to find out.

He reached for his atlas and began explaining the longitudes; Félicité's consternation provoked a fine pedantic smile. Finally he marked with his pencil a black, imperceptible point in the indentations of an oval spot, and said as he did so, "Here it is." She went over the map; the maze of colored lines wearied her eyes without conveying anything; and on an invitation from Bourais to tell him her difficulty she begged him to show her the house where Victor was living. Bourais threw up his arms, sneezed, and laughed immensely: a simplicity like hers was a positive joy. And Félicité did not understand the reason; how could she when she expected, very likely, to see the actual image of her nephew—so stunted was her mind!

A fortnight afterwards Liébard came into the kitchen at market time as usual and handed her a letter from her brother-in-law. As neither of them could read she took it to her mistress.

Mme Aubain, who was counting the stitches in her knitting, put the work down by her side, broke the seal of the letter, started, and said in a low voice, with a look of meaning:

"It is bad news . . . that they have to tell you. Your nephew . . ."

He was dead. The letter said no more.

Félicité fell onto a chair, leaning her head against the wainscot; and she closed her eyelids, which suddenly flushed pink. Then with bent forehead, hands hanging, and fixed eyes, she said at intervals:

"Poor little lad! poor little lad!"

Liébard watched her and heaved sighs. Mme Aubain trembled a little. She suggested that Félicité should go to see her sister at Trouville. Félicité answered by a gesture that she had no need.

There was a silence. The worthy Liébard thought it was time for them to withdraw.

Then Félicité said:

"They don't care, not they!"

Her head dropped again; and she took up mechanically, from time to time, the long needles on her worktable.

Women passed in the yard with a barrow of dripping linen.

As she saw them through the windowpanes she remembered her washing; she had put it to soak the day before, today she must wring it out; and she left the room.

Her plank and tub were at the edge of the Toucques. She threw a pile of linen on the bank, rolled up her sleeves, and taking her wooden beater dealt lusty blows whose sound carried to the neighboring gardens. The meadows were empty, the river stirred in the wind; and down below long grasses wavered, like the hair of corpses floating in the water. She kept her grief down and was very brave until the evening; but once in her room she surrendered to it utterly, lying stretched on the mattress with her face in the pillow and her hands clenched against her temples.

Much later she heard, from the captain himself, the circumstances of Victor's end. They had bled him too much at the hospital for yellow fever. Four doctors held him at once. He had died instantly, and the chief had said:

"Bah! there goes another!"

His parents had always been brutal to him. She preferred not to see them again; and they made no advances, either because they forgot her or from the callousness of the wretchedly poor.

Virginie began to grow weaker. Tightness in her chest, coughing, continual fever, and veinings on her cheekbones betrayed some deep-seated complaint. M. Poupart had advised a stay in Provence. Mme Aubain determined on it, and would have brought her daughter home at once but for the climate of Pont-l'Évêque.

She made an arrangement with a jobmaster, and he drove her to the convent every Tuesday. There is a terrace in the garden, with a view over the Seine. Virginie took walks there over the fallen vine leaves, on her mother's arm. A shaft of sunlight through the clouds made her blink sometimes, as she gazed at the sails in the distance and the whole horizon from the castle of Tancarville to the lighthouses at Havre. Afterwards they rested in the arbor. Her mother had secured a little cask of excellent Malaga; and Virginie, laughing at the idea of getting tipsy, drank a thimbleful of it, no more.

Her strength came back visibly. The autumn glided gently away. Félicité reassured Mme Aubain. But one evening, when she had been out on a commission in the neighborhood, she found M. Poupart's gig at the door. He was in the hall, and Mme Aubain was tying her bonnet.

"Give me my foot warmer, purse, gloves! Quicker, come!"

Virginie had inflammation of the lungs; perhaps it was hopeless.

"Not yet!" said the doctor, and they both got into the carriage under whirling flakes of snow. Night was coming on and it was very cold.

Félicité rushed into the church to light a taper. Then she ran after the gig, came up with it in an hour, and jumped lightly in behind. As she hung on by the fringes a thought came into her mind: "The courtyard has not been shut up; supposing burglars got in!" And she jumped down.

At dawn next day she presented herself at the doctor's. He had come in and started for the country again. Then she waited in the inn, thinking that a letter would come by some hand or other. Finally, when it was twilight, she took the Lisieux coach.

The convent was at the end of a steep lane. When she was about halfway up it she heard strange sounds—a death bell tolling. "It is for someone else," thought Félicité, and she pulled the knocker violently.

After some minutes there was a sound of trailing slippers, the door opened ajar, and a nun appeared.

The good sister, with an air of compunction, said that "she had just passed away." On the instant the bell of St. Leonard's tolled twice as fast.

Félicité went up to the second floor.

From the doorway she saw Virginie stretched on her back, with her hands joined, her mouth open, and head thrown back under a black crucifix that leaned toward her, between curtains that hung stiffly, less pale than was her face. Mme Aubain, at the foot of the bed which she clasped with her arms, was choking with sobs of agony. The mother superior stood on the right. Three candlesticks on the chest of drawers made spots of red, and the mist came whitely through the windows. Nuns came and took Mme Aubain away.

For two nights Félicité never left the dead child. She repeated the same prayers, sprinkled holy water over the sheets, came and sat down again, and watched her. At the end of the first vigil she noticed that the face had grown yellow, the lips turned blue, the nose was sharper, and the eyes sunk in. She kissed them several times, and would not have been immensely surprised if Virginie had opened them again; to minds like hers the supernatural is quite simple. She made the girl's toilette, wrapped her in her shroud, lifted her down into her bier, put a garland on her. head, and spread out her hair. It was fair, and extraordinarily long for her age. Félicité cut off a big lock and slipped half of it into her bosom, determined that she should never part with it.

The body was brought back to Pont-l'Évêque, as Mme Aubain intended; she followed the hearse in a closed carriage.

It took another three quarters of an hour after the Mass to reach the cemetery. Paul walked in front, sobbing. M. Bourais was behind, and then came the chief residents, the women shrouded in black mantles, and Félicité. She thought of her nephew; and because she had not been able to pay these honors to him her grief was doubled, as though the one were being buried with the other.

Mme Aubain s despair was boundless. It was against God that she first rebelled, thinking it unjust of Him to have taken her daughter from her—she had never done evil and her conscience was so clear! Ah, no! —she ought to have taken Virginie off to the south. Other doctors would have saved her. She accused herself now, wanted to join her child, and broke into cries of distress in the middle of her dreams. One dream haunted her above all. Her husband, dressed as a sailor, was returning from a long voyage, and shedding tears he told her that he had been ordered to take Virginie away. Then they consulted how to hide her somewhere.

She came in once from the garden quite upset. A moment ago—and she pointed out the place—the father and daughter had appeared to her, standing side by side, and they did nothing, but they looked at her.

For several months after this she stayed inertly in her room. Félicité lectured her gently; she must live for her son's sake, and for the other, in remembrance of "her."

"Her," answered Mme Aubain, as though she were just waking up. "Ah, yes! . . . yes! . . . You do not forget her!" This was an allusion to the cemetery, where she was strictly forbidden to go.

Félicité went there every day.

Precisely at four she skirted the houses, climbed the hill, opened the gate, and came to Virginie's grave. It was a little column of pink marble with a stone underneath and a garden plot enclosed by chains. The beds were hidden under a coverlet of flowers. She watered their leaves, freshened the gravel, and knelt down to break up the earth better. When Mme Aubain was able to come there she felt a relief and a sort of consolation.

Then years slipped away, one like another, and their only episodes were the great festivals as they recurred—Easter, the Assumption, All Saints' Day. Household occurrences marked dates that were referred to afterwards. In 1825, for instance, two glaziers whitewashed the hall; in 1827 a piece of the roof fell into the courtyard and nearly killed a man. In the summer of 1828 it was Madame's turn to offer the consecrated bread; Bourais, about this time, mysteriously absented himself; and one by one the old acquaintances passed away: Guyot, Liébard, Mme Lechaptois, Robelin, and Uncle Gremanville, who had been paralyzed for a long time.

One night the driver of the mail coach announced the Revolution of July in Pont-l'Évêque. A new subprefect was appointed a few days later—Baron de Larsonnière, who had been consul in America, and brought with him, besides his wife, a sister-in-law and three young ladies, already growing up. They were to be seen about on their lawn, in loose blouses, and they had a Negro and a parrot. They paid a call on Mme Aubain which she did not fail to return. The moment they were seen in the distance Félicité ran to let her mistress know. But only one thing could really move her feelings—the letters from her son.

He was swallowed up in a tavern life and could follow no career. She paid his debts, he made new ones; and the sighs that Mme Aubain uttered as she sat knitting by the window reached Félicité at her spinning wheel in the kitchen.

They took walks together along the espaliered wall, always talking of Virginie and wondering if such and such a thing would have pleased her and what, on some occasion, she would have been likely to say.

All her small belongings filled a cupboard in the two-bedded room. Mme Aubain inspected them as seldom as she could. One summer day she made up her mind to it—and some moths flew out of the wardrobe.

Virginie's dresses were in a row underneath a shelf, on which there were three dolls, some hoops, a set of toy pots and pans, and the basin that she used. They took out her petticoats as well, and the stockings and handkerchiefs, and laid them out on the two beds before folding them up again. The sunshine lit up these poor things, bringing out their stains and the creases made by the body's movements. The air was warm and blue, a blackbird warbled, life seemed bathed in a deep sweetness. They found a little plush hat with thick, chestnut-colored pile; but it was eaten all over by moths. Félicité begged it for her own. Their eyes met fixedly and filled with tears; at last the mistress opened her arms, the servant threw herself into them, and they embraced each other, satisfying their grief in a kiss that made them equal.

It was the first time in their lives, Mme Aubain's nature not being expansive. Félicité was as grateful as though she had received a favor, and cherished her mistress from that moment with the devotion of an animal and a religious worship.

The kindness of her heart unfolded.

When she heard the drums of a marching regiment in the street she posted herself at the door with a pitcher of cider and asked the soldiers to drink. She nursed cholera patients and protected the Polish refugees; one of these even declared that he wished to marry her. They quarreled, however; for when she came back from the Angelus one morning she found that he had got into her kitchen and made himself a vinegar salad which he was quietly eating.

After the Poles came Father Colmiche, an old man who was supposed to have committed atrocities in '93. He lived by the side of the river in the ruins of a pigsty. The little boys watched him through the cracks in the wall, and threw pebbles at him which fell on the pallet where he lay constantly shaken by a catarrh; his hair was very long, his eyes inflamed, and there was a tumor on his arm bigger than his head. She got him some linen and tried to clean up his miserable hole; her dream was to establish him in the bakehouse, without letting him annoy Madame. When the tumor burst she dressed it every day; sometimes she brought him cake, and would put him in the sunshine on a truss of straw. The poor old man, slobbering and trembling, thanked her in his worn-out voice, was terrified that he might lose her, and stretched out his hands when he saw her go away. He died; and she had a Mass said for the repose of his soul.

That very day a great happiness befell her; just at dinnertime appeared Mme de Larsonnière's Negro, carrying the parrot in its cage, with perch, chain, and padlock. A note from the baroness informed Mme Aubain that her husband had been raised to a prefecture and they were starting that evening; she begged her to accept the bird as a memento and mark of her regard.

For a long time he had absorbed Félicité's imagination, because he came from America; and that name reminded her of Victor, so much so that she made inquiries of the Negro. She had once gone so far as to say "How Madame would enjoy having him!"

The Negro repeated the remark to his mistress; and as she could not take the bird away with her she chose this way of getting rid of him.

IV

His name was Loulou. His body was green and the tips of his wings rose-pink; his forehead was blue and his throat golden.

But he had the tiresome habits of biting his perch, tearing out his feathers, sprinkling his dirt about, and spattering the water of his tub. He annoyed Mme Aubain, and she gave him to Félicité for good.

She endeavored to train him; soon he could repeat, "Nice boy! Your servant, sir! Good morning, Marie!" He was placed by the side of the door, and astonished several people by not answering to the name Jacquot, for all parrots are called Jacquot. People compared him to a turkey and a log of wood, and stabbed Félicité to the heart each time. Strange obstinacy on Loulou's part!—directly you looked at him he refused to speak.

None the less he was eager for society; for on Sundays, while the Rochefeuille ladies, M. de Houppeville, and new familiars—Onfroy the apothecary, Monsieur Varin, and Captain Mathieu—were playing their game of cards, he beat the windows with his wings and threw himself about so frantically that they could not hear each other speak.

Bourais' face, undoubtedly, struck him as extremely droll. Directly he saw it he began to laugh—and laugh with all his might. His peals rang through the courtyard and were repeated by the echo; the neighbors came to their windows and laughed too; while M. Bourais, gliding along under the wall to escape the parrot's eye, and hiding his profile with his hat, got to the river and then entered by the garden gate. There was a lack of tenderness in the looks which he darted at the bird.

Loulou had been slapped by the butcher boy for making so free as to plunge his head into his basket; and since then he was always trying to nip him through his shirt. Fabu threatened to wring his neck, although he was not cruel, for all his tattooed arms and large whiskers. Far from it; he really rather liked the parrot, and in a jovial humor even wanted to teach him to swear. Félicité, who was alarmed by such proceedings, put the bird in the kitchen. His little chain was taken off and he roamed about the house.

His way of going downstairs was to lean on each step with the curve of his beak, raise the right foot, and then the left; and Félicité was afraid that these gymnastics brought on fits of giddiness. He fell ill and could not talk or eat any longer. There was a growth under his tongue, such as fowls have sometimes. She cured him by tearing the pellicle off with her fingernails. M. Paul was thoughtless enough one day to blow some cigar smoke into his nostrils, and another time when Mme Lormeau was teasing him with the end of her umbrella he snapped at the ferrule. Finally he got lost.

Félicité had put him on the grass to refresh him, and gone away for a minute, and when she came back— no sign of the parrot! She began by looking for him in the shrubs, by the waterside, and over the roofs, without listening to her mistress's cries of "Take care, do! You are out of your wits!" Then she investigated all the gardens in Pont-l'Évêque, and stopped the passers-by. "You don't ever happen to have seen my parrot, by any chance, do you?" And she gave a description of the parrot to those who did not know him. Suddenly, behind the mills at the foot of the hill she thought she could make out something green that fluttered. But on the top of the hill there was nothing. A hawker assured her that he had come across the parrot just before, at Saint-Melaine, in Mère Simon's shop. She rushed there; they had no idea of what she meant. At last she came home exhausted, with her slippers in shreds and despair in her soul; and as she was sitting in the middle of the garden seat at Madame's side, telling the whole story of her efforts, a light weight dropped on to her shoulder—it was Loulou! What on earth had he been doing? Taking a walk in the neighborhood, perhaps!

She had some trouble in recovering from this, or rather never did recover. As the result of a chill she had an attack of quinsy, and soon afterwards an earache. Three years later she was deaf; and she spoke very loud, even in church. Though Félicité's sins might have been published in every corner of the diocese without dishonor to her or scandal to anybody, his reverence the priest thought it right now to hear her confession in the sacristy only.

Imaginary noises in the head completed her upset. Her mistress often said to her, "Heavens! how stupid you are!" "Yes, Madame," she replied, and looked about for something.

Her little circle of ideas grew still narrower; the peal of church bells and the lowing of cattle ceased to exist for her. All living beings moved as silently as ghosts. One sound only reached her ears now—the parrot's voice.

Loulou, as though to amuse her, reproduced the click-clack of the turnspit, the shrill call of a man selling fish, and the noise of the saw in the joiner's house opposite; when the bell rang he imitated Mme Aubain's "Félicité! the door! the door!"

They carried on conversations, he endlessly reciting the three phrases in his repertory, to which she replied with words that were just as disconnected but uttered what was in her heart. Loulou was almost a son and a lover to her in her isolated state. He climbed up her fingers, nibbled at her lips, and clung to her kerchief; and when she bent her forehead and shook her head gently to and fro, as nurses do, the great wings of her bonnet and the bird's wings quivered together.

When the clouds massed and the thunder rumbled Loulou broke into cries, perhaps remembering the downpour in his native forests. The streaming rain made him absolutely mad; he fluttered wildly about, dashed up to the ceiling, upset everything, and went out through the window to dabble in the garden; but he was back quickly to perch on one of the firedogs and hopped about to dry himself, exhibiting his tail and his beak in turn.

One morning in the terrible winter of 1837 she had put him in front of the fireplace because of the cold. She found him dead, in the middle of his cage: head downwards, with his claws in the wires. He had died from congestion, no doubt. But Félicité thought he had been poisoned with parsley, and though there was no proof of any kind her suspicions inclined to Fabu.

She wept so piteously that her mistress said to her, "Well, then, have him stuffed!"

She asked advice from the chemist, who had always been kind to the parrot. He wrote to Havre, and a person called Fallacher undertook the business. But as parcels sometimes got lost in the coach she decided to take the parrot as far as Honfleur herself.

Along the sides of the road were leafless apple trees, one after the other. Ice covered the ditches. Dogs barked about the farms; and Félicité, with her hands under her cloak, her little black sabots and her basket, walked briskly in the middle of the road.

She crossed the forest, passed High Oak, and reached St. Gatien.

A cloud of dust rose behind her, and in it a mail coach, carried away by the steep hill, rushed down at full gallop like a hurricane. Seeing this woman who would not get out of the way, the driver stood up in front and the postilion shouted too. He could not hold in his four horses, which increased their pace, and the two leaders were grazing her when he threw them to one side with a jerk of the reins. But he was wild with rage, and lifting his arm as he passed at full speed, gave her such a lash from waist to neck with his big whip that she fell on her back.

Her first act, when she recovered consciousness, was to open her basket. Loulou was happily none the worse. She felt a burn in her right cheek, and when she put her hands against it they were red; the blood was flowing.

She sat down on a heap of stones and bound up her face with her handkerchief. Then she ate a crust of bread which she had put in the basket as a precaution, and found a consolation for her wound in gazing at the bird.

When she reached the crest of Ecquemauville she saw the Honfleur lights sparkling in the night sky like a company of stars; beyond, the sea stretched dimly. Then a faintness overtook her and she stopped; her wretched childhood, the disillusion of her first love, her nephew's going away, and Virginie's death all came back to her at once like the waves of an oncoming tide, rose to her throat, and choked her.

Afterwards, at the boat, she made a point of speaking to the captain, begging him to take care of the parcel, though she did not tell him what was in it.

Fellacher kept the parrot a long time. He was always promising it for the following week. After six months he announced that a packing case had started, and then nothing more was heard of it. It really seemed as though Loulou was never coming back. "Ah, they have stolen him!" she thought.

He arrived at last, and looked superb. There he was, erect upon a branch which screwed into a mahogany socket, with a foot in the air and his head on one side, biting a nut which the bird stuffer—with a taste for impressiveness—had gilded.

Félicité shut him up in her room. It was a place to which few people were admitted, and held so many religious objects and miscellaneous things that it looked like a chapel and bazaar in one.

A big cupboard impeded you as you opened the door. Opposite the window commanding the garden a little round one looked into the court; there was a table by the folding bed with a water jug, two combs, and a cube of blue soap in a chipped plate. On the walls hung rosaries, medals, several benign Virgins, and a holy-water vessel made out of coconut; on the chest of drawers, which was covered with a cloth like an altar, was the shell box that Victor had given her, and after that a watering can, a toy balloon, exercise books, the illustrated geography, and a pair of young lady's boots; and, fastened by its ribbons to the nail of the looking glass, hung the little plush hat! Félicité carried observances of this kind so far as to keep one of Monsieur's frock coats. All the old rubbish which Mme Aubain did not want any longer she laid hands on for her room. That was why there were artificial flowers along the edge of the chest of drawers and a portrait of the Comte d'Artois in the little window recess.

With the aid of a bracket Loulou was established over the chimney, which jutted into the room. Every morning when she woke up she saw him there in the dawning light, and recalled old days and the smallest details of insignificant acts in a deep quietness which knew no pain.

Holding, as she did, no communication with anyone, Félicité lived as insensibly as if she were walking in her sleep. The Corpus Christi processions roused her to life again. Then she went round begging mats and candlesticks from the neighbors to decorate the altar they put up in the street.

In church she was always gazing at the Holy Ghost in the window, and observed that there was something of the parrot in him. The likeness was still clearer, she thought, on a crude color print representing the baptism of Our Lord. With his purple wings and emerald body he was the very image of Loulou.

She bought him, and hung him up instead of the Comte d'Artois, so that she could see them both together in one glance. They were linked in her thoughts; and the parrot was consecrated by his asso-

ciation with the Holy Ghost, which became more vivid to her eye and more intelligible. The Father could not have chosen to express Himself through a dove, for such creatures cannot speak; it must have been one of Loulou's ancestors, surely. And though Félicité looked at the picture while she said her prayers she swerved a little from time to time toward the parrot.

She wanted to join the Ladies of the Virgin, but Mme Aubain dissuaded her.

And then a great event loomed up before them—Paul's marriage.

He had been a solicitor's clerk to begin with, and then tried business, the Customs, the Inland Revenue, and made efforts, even, to get into the Rivers and Forests. By an inspiration from heaven he had suddenly, at thirty-six, discovered his real line—the Registrar's Office. And there he showed such marked capacity that an inspector had offered him his daughter's hand and promised him his influence.

So Paul, grown serious, brought the lady to see his mother.

She sniffed at the ways of Pont-l'Évêque, gave herself great airs, and wounded Félicité's feelings. Mme Aubain was relieved at her departure.

The week after came news of M. Bourais' death in an inn in Lower Brittany. The rumor of suicide was confirmed, and doubts arose as to his honesty. Mme Aubain studied his accounts, and soon found out the whole tale of his misdoings—embezzled arrears, secret sales of wood, forged receipts, etc. Besides that he had an illegitimate child, and "relations with a person at Dozulé."

These shameful facts distressed her greatly. In March, 1853, she was seized with a pain in the chest;

her tongue seemed to be covered with film, and leeches did not ease the difficult breathing. On the ninth evening of her illness she died, just at seventy-two.

She passed as being younger, owing to the bands of brown hair which framed her pale, pockmarked face. There were few friends to regret her, for she had a stiffness of manner which kept people at a distance.

But Félicité mourned for her as one seldom mourns for a master. It upset her ideas and seemed contrary to the order of things, impossible and monstrous, that Madame should die before her.

Ten days afterwards, which was the time it took to hurry there from Besançon, the heirs arrived. The daughter-in-law ransacked the drawers, chose some furniture, and sold the rest; and then they went back to their registering.

Madame's armchair, her small round table, her foot warmer, and the eight chairs were gone! Yellow patches in the middle of the panels showed where the engravings had hung. They had carried off the two little beds and the mattresses, and all Virginie's belongings had disappeared from the cupboard. Félicité went from floor to floor dazed with sorrow.

The next day there was a notice on the door, and the apothecary shouted in her ear that the house was for sale.

She tottered, and was obliged to sit down. What distressed her most of all was to give up her room, so suitable as it was for poor Loulou. She enveloped him with a look of anguish when she was imploring the Holy Ghost, and formed the idolatrous habit of kneeling in front of the parrot to say her prayers. Some-

times the sun shone in at the attic window and caught his glass eye, and a great luminous ray shot out of it and put her in an ecstasy.

She had a pension of fifteen pounds a year which her mistress had left her. The garden gave her a supply of vegetables. As for clothes, she had enough to last her to the end of her days, and she economized in candles by going to bed at dusk.

She hardly ever went out, as she did not like passing the dealer's shop, where some of the old furniture was exposed for sale. Since her fit of giddiness she dragged one leg; and as her strength was failing Mère Simon, whose grocery business had collapsed, came every morning to split the wood and pump water for her.

Her eyes grew feeble. The shutters ceased to be thrown open. Years and years passed, and the house was neither let nor sold.

Félicité never asked for repairs because she was afraid of being sent away. The boards on the roof rotted; her bolster was wet for a whole winter. After Easter she spat blood.

Then Mère Simon called in a doctor. Félicité wanted to know what was the matter with her. But she was too deaf to hear, and the only word which reached her was "pneumonia." It was a word she knew, and she answered softly, "Ah! like Madame," thinking it natural that she should follow her mistress.

The time for the festal shrines was coming near. The first one was always at the bottom of the hill, the second in front of the post office, and the third toward the middle of the street. There was some rivalry in the matter of this one, and the women of the parish ended by choosing Mme Aubain's courtyard.

The hard breathing and fever increased. Félicité was vexed at doing nothing for the altar. If only she could at least have put something there! Then she thought of the parrot. The neighbors objected that it would not be decent. But the priest gave her permission, which so intensely delighted her that she begged him to accept Loulou, her sole possession, when she died.

From Tuesday to Saturday, the eve of the festival, she coughed more often. By the evening her face had shriveled, her lips stuck to her gums, and she had vomitings; and at twilight next morning, feeling herself very low, she sent for a priest.

Three kindly women were round her during the extreme unction. Then she announced that she must speak to Fabu. He arrived in his Sunday clothes, by no means at his ease in the funeral atmosphere.

"Forgive me," she said, with an effort to stretch out her arm: "I thought it was you who had killed him."

What did she mean by such stories? She suspected him of murder—a man like him! He waxed indignant, and was on the point of making a row.

"There," said the woman, "she is no longer in her senses, you can see it well enough!"

Félicité spoke to shadows of her own from time to time. The women went away, and Mère Simon had breakfast. A little later she took Loulou and brought him close to Félicité with the words:

"Come, now, say good-by to him!"

Loulou was not a corpse, but the worms devoured him; one of his wings was broken, and the tow was coming out of his stomach. But she was blind now; she kissed him on the forehead and kept him close

against her cheek. Mère Simon took him back from her to put him on the altar.

V

Summer scents came up from the meadows; flies buzzed; the sun made the river glitter and heated the slates. Mère Simon came back into the room and fell softly asleep.

She woke at the noise of bells; the people were coming out from vespers. Félicité's delirium subsided. She thought of the procession and saw it as if she had been there.

All the school children, the church singers, and the firemen walked on the pavement, while in the middle of the road the verger armed with his hallebard and the beadle with a large cross advanced in front. Then came the schoolmaster, with an eye on the boys, and the sister, anxious about her little girls; three of the daintiest, with angelic curls, scattered rose petals in the air; the deacon controlled the band with outstretched arms; and two censer bearers turned back at every step toward the Holy Sacrament, which was borne by monsieur the curé, wearing his beautiful chasuble, under a canopy of dark-red velvet held up by four churchwardens. A crowd of people pressed behind, between the white cloths covering the house walls, and they reached the bottom of the hill.

A cold sweat moistened Félicité's temples. Mère Simon sponged her with a piece of linen, saying to herself that one day she would have to go that way.

The hum of the crowd increased, was very loud for an instant, and then went further away.

A fusillade shook the windowpanes. It was the postilions saluting the monstrance. Félicité rolled her eyes and said as audibly as she could: "Does he look well?" The parrot was weighing on her mind.

Her agony began. A death rattle that grew more and more convulsed made her sides heave. Bubbles of froth came at the corners of her mouth and her whole body trembled.

Soon the booming of the ophicleides, the high voices of the children, and the deep voices of the men were distinguishable. At intervals all was silent, and the tread of feet, deadened by the flowers they walked on, sounded like a flock pattering on grass.

The clergy appeared in the courtyard. Mère Simon clambered on to a chair to reach the attic window, and so looked down straight upon the shrine. Green garlands hung over the altar, which was decked with a flounce of English lace. In the middle was a small frame with relics in it; there were two orange trees at the corners, and all along stood silver candlesticks and china vases, with sunflowers, lilies, peonies, foxgloves, and tufts of hortensia. This heap of blazing color slanted from the level of the altar to the carpet which went on over the pavement; and some rare objects caught the eye. There was a silver-gilt sugar basin with a crown of violets; pendants of Alençon stone glittered on the moss, and two Chinese screens displayed their landscapes. Loulou was hidden under roses, and showed nothing but his blue forehead, like a plaque of lapis lazuli.

The churchwardens, singers, and children took their places round the three sides of the court. The priest went slowly up the steps, and placed his great, radiant golden sun upon the lace. Everyone knelt down. There was a deep silence; and the censers glided to and fro on the full swing of their chains.

An azure vapor rose up into Félicité's room. Her nostrils met it; she inhaled it sensuously, mystically; and then closed her eyes. Her lips smiled. The beats of her heart lessened one by one, vaguer each time and softer, as a fountain sinks, an echo disappears; and when she sighed her last breath she thought she saw an opening in the heavens, and a gigantic parrot hovering above her head.

Guy de Maupassant
1850-1893

WHEN the literary great were gathering at Flaubert's house, a young man, conspicuous for physique rather than culture, used to come in from rowing on the Seine to listen to the conversation. He was Guy de Maupassant, and he too wanted to write, but Flaubert saw no particular promise in him, and the others thought him only an athlete. For seven years, however, just because he happened to be a friend of Maupassant's mother, Flaubert put the young man through a severe apprenticeship, and what was the astonishment of all when Maupassant's first published story came out a masterpiece! The story was the famous "Boule de Suif" ("Ball-of-Fat").

Where Flaubert wrote a single story, Maupassant wrote a dozen. Where the master strained for a single effect, the pupil was a fountain of freedom and variety. Maupassant wrote almost three hundred short stories in ten years, rapid, concise tales, strong, brutal, often obscene. He wrote only of what he perceived through his senses—fields, bodies, clothes, food. No theories or moral prejudices clouded the crystal-clear vision of his best work. He too had a great influence on the generation of writers to come, and to many he still remains the perfect master of the short story.

Maupassant lived and loved too hard, and a few years before he died, he was committed to an insane asylum.

Two Little Soldiers

BY GUY DE MAUPASSANT

EVERY Sunday, the moment they were dismissed, the two little soldiers made off. Once outside the barracks, they struck out to the right through Courbevoie, walking with long rapid strides, as though they were on a march.

When they were beyond the last of the houses, they slackened pace along the bare, dusty roadway which goes toward Bézons.

They were both small and thin, and looked quite lost in their coats, which were too big and too long. Their sleeves hung down over their hands, and they found their enormous red breeches, which compelled them to waddle, very much in the way. Under their stiff, high helmets their faces had little character—two poor, sallow Breton faces, simple with an almost animal simplicity, and with gentle and quiet blue eyes.

They never conversed during these walks, but went straight on, each with the same thought in his head. This thought atoned for the lack of conversation; it was this—that just inside the little wood near Les Champioux they had found a place which reminded them of their own country, where they could feel happy again.

When they arrived under the trees where the roads from Colombes and from Chatou cross, they would take off their heavy helmets and wipe their foreheads. They always halted on the Bézons bridge to look at the Seine, and would remain there two or three minutes, bent double, leaning on the parapet.

Sometimes they would gaze out over the great basin of Argenteuil, where the skiffs might be seen scudding, with their white, careening sails, recalling perhaps the look of the Breton waters, the harbor of Vanne, near which they lived, and the fishing boats standing out across the Morbihan to the open sea.

Just beyond the Seine they bought their provisions from a sausage merchant, a baker, and a wineseller. A piece of blood pudding, four sous' worth of bread, and a liter of *petit bleu* constituted the provisions, which they carried off in their handkerchiefs. After they had left Bézons they traveled slowly and began to talk.

In front of them a barren plain studded with clumps of trees led to the wood, to the little wood which had seemed to them to resemble the one at Kermarivan. Grainfields and hayfields bordered the narrow path, which lost itself in the young green-ness of the crops, and Jean Kerderen would always say to Luc le Ganidec: "It looks like it does near Plouni-von."

"Yes; exactly."

Side by side they strolled, their souls filled with vague memories of their own country, with awakened images as naïve as the pictures on the colored broadsheets which you buy for a penny. They kept on recognizing, as it were, now a corner of a field, a hedge, a bit of moorland, now a crossroad, now a granite cross. Then, too, they would always stop beside a certain landmark, a great stone, because it looked something like the cromlech at Locneuven.

Every Sunday on arriving at the first clump of trees Luc le Ganidec would cut a switch, a hazel switch, and begin gently to peel off the bark, thinking meanwhile of the folk at home. Jean Kerderen carried the provisions.

From time to time Luc would mention a name, or recall some deed of their childhood in a few brief words, which caused long thoughts. And their own country, their dear, distant country, recaptured them little by little, seizing on their imaginations, and sending to them from afar her shapes, her sounds, her well-known prospects, her odors—odors of the green lands where the salt sea air was blowing.

No longer conscious of the ex-halations of the Parisian stables, on which the earth of the *banlieue* fattens, they scented the perfume of the flowering broom, which the salt breeze of the open sea plucks and bears away. And the sails of the boats from the riverbanks seemed like the white wings of the coasting vessels seen beyond the great plain which extended from their homes to the very margin of the sea.

They walked with short steps, Luc le Ganidec and Jean Kerderen, content and sad, haunted by a sweet melancholy, by the lingering, ever-present sorrow of a caged animal who remembers his liberty.

By the time that Luc had stripped the slender wand of its bark they reached the corner of the wood where every Sunday they took breakfast. They found the two bricks which they kept hidden in the thicket, and kindled a little fire of twigs, over which to roast the blood pudding at the end of a bayonet.

When they had had breakfast, eaten their bread to the last crumb, and drunk their wine to the last drop, they remained seated side by side upon the grass, saying nothing, their eyes on the distance, their eye-lids drooping, their fingers crossed as at Mass, their red legs stretched out beside the poppies of the field. And the leather of their helmets and the brass of their buttons glittered in the ardent sun, making the larks, which sang and hovered above their heads, cease in mid-song.

Toward noon they began to turn their eyes from time to time in the direction of the village of Bézons, because the girl with the cow was coming. She passed by them every Sunday on her way to milk and change the pasture of her cow—the only cow in this district which ever went out of the stable to grass. It was pastured in a narrow field along the edge of the wood a little farther on.

They soon perceived the girl, the only human being within vision, and were gladdened by the brilliant reflections thrown off by the tin milk pail under the rays of the sun. They never talked about her. They were simply glad to see her, without understanding why.

She was a big strong wench with red hair, burned by the heat of sunny days, a sturdy product of the environs of Paris.

Once, finding them seated in the place, she said:

"Good morning. You two are always here, aren't you?"

Luc le Ganidec, the bolder, stammered:

"Yes, we come to rest."

That was all. But the next Sunday she laughed on seeing them, laughed with a protecting benevolence and a feminine keenness which knew well enough that they were bashful. And she asked:

"What are you doing there? Are you trying to see the grass grow?"

Luc was cheered up by this, and smiled likewise: "Maybe we are."

"That's pretty slow work," said she.

He answered, still laughing: "Well, yes, it is."

She went on. But coming back with a milk pail full of milk, she stopped again before them, and said:

"Would you like a little? It will taste like home."

With the instinctive feeling that they were of the same peasant race as she, being herself perhaps also far away from home, she had divined and touched the spot.

They were both touched. Then with some difficulty, she managed to make a little milk run into the neck of the glass bottle in which they carried their wine. And Luc drank first, with little swallows, stopping every minute to see whether he had drunk more than his half. Then he handed the bottle to Jean.

She stood upright before them, her hands on her hips, her pail on the ground at her feet, glad at the pleasure which she had given.

Then she departed, shouting:

"*Allons,* adieu! Till next Sunday!"

And as long as they could see her at all, they followed with their eyes her tall silhouette, which faded, growing smaller and smaller, seeming to sink into the verdure of the fields.

When they were leaving the barracks the week after, Jean said to Luc:

"Oughtn't we to buy her something good?"

They were in great embarrassment before the problem of the choice of a delicacy for the girl with the cow. Luc was of the opinion that a little tripe would be the best, but Jean prefered some *berlingots* because he was fond of sweets. His choice fairly made him enthusiastic, and they bought at a grocer's two sous' worth of white and red candies.

They ate their breakfast more rapidly than usual, being nervous with expectation.

Jean saw her first. "There she is!" he cried. Luc added: "Yes, there she is."

While yet some distance off she laughed at seeing them. Then she cried:

"Is everything going as you like it?"

And in unison they asked:

"Are you getting on all right?"

Then she conversed, talked to them of simple things in which they felt an interest—of the weather, of the crops, and of her master.

They were afraid to offer her the candies, which were slowly melting away in Jean's pocket.

At last Luc grew bold, and murmured:

"We have brought you something."

She demanded, "What is it? Tell me."

Then Jean, blushing up to his ears, managed to get at the little paper cornucopia, and held it out.

She began to eat the little bon-bons, rolling them from one cheek to the other where they made little round lumps. The two soldiers, seated before her, gazed at her with emotion and delight.

Then she went to milk her cow, and once more gave them some milk on coming back.

They thought of her all the week; several times they even spoke of her. The next Sunday she sat down with them for a little longer talk; and all three, seated side by side, their eyes lost in the distance, clasping their knees with their hands, told the small doings, the minute details of life in the villages where they had been born, while over there the cow, seeing that the milkmaid had stopped on her way, stretched out toward her its heavy head with its dripping nostrils, and gave a long low to call her.

Soon the girl consented to eat a bit of bread with them and drink a mouthful of wine. She often brought them plums in her pocket, for the season of plums had come. Her pres-ence sharpened the wits of the two little Breton soldiers, and they chat-tered like two birds.

But, one Tuesday, Luc le Ganidec asked for leave—a thing which had never happened before—and he did not return until ten o'clock at night. Jean racked his brains uneasily for a reason for his comrade's going out in this way.

The next Thursday Luc, having borrowed ten sous from his bed-fellow, again asked and obtained per-mission to leave the barracks for several hours. When he set off with Jean on their Sunday walk his man-ner was very queer, quite restless, and quite changed. Kerderen did not understand, but he vaguely suspected something without divining what it could be.

They did not say a word to one another until they reached their usual halting place, where, from their constant sitting in the same spot, the grass was quite worn away. They ate their breakfast slowly. Neither of them felt hungry.

Before long the girl appeared. As on every Sunday, they watched her coming. When she was quite near, Luc rose and made two steps forward. She put her milk pail on the ground and kissed him. She kissed him pas-sionately, throwing her arms about his neck, without noticing Jean, with-out remembering that he was there, without even seeing him.

And he sat there desperate, poor Jean, so desperate that he did not understand, his soul quite over-whelmed, his heart bursting, but not yet understanding himself. Then the girl seated herself beside Luc, and they began to chatter.

Jean did not look at them. He now divined why his comrade had gone out twice during the week, and he felt within him a burning grief, a kind of wound, that sense of rend-ing which is caused by treason.

Luc and the girl went off together to change the position of the cow. Jean followed them with his eyes. He saw them departing side by side. The red breeches of his comrade made a bright spot on the road. It was Luc who picked up the mallet and hammered down the stake to which they tied the beast.

The girl stooped to milk her, while he stroked the cow's sharp spine with a careless hand. Then they left the milk pail on the grass, and went deep into the wood.

Jean saw nothing but the wall of leaves where they had entered; and he felt himself so troubled that if he had tried to rise he would certainly have fallen. He sat motionless, stupefied by astonishment and suffering, with an agony which was simple but deep. He wanted to cry, to run away, to hide himself, never to see anybody any more.

Soon he saw them issuing from the thicket. They returned slowly, holding each other's hands as in the villages do those who are promised. It was Luc who carried the pail.

They kissed one another again before they separated, and the girl went off after having thrown Jean a friendly "Good evening" and a smile which was full of meaning. Today she no longer thought of offering him any milk.

The two little soldiers sat side by side, motionless as usual, silent and calm, their placid faces betraying nothing of all which troubled their hearts. The sun fell on them. Sometimes the cow lowed, looking at them from afar.

At their usual hour they rose to go back. Luc cut a switch. Jean carried the empty bottle to return it to the wineseller at Bézons. Then they sallied out upon the bridge, and, as they did every Sunday, stopped several minutes in the middle to watch the water flowing.

Jean leaned, leaned more and more, over the iron railing, as though he saw in the current something which attracted him. Luc said: "Are you trying to drink?" Just as he uttered the last word Jean's head overbalanced his body, his legs described a circle in the air, and the little blue and red soldier fell in a heap, struck the water, and disappeared.

Luc, his tongue paralyzed with anguish, tried in vain to shout. Farther down he saw something stir; then the head of his comrade rose to the surface of the river and sank immediately. Farther still he again perceived a hand, a single hand, which issued from the stream and then disappeared. That was all.

The bargemen who dragged the river did not find the body that day.

Luc set out alone for the barracks, going at a run, his soul filled with despair. He told of the accident, with tears in his eyes, and a husky voice, blowing his nose again and again: "He leaned over—he—he leaned over—so far—so far that his head turned a somersault; and—and—so he fell—he fell ——"

Choked with emotion, he could say no more. If he had only known!

Alphonse Daudet
1840-1897

DAUDET, "great little novelist," as he was called, had the light touch. He was strongly influenced, like all his French contemporaries, by Flaubert, but his own sweetness and charm showed through in spite of himself. He was also a follower of Dickens, and was accused of imitating him. In fact his first novel, about the miseries of an unhappy childhood, is in typical Dickens style. But the special grace of it remains pure Daudet. His stories are sentimental, comical, pathetic, a mixture of laughter and tears, and—particularly *Lettres de mon moulin*—have probably done more than any others to make French endurable to beginning students.

Daudet was born in Nîmes, the son of a silk manufacturer, had his schooling in Lyon, and as a young man went to Paris. Here he became more Parisian than the Parisians. As secretary to the Duc de Morny he was very much of the *haut monde*. He lived an intense artistic life, and his marriage to Julia Allard, also a writer, was one of complete intellectual harmony.

On Daudet, as on Maupassant and Flaubert, the Franco-Prussian War left its mark. "The Last Lesson" concerns those tragic days of the 1870's, but it might as easily have been the 1940's.

The Last Lesson

BY ALPHONSE DAUDET

I STARTED for school very late that morning and was in great dread of a scolding, especially because M. Hamel had said that he would question us on participles, and I did not know the first word about them. For a moment I thought of running away and spending the day out-of-doors. It was so warm, so bright! The birds were chirping at the edge of the woods; and in the open field back of the sawmill the Prussian soldiers were drilling. It was all much more tempting than the rule for participles, but I had the strength to resist, and hurried off to school.

When I passed the town hall there was a crowd in front of the bulletin board. For the last two years all our bad news had come from there— the lost battles, the draft, the orders of the commanding officer—and I thought to myself, without stopping: "What can be the matter now?"

Then, as I hurried by as fast as I could go, the blacksmith, Wachter, who was there, with his apprentice, reading the bulletin, called after me: "Don't go so fast, bub; you'll get to your school in plenty of time!"

I thought he was making fun of me, and reached M. Hamel's little garden all out of breath.

Usually, when school began, there was a great bustle, which could be heard out in the street, the opening and closing of desks, lessons repeated in unison, very loud, with our hands over our ears to understand better, and the teacher's great ruler rapping on the table. But now it was all so still! I had counted on the commotion to get to my desk without being seen; but, of course, that day everything had to be as quiet as Sunday morning. Through the window I saw my classmates, already in their places, and M. Hamel walking up and down with his terrible iron ruler under his arm. I had to open the door and go in before everybody. You can imagine how I blushed and how frightened I was.

But nothing happened. M. Hamel saw me and said very kindly: "Go to your place quickly, little Franz. We were beginning without you."

I jumped over the bench and sat down at my desk. Not till then, when I had got a little over my fright, did I see that our teacher had on his beautiful green coat, his frilled shirt, and the little black silk cap, all embroidered, that he never wore except on inspection and prize days. Besides, the whole school seemed so strange and solemn. But the thing that surprised me most was to see, on the back benches that were always empty, the village people sitting quietly like ourselves; old Hauser, with his three-cornered hat, the former mayor, the former postmaster, and several others besides. Everybody looked sad; and Hauser had brought an old primer, thumbed at the edges, and he held it open on his knees with his great spectacles lying across the pages.

While I was wondering about it all, M. Hamel mounted his chair, and, in the same grave and gentle tone which he had used to me, said:

"My children, this is the last lesson I shall give you. The order has come from Berlin to teach only German in the schools of Alsace and Lorraine. The new master comes tomorrow. This is your last French lesson. I want you to be very attentive."

What a thunderclap these words were to me!

Oh, the wretches; that was what they had put up at the town hall!

My last French lesson! Why, I hardly knew how to write! I should never learn any more! I must stop there, then! Oh, how sorry I was for not learning my lessons, for seeking birds' eggs, or going sliding on the Saar! My books, that had seemed such a nuisance a while ago, so heavy to carry, my grammar, and my history of the saints, were old friends now that I couldn't give up. And M. Hamel, too; the idea that he was going away, that I should never see him again, made me forget all about his ruler and how cranky he was.

Poor man! It was in honor of this last lesson that he had put on his fine Sunday clothes, and now I understood why the old men of the village were sitting there in the back

of the room. It was because they were sorry, too, that they had not gone to school more. It was their way of thanking our master for his forty years of faithful service and of showing their respect for the country that was theirs no more.

While I was thinking of all this, I heard my name called. It was my turn to recite. What would I not have given to be able to say that dreadful rule for the participle all through, very loud and clear, and without one mistake? But I got mixed up on the first words and stood there, holding on to my desk, my heart beating, and not daring to look up. I heard M. Hamel say to me:

"I won't scold you, little Franz; you must feel bad enough. See how it is! Every day we have said to ourselves: 'Bah! I've plenty of time. I'll learn it tomorrow.' And now you see where we've come out. Ah, that's the great trouble with Alsace; she puts off learning till tomorrow. Now those fellows out there will have the right to say to you: 'How is it; you pretend to be Frenchmen, and yet you can neither speak nor write your own language?' But you are not the worst, poor little Franz. We've all a great deal to reproach ourselves with.

"Your parents were not anxious enough to have you learn. They preferred to put you to work on a farm or at the mills, so as to have a little more money. And I? I've been to blame also. Have I not often sent you to water my flowers instead of learning your lessons? And when I wanted to go fishing, did I not just give you a holiday?"

Then, from one thing to another, M. Hamel went on to talk of the French language, saying that it was the most beautiful language in the world—the clearest, the most logical; that we must guard it among us and never forget it, because when a people are enslaved, as long as they hold fast to their language it is as if they had the key to their prison. Then he opened a grammar and read us our lesson. I was amazed to see how well I understood it. All he said seemed so easy, so easy! I think, too, that I had never listened so carefully, and that he had never explained everything with so much patience. It seemed almost as if the poor man wanted to give us all he knew before going away, and to put it all into our heads at one stroke.

After the grammar, we had a lesson in writing. That day M. Hamel had new copies for us, written in a beautiful round hand: France, Alsace, France, Alsace. They looked like little flags floating everywhere in the schoolroom, hung from the rod at the top of our desks. You ought to have seen how everyone set to work, and how quiet it was! The only sound was the scratching of the pens over the paper. Once some beetles flew in; but nobody paid any attention to them, not even the littlest ones, who worked right on tracing their fishhooks, as if that was French, too. On the roof the pigeons cooed very low, and I thought to myself:

"Will they make them sing in German, even the pigeons?"

Whenever I looked up from my writing I saw M. Hamel sitting motionless in his chair and gazing first at one thing, then at another, as if he wanted to fix in his mind just how everything looked in that little schoolroom. Fancy! For forty years he had been there in the same place, with his garden outside the window and his class in front of him, just like that. Only the desks and benches had been worn smooth; the walnut trees in the garden were taller, and the hop vine that he had planted himself twined about the windows to the roof. How it must have broken his heart to leave it all, poor man; to hear his sister moving about in the room above, packing their trunks! For they must leave the country next day.

But he had the courage to hear every lesson to the very last. After the writing, we had a lesson in history, and then the babies chanted their ba, be, bi, bo, bu. Down there at the back of the room old Hauser had put on his spectacles and, holding his primer in both hands, spelled the letters with them. You could see that he, too, was crying; his voice trembled with emotion, and it was so funny to hear him that we all wanted to laugh and cry. Ah, how well I remember it, that last lesson!

All at once the church clock struck twelve. Then the Angelus. At the same moment the trumpets of the Prussians, returning from drill, sounded under our windows. M. Hamel stood up, very pale, in his chair. I never saw him look so tall.

"My friends," said he, "I—I——" But something choked him. He could not go on.

Then he turned to the blackboard, took a piece of chalk, and, bearing down with all his might, he wrote as large as he could:

"Vive la France!"

Then he stopped and leaned his head against the wall, and, without a word, he made a gesture to us with his hand:

"School is dismissed—you may go."

Anatole France
1844-1924

ANATOLE FRANCE, born Jacques Anatole Thibault, was the son of a bookseller of the Quai Malaquai. His father, a Royalist and a devout Catholic, sent him to an aristocratic Jesuit school where he got an excellent grounding in the classics. But France always claimed it was the Seine booksellers who really educated him, and in spite of his Catholic training, Voltaire and Renan became his ideals. Naturally indolent, he took neither writing nor anything else seriously. During the Franco-Prussian War he served in the army at the siege of Paris, and diverted himself by playing the flute and reading Virgil.

France's early writing was devoted to publishers' blurbs and a weekly magazine article. Although he was later to dominate the French literary scene for a period of thirty years, he might well have died in comparative obscurity had he not come under the influence of a certain strong-minded woman. In 1883 he met Mme Arman de Caillavet, who drove him to work and propelled him into that position of eminence in the social and literary world which he was to hold for so long. For twenty-five years she saw to it that he wrote six days a week. On Sundays she "received," and France "conversed." In fact, he became almost as renowned for his conversation as for his writing. Under her strenuous discipline he wrote the greater part of his best work. "Without her help I should write no books," he said in the dedication of *Crainquebille*.

Though a contemporary of Zola, Turgenev, and Flaubert, France was not so deeply serious. He was the stylist par excellence. "I have passed my life," he said, "twisting dynamite into curlpapers." His world fame receded considerably after 1919. . . . "Our Lady's Juggler" was the inspiration for Massenet's opera *Le Jongleur de Notre Dame*, and his funeral in 1924 was said to have brought out the biggest crowd in Paris after the Victory Parade of 1919. . . . "Our Lady's Juggler" was the inspiration for Massenet's opera *Le Jongleur de Notre Dame*.

Our Lady's Juggler

BY ANATOLE FRANCE

In the days of King Louis there was a poor juggler in France, a native of Compiègne, Barnaby by name, who went about from town to town, performing feats of skill and strength. On fair days he would unfold an old worn-out carpet in the public square, and when by means of a jovial address, which he had learned of a very ancient juggler, and which he never varied in the least, he had drawn together the children and loafers, he assumed extraordinary attitudes, and balanced a tin plate on the tip of his nose. At first the crowd would feign indifference.

But when, supporting himself on his hands face downwards, he threw into the air six copper balls, which glittered in the sunshine, and caught them again with his feet; or when, throwing himself backwards until his heels and the nape of the neck met, giving his body the form of a perfect wheel, he would juggle in this posture with a dozen knives, a murmur of admiration would escape the spectators, and pieces of money rain down upon the carpet.

Nevertheless, like the majority of those who live by their wits, Barnaby of Compiègne had a great struggle to make a living.

Earning his bread in the sweat of his brow, he bore rather more than his share of the penalties consequent upon the misdoings of our father Adam.

Again, he was unable to work as constantly as he would have been willing to do. The warmth of the sun and the broad daylight were as necessary to enable him to display his brilliant parts as to the trees if flower and fruit should be expected of them. In wintertime he was nothing more than a tree stripped of its leaves, and as it were dead. The frozen ground was hard to the juggler, and, like the grasshopper of which Marie de France tells us, the inclement season caused him to suffer both cold and hunger. But as he was simple-natured he bore his ills patiently.

He had never meditated on the origin of wealth, nor upon the inequality of human conditions. He believed firmly that if this life should prove hard, the life to come could not fail to redress the balance, and this hope upheld him. He did not resemble those thievish and miscreant Merry Andrews who sell their souls to the devil. He never blasphemed God's name; he lived uprightly, and although he had no wife

From *Mother of Pearl* by Anatole France. By permission of Dodd, Mead & Company and John Lane, The Bodley Head, Ltd., of London.

of his own, he did not covet his neighbor's, since woman is ever the enemy of the strong man, as it appears by the history of Samson recorded in the Scriptures.

In truth, his was not a nature much disposed to carnal delights, and it was a greater deprivation to him to forsake the tankard than the Hebe who bore it. For whilst not wanting in sobriety, he was fond of a drink when the weather waxed hot. He was a worthy man who feared God, and was very devoted to the Blessed Virgin.

Never did he fail, on entering a church, to fall upon his knees before the image of the Mother of God, and offer up this prayer to her: "Blessed Lady, keep watch over my life until it shall please God that I die, and when I am dead, ensure to me the possession of the joys of paradise."

Now, on a certain evening after a dreary wet day, as Barnaby pursued his road, sad and bent, carrying under his arm his balls and knives wrapped up in his old carpet, on the watch for some barn where, though he might not sup, he might sleep, he perceived on the road, going in the same direction as himself, a monk, whom he saluted courteously. And as they walked at the same rate they fell into conversation with one another.

"Fellow traveler," said the monk, "how comes it about that you are clothed all in green? Is it perhaps in order to take the part of a jester in some mystery play?"

"Not at all, good father," replied Barnaby. "Such as you see me, I am called Barnaby, and for my calling I am a juggler. There would be no pleasanter calling in the world if it would always provide one with daily bread."

"Friend Barnaby," returned the monk, "be careful what you say. There is no calling more pleasant than the monastic life. Those who lead it are occupied with the praises of God, the Blessed Virgin, and the saints; and, indeed, the religious life is one ceaseless hymn to the Lord."

Barnaby replied, "Good father, I own that I spoke like an ignorant man. Your calling cannot be in any respect compared to mine, and although there may be some merit in dancing with a penny balanced on a stick on the tip of one's nose, it is not a merit which comes within hail of your own. Gladly would I, like you, good father, sing my office day by day, and especially, the office of the most Holy Virgin, to whom I have vowed a singular devotion. In order to embrace the monastic life I would willingly abandon the art by which from Soissons to Beauvais I am well known in upwards of six hundred towns and villages."

The monk was touched by the juggler's simplicity, and as he was not lacking in discernment, he at once recognized in Barnaby one of those men of whom it is said in the Scriptures: Peace on earth to men of good will. And for this reason he replied, "Friend Barnaby, come with me, and I will have you admitted into the monastery of which I am prior. He who guided Saint Mary of Egypt in the desert set me upon your path to lead you into the way of salvation."

It was in this manner, then, that Barnaby became a monk. In the monastery into which he was received the religious vied with one another in the worship of the Blessed Virgin, and in her honor each employed all the knowledge and all the skill which God had given him.

The prior on his part wrote books dealing according to the rules of scholarship with the virtues of the Mother of God.

Brother Maurice, with a deft hand, copied out these treatises upon sheets of vellum.

Brother Alexander adorned the leaves with delicate miniature paintings. Here were displayed the Queen of Heaven seated upon Solomon's throne, and while four lions were on guard at her feet, around the nimbus which encircled her head hovered seven doves, which are the seven gifts of the Holy Spirit, the gifts, namely, of Fear, Piety, Knowledge, Strength, Counsel, Understanding, and Wisdom. For her companions she had six virgins with hair of gold, namely, Humility, Prudence, Seclusion, Submission, Virginity, and Obedience.

At her feet were two little naked figures, perfectly white, in an attitude of supplication. These were souls imploring her all-powerful intercession for their soul's health, and we may be sure not imploring in vain.

Upon another page facing this, Brother Alexander represented Eve, so that the Fall and the Redemption could be perceived at one and the same time—Eve the Wife abased, and Mary the Virgin exalted.

Furthermore, to the marvel of the beholder, this book contained presentments of the Well of Living Waters, the Fountain, the Lily, the Moon, the Sun, and the Garden enclosed of which the Song of Songs tells us, the Gate of Heaven and the City of God, and all these things were symbols of the Blessed Virgin.

Brother Marbode was likewise one of the most loving children of Mary.

He spent all his days carving images in stone, so that his beard, his eyebrows, and his hair were white with dust, and his eyes continually swollen and weeping; but his strength and cheerfulness were not diminished, although he was now well gone in years, and it was clear that the Queen of Paradise still cherished her servant in his old age. Marbode represented her seated upon a throne, her brow encircled with an orb-shaped nimbus set with pearls. And he took care that the folds of her dress should cover the feet of her, concerning whom the prophet declared: My beloved is as a garden enclosed.

Sometimes, too, he depicted her in the semblance of a child full of grace, and appearing to say, "Thou art my God, even from my mother's womb."

In the priory, moreover, were poets who composed hymns in Latin, both in prose and verse, in honor of the Blessed Virgin Mary, and amongst the company was even a brother from Picardy who sang the miracles of Our Lady in rhymed verse and in the vulgar tongue.

Being a witness of this emulation in praise and the glorious harvest of their labors, Barnaby mourned his own ignorance and simplicity.

"Alas!" he sighed, as he took his solitary walk in the little shelterless garden of the monastery, "wretched wight that I am, to be unable, like my brothers, worthily to praise the Holy Mother of God, to whom I have vowed my whole heart's affection. Alas! alas! I am but a rough man and unskilled in the arts, and I can render you in service, Blessed Lady, neither edifying sermons, nor in-

genious paintings, nor statues truth-
fully sculptured, nor verses whose
march is measured to the beat of
feet. No gift have I, alas!"

After this fashion he groaned and
gave himself up to sorrow. But one
evening, when the monks were
spending their hour of liberty in conversation, he heard one of them tell
the tale of a religious man who
could repeat nothing other than the
Ave Maria. This poor man was
despised for his ignorance; but after
his death there issued forth from
his mouth five roses in honor of the
five letters of the name Mary
(Marie), and thus his sanctity was
made manifest.

Whilst he listened to this narra-
tive, Barnaby marveled yet once
again at the loving-kindness of the
Virgin; but the lesson of that blessed
death did not avail to console him,
for his heart overflowed with zeal,
and he longed to advance the glory
of his Lady, who is in heaven.

How to compass this he sought,
but could find no way, and day by
day he became the more cast down,
when one morning he awakened
filled full with joy, hastened to the
chapel, and remained there alone
for more than an hour. After dinner
he returned to the chapel once
more.

And, starting from that moment,
he repaired daily to the chapel at
such hours as it was deserted, and
spent within it a good part of the
time which the other monks devoted
to the liberal and mechanical arts.
His sadness vanished, nor did he any
longer groan.

A demeanor so strange awakened
the curiosity of the monks.

These began to ask one another
for what purpose Brother Barnaby
could be indulging so persistently
in retreat.

The prior, whose duty it is to let
nothing escape him in the behavior
of his children in religion, resolved
to keep a watch over Barnaby during his withdrawals to the chapel.
One day, then, when he was shut
up there after his custom, the prior,
accompanied by two of the older
monks, went to discover through the
chinks in the door what was going
on within the chapel.

They saw Barnaby before the altar
of the Blessed Virgin, head downwards, with his feet in the air, and
he was juggling with six balls of
copper and a dozen knives. In honor
of the Holy Mother of God he was
performing those feats, which afore-
time had won him most renown.
Not recognizing that the simple fellow was thus placing at the service
of the Blessed Virgin his knowledge
and skill, the two old monks exclaimed against the sacrilege.

The prior was aware how stain-
less was Barnaby's soul, but he concluded that he had been seized
with madness. They were all three
preparing to lead him swiftly from
the chapel, when they saw the
Blessed Virgin descend the steps of
the altar and advance to wipe away
with a fold of her azure robe the
sweat which was dropping from her
juggler's forehead.

Then the prior, falling upon his
face upon the pavement, uttered
these words, "Blessed are the simple-
hearted, for they shall see God."

"Amen!" responded the old
brethren, and kissed the ground.

Hans Christian Andersen
1805-1875

HANS ANDERSEN's life is like one of his own fairy stories, strange and a little sad. He was born in the small island town of Odense, in Denmark. His father was a poor shoemaker, very young and sickly, and the little family of three lived, ate, and slept in one room. When Hans was eleven his father died, and the little boy, left to his own devices, promptly stopped going to school. He built himself a toy theater, made puppets and clothed them, and read all the plays he could put his hands on, including most of Shakespeare.

His mother wanted Hans to be a tailor, but he preferred to be an opera singer, and at fourteen ran away to Copenhagen, where he hoped to make his fortune. But he was never a success in Copenhagen, neither then nor later. When he found that he had no voice, he turned to dancing, and the director of the Royal Theater, where he tried out as a dancer, took a fancy to the eccentric boy. In time King Ferdinand VI became interested and sent Hans to a fine school. But he was an unwilling student, and his school years were bitter and dark. In his young manhood he wrote plays and poetry, again without much success. He traveled on a stipend from the King and wrote about the countries he visited.

Not until after his first book of *Fairy Tales* was published in 1835 did he become famous, and even then Copenhagen mocked him. "Totally devoid of variety," said the Danish critics. All over the world, however, Hans Christian Andersen's name had by now become celebrated. When he visited England, Charles Dickens was his host. Yet Hans had not made good in the city of his choice and still believed himself a failure. To the end he disdained his fairy stories. . . . Although some of them are old tales retold, most of the fairy tales, including "The Steadfast Tin Soldier," were his own invention.

The Steadfast Tin Soldier

BY HANS CHRISTIAN ANDERSEN

THERE were once five and twenty tin soldiers, all brothers, for they were the offspring of the same old tin spoon. Each man shouldered his gun, kept his eyes well to the front, and wore the smartest red and blue uniform imaginable. The first thing they heard in their new world, when the lid was taken off the box, was a little boy clapping his hands and crying, "Soldiers, soldiers!" It was his birthday and they had just been given to him; so he lost no time in setting them up on the table. All the soldiers were exactly alike, with one exception, and he differed from the rest in having only one leg. For he was made last, and there was not quite enough tin left to finish him. However, he stood just as well on his one leg as the others on two; in fact, he is the very one who is to become famous. On the table where they were being set up were many other toys; but the chief thing which caught the eye was a delightful paper castle. You could see through the tiny windows, right into the rooms. Outside there were some little trees surrounding a small mirror, representing a lake, whose surface reflected the waxen swans which were swimming about on it. It was altogether charming, but the prettiest thing of all was a little maiden standing at the open door of the castle. She, too, was cut out of paper, but she wore a dress of the lightest gauze, with a dainty little blue ribbon over her shoulders, by way of a scarf, set off by a brilliant spangle as big as her whole face. The little maid was stretching out both arms, for she was a dancer, and in the dance one of her legs was raised so high into the air that the tin soldier could see absolutely nothing of it, and supposed that she, like himself, had but one leg.

"That would be the very wife for me!" he thought; "but she is much too grand; she lives in a palace, while I only have a box, and then there are five and twenty of us to share it. No, that would be no place for her! but I must try to make her acquaintance!" Then he lay down full length behind a snuffbox, which stood on the table. From that point he could have a good look at the lady, who continued to stand on one leg without losing her balance.

Late in the evening the other soldiers were put into their box, and the people of the house went to bed. Now was the time for the toys to play; they amused themselves with paying visits, fighting battles, and giving balls. The tin soldiers rustled about in their box, for they wanted to join the games, but they could not get the lid off. The nutcrackers turned somersaults, and the pencil scribbled nonsense on the slate. There was such a noise that the canary woke up and joined in, but his remarks were in verse. The only two who did not move were the tin soldier and the little dancer. She stood as stiff as ever on tiptoe, with her arms spread out; he was equally firm on his one leg, and he did not take his eyes off her for a moment.

Then the clock struck twelve, when pop! up flew the lid of the snuffbox, but there was no snuff in it, no! There was a little black goblin, a sort of Jack-in-the-box.

"Tin soldier!" said the goblin, "have the goodness to keep your eyes to yourself."

But the tin soldier feigned not to hear.

"Ah! you just wait till tomorrow," said the goblin.

In the morning when the children got up they put the tin soldier on the window frame, and, whether it was caused by the goblin or by a puff of wind, I do not know, but all at once the window burst open, and the soldier fell head foremost from the third story.

It was a terrific descent, and he landed at last, with his leg in the air, and rested on his cap, with his bayonet fixed between two paving stones. The maidservant and the little boy ran down at once to look for him; but although they almost trod on him, they could not see him. Had the soldier only called out, "Here I am," they would easily have found him, but he did not think it proper to shout when he was in uniform.

Presently it began to rain, and the drops fell faster and faster, till

there was a regular torrent. When it was over two street boys came along.

"Look out!" said one; "there is a tin soldier! He shall go for a sail."

So they made a boat out of a newspaper and put the soldier into the middle of it, and he sailed away down the gutter; both boys ran alongside, clapping their hands. Good heavens! what waves there were in the gutter, and what a current, but then it certainly had rained cats and dogs. The paper boat danced up and down, and now and then whirled round and round. A shudder ran through the tin soldier, but he remained undaunted, and did not move a muscle, only looked straight before him with his gun shouldered. All at once the boat drifted under a long wooden tunnel, and it became as dark as it was in his box.

"Where on earth am I going now!" thought he. "Well, well, it is all the fault of that goblin! Oh, if only the little maiden were with me in the boat it might be twice as dark for all I should care!"

At this moment a big water rat, who lived in the tunnel, came up.

"Have you a pass?" asked the rat. "Hand up your pass!"

The tin soldier did not speak, but clung still tighter to his gun. The boat rushed on, the rat close behind. Phew, how he gnashed his teeth and shouted to the bits of stick and straw, "Stop him, stop him, he hasn't paid his toll; he hasn't shown his pass!" But the current grew stronger and stronger, the tin soldier could already see daylight before him at the end of the tunnel; but he also heard a roaring sound, fit to strike terror to the bravest heart. Just imagine! Where the tunnel ended the stream rushed straight into the big canal. That would be just as dangerous for him as it would be for us to shoot a great rapid.

He was so near the end now that it was impossible to stop. The boat dashed out; the poor tin soldier held himself as stiff as he could; no one should say of him that he even winced.

The boat swirled round three or four times, and filled with water to the edge; it must sink. The tin soldier stood up to his neck in water, and the boat sank deeper and deeper. The paper became limper and limper, and at last the water went over his head—then he thought of the pretty little dancer, whom he was never to see again, and this refrain rang in his ears:

Onward! Onward! Soldier!
For death thou canst not shun.

At last the paper gave way entirely and the soldier fell through —but at the same moment he was swallowed by a big fish.

Oh, how dark it was inside the fish, it was worse than being in the tunnel even; and then it was so narrow! But the tin soldier was as dauntless as ever, and lay full length, shouldering his gun.

The fish rushed about and made the most frantic movements. At last it became quite quiet, and after a time, a flash like lightning pierced it. The soldier was once more in the broad daylight, and someone called out loudly, "A tin soldier!" The fish had been caught, taken to market, sold, and brought into the kitchen, where the cook cut it open with a large knife. She took the soldier up by the waist, with two fingers, and carried him into the parlor, where everyone wanted to see the wonderful man who had traveled about in the stomach of a fish; but the tin sol-

dier was not at all proud. They set him up on the table, and, wonder of wonders! he found himself in the very same room that he had been in before. He saw the very same children, and the toys were still standing on the table, as well as the beautiful castle with the pretty little dancer.

She still stood on one leg, and held the other up in the air. You see she also was unbending. The soldier was so much moved that he was ready to shed tears of tin, but that would not have been fitting. He looked at her, and she looked at him, but they said never a word. At this moment one of the little boys took up the tin soldier, and without rhyme or reason, threw him into the fire. No doubt the little goblin in the snuffbox was to blame for that. The tin soldier stood there, lighted up by the flame, and in the most horrible heat; but whether it was the heat of the real fire, or the warmth of his feelings, he did not know. He had lost all his gay color; it might have been from his perilous journey, or it might have been from grief, who can tell?

He looked at the little maiden, and she looked at him; and he felt that he was melting away, but he still managed to keep himself erect, shouldering his gun bravely.

A door was suddenly opened, the draft caught the little dancer, and she fluttered like a sylph, straight into the fire, to the soldier, blazed up, and was gone!

By this time the soldier was reduced to a mere lump, and when the maid took away the ashes next morning she found him, in the shape of a small tin heart. All that was left of the dancer was her spangle, and that was burned as black as coal.

Friedrich Gerstäcker
1816-1872

ON THE German horizon, dominated by the giant figures of
Goethe and Schiller and Heine, Friedrich Gerstäcker stands
up, a smallish figure beside those others, but an erect one.
Unlike his parochial countrymen of that day, Gerstäcker liked
to travel. Adventure was his métier, Robinson Crusoe his
immediate inspiration. As early as 1837 he was in America,
and wrote about what he saw, opening up vistas to the stay-
at-home Germans. "Germelshausen" is a tale of travel, too,
but of a region farther away than even Gerstäcker ventured.
In this story of the village that appears only every hundred
years, there is the spooky touch of an early Kafka.

Germelshausen

BY FRIEDRICH GERSTÄCKER

In the autumn of the year 184- a strapping young fellow, knapsack on back and stick in hand, was walking with slow and easy stride along the broad highroad that leads up from Marisfeld to Wichtelhausen.

He was not one of those journeyman artisans who travel about from place to place, seeking work; anyone could see that at the first glance, even if the small, neatly made leather portfolio, which he carried strapped on his knapsack, had not betrayed his calling. There was certainly no denying the fact that he was an artist.

His black, broad-brimmed hat cocked jauntily on one side, his long, fair, curly hair, his downy beard, full but youthful still—everything announced it, even the somewhat threadbare black velvet jacket, which seemed likely to be a little too warm for him on this bright warm morning. He had unbuttoned it, and the white shirt underneath—for he wore no waistcoat—was but loosely held together round his neck by a black silk scarf.

He might have been about a mile distant from Marisfeld when the bell of the village church rang out, and he halted, leaning upon his stick and listening intently to the full tones of the bell, which sounded wondrously sweet to him across the breezes.

The sounds had long since died away, and yet he still stood there, gazing dreamily out over the hill slopes. His heart was at home with his loved ones in the dear little village among the Taurus Mountains, with his mother and his sisters, and it almost seemed as if a tear was like to spring to his eye.

But his light and merry heart would not suffer the intrusion of sad and melancholy thought. He only took off his hat, waved a loving, smiling greeting in the direction in which he knew his home lay, and then gripping his stout stick more firmly he gaily stepped out along the road, continuing the journey he had already begun.

Meanwhile the sun was beating down with considerable warmth upon the broad, monotonous highway, which was covered with a thick layer of dust; and our traveler had already for some time been casting glances to right and left to see if he could anywhere discover some pleasanter footpath.

At one point, indeed, a road did branch off to the right, but it looked to him unpromising, and besides, it would lead him too far out of his

This translation is used by permission of George G. Harrap of London.

way; so he stuck to his original track a little longer, until he at length came to a limpid mountain stream, across which he could discern the ruins of an old stone bridge.

Away on the other side ran a grassy path, leading farther into the valley; so, with no definite purpose in view—for he was only passing through the beautiful Werra Valley to enrich his portfolio—he crossed the brook dry-shod by leaping from one great stone to another, and so reached the close-cropped meadow on the other side, where he advanced rapidly on the springy turf under the shadow of the thick alder bushes, well content with the change.

"Now I have the advantage," he said to himself with a laugh, "of not knowing whither I am bound. There is no tiresome sign post here telling one miles beforehand what is the name of the next village, and invariably giving the wrong distance. How ever do people in these parts measure their miles, I should like to know!

"How wonderfully quiet it is in this valley! To be sure, on Sundays farmers have nothing to do out-of-doors, and since they have to walk behind their plow or by their cart the whole week, they don't care much about going for a walk when Sunday comes; they first of all make up for their arrears of sleep in church during the morning, and after dinner stretch their legs under the table in the tavern. Tavern! hm, a glass of beer wouldn't be such a bad thing in this heat; but until I can get it this clear stream will quench my thirst just as well."

And with that he flung off knapsack and hat, knelt down at the waterside, and drank to his heart's content.

Somewhat cooled by his drink, his glance fell on an old, strangely gnarled willow tree, which he rapidly sketched with practiced hand; and then, completely rested and refreshed, he took up his knapsack again and continued his way, regardless as to where it would lead him.

He had wandered on thus for perhaps an hour or so, jotting down in his sketchbook here a crag, there a peculiar clump of alder bushes, or again a knotty oak branch; the sun had meanwhile mounted higher and higher, and he had just made up his mind to quicken his steps in order at least not to miss his dinner in the next village, when before him in the valley, sitting close to the brook and by an old stone, on which perhaps in times gone by there had stood a sacred shrine, he caught sight of a peasant girl, who was gazing down the road along which he came.

As he was hidden by the alders, he had been able to see her before she saw him; but following the bank of the stream, he had hardly passed beyond the bushes which had hitherto concealed him from her sight, when she leaped to her feet and flew toward him with a cry of pleasure.

Arnold, as the young painter was called, stood amazed, and was soon aware that a beautiful girl of hardly seventeen years, dressed in a peculiar but extremely pretty peasant's costume, was running up to him with outstretched arms.

Arnold of course saw at once that she had mistaken him for someone else, and that this joyful greeting was not meant for him; and the girl no sooner recognized him than she stood stock-still with horror, turned pale at first and then red all over, and finally said with shy embarrassment: "Do not be offended, stranger! I—I thought——"

"That it was your sweetheart, my dear child, didn't you?" laughed the young man. "And now you are vexed that a different person, an uninteresting stranger, has met you! Don't be angry because I am not he."

"Ah, how can you say such things?" said the girl in a distressed whisper. "Why should I be angry?— oh! but if you only knew how delighted I was!"

"Then he certainly does not deserve that you should wait any longer for him," said Arnold, who now for the first time noticed the truly wonderful charm of the graceful peasant girl. "Were I in his place, you would not have had to wait for me in vain for a single moment."

"You do say such strange things," said the girl, abashed. "If he could have come he would certainly be here by now. Perhaps he is ill, or— even dead," she added slowly and with a sigh that came from the depths of her heart.

"And has he let you have no news of himself all this time?"

"No, all this long, long time."

"Then his home is perhaps a long way from here?"

"A long way? Why, yes; quite a great distance from here," said the girl. "In Bischofsroda."

"Bischofsroda?" cried Arnold. "I spent four weeks there only recently, and I know every child in the whole village. What is his name?"

"Heinrich — Heinrich Vollgut," said the girl shyly; "the mayor's son in Bischofsroda."

"Hm," mused Arnold, "I was in and out of the mayor's house, but *his* name was Bauerling, as far as I know, and I never heard the name of Vollgut in the whole village."

"Probably you didn't know all the people there," argued the girl, and over the sorrowful expression which clouded her sweet face there stole a soft, roguish smile, which became her as well and much better than her previous melancholy.

"Well, but from Bischofsroda," said the young man, "you can get here over the mountains easily in two hours, at most in three."

"And yet he is not here," said the girl, sighing deeply again, "though he promised so faithfully."

"Then he'll come, sure enough," Arnold assured her with hearty conviction; "for once anyone has given you a promise, he must surely have a heart of stone if he went back on his word—and that I am sure your Heinrich has not got."

"No," she answered resolutely; "but now I cannot wait any longer for him, as I have to be home for dinner, or else Father will scold me."

"And where is your home?"

"Straight down there in the valley. Hark! there's the bell; they are just coming out of church."

Arnold listened, and at no great distance off he could hear the slow pealing of a bell, but the sound came to him not deep and full, but sharp and discordant, and when he turned his eyes toward the spot it seemed to him almost as if a thick mountain mist lay over that part of the valley.

"Your bell is cracked," he laughed; "it doesn't ring true."

"Yes, I know that," answered the girl calmly; "it has not a pleasant sound, and we should have had it recast long ago, but we are always short of money and time, for hereabouts there are no bellcasters. Yet, what does it matter? We know it all right, and we know what it means when it rings—so even though it is cracked it serves its purpose."

"And what is the name of your village?"

"Germelshausen."

"And can I get to Wichtelhausen from there?"

"Quite easily; by the footpath it takes hardly half an hour—perhaps, indeed, not so much, if you put your best foot forward."

"Then I'll go with you through the village, sweetheart, and if you have a good inn in the place I'll have my dinner there too."

"The inn is only too good," said the maiden with a sigh, as she cast a glance backward to see if her ex-pected lover might not yet be coming.

"Can any inn be too good?"

"For the farmer, yes," said the girl gravely, as she walked slowly by his side along the valley. "Of an evening after his work he still has much to do in the house, and this he neglects if he sits in the public house till late at night."

"But I at any rate have nothing more to neglect today."

"Yes, with townfolk it is rather different; they don't do anything, and consequently haven't got much to neglect either. Yet the farmer has to earn bread for them."

"Well, not exactly so," said Arnold with a laugh. "He has to grow it, I grant you, but we have to earn it for ourselves; and a hard job it is too, many a time, for what the farmer does he sees that he is well paid for it."

"But you don't work, anyhow?"

"Why not, pray?"

"Your hands don't look like it."

"Then I will show you at once how I work and what I work at," laughed Arnold. "Just you sit down on that flat stone under the old lilac tree——"

"And what am I to do there?"

"Just sit down," cried the young painter, who threw off his knapsack and took out his sketchbook and pencil.

"But I must go home."

"I shall be done in five minutes. I should very much like to take a re-minder of you away into the world with me; even your Heinrich will have no objection to that!"

"A reminder of me? What a funny man you are!"

"I will take your portrait away with me."

"You are a painter, then?"

"Yes."

"What a lucky thing! Then you might set to work and touch up the pictures in Germelshausen Church; they look so very poor and shabby."

"What is your name?" was Arnold's next question. He had meanwhile opened his portfolio and was rapidly sketching in the girl's charming features.

"Gertrud."

"And what is your father?"

"The mayor of the village. If you are a painter, you must not go to the inn either; I will take you straight home with me, and after dinner you can talk over the whole matter with Father."

"Oh, the pictures in the church?" said Arnold, laughing.

"Of course," said the girl gravely; "and then you must stay with us a long, long time until—our day comes again and the pictures are finished."

"Well, we'll talk about that later, Gertrud," said the young painter, busily plying his pencil the while; "but won't your Heinrich be angry if I am often—very often with you, and if I talk with you a good deal?"

"Heinrich?" said she. "Oh, he won't come now."

"Not today, no; but perhaps to-morrow."

"No," said Gertrud, quite calmly; "as he wasn't there by eleven o'clock, he will stay away until our day comes again."

"Your day? What do you mean by that?"

The girl looked at him with wide-open, earnest eyes, but gave no answer to his question, and her gaze, turning to the clouds floating away high over their heads, fastened upon them with a peculiar expression of pain and melancholy.

Gertrud's beauty at this moment was truly the beauty of an angel, and Arnold forgot all else in the interest which he was taking in the completion of her picture. Nor had he much more time left. The girl suddenly stood up, and tossing a kerchief over her head to shield her from the sun's rays, she said:

"Go I must; the day is so short, and they are expecting me at home."

But Arnold had finished his little picture, and indicating with a few bold strokes the folds of her dress, he held out the sketch to her and said:

"Have I caught your likeness?"

"It is myself!" gasped Gertrud, almost in fright.

"Well, who else could it be?" laughed Arnold.

"And do you wish to keep the picture and take it away with you?" asked the girl shyly, almost wistfully.

"Why, certainly I do," cried the young man, "and then when I am far, far away from here I shall think of you hard, and often."

"But will my father allow that?"

"Allow me to think of you? Is he capable of forbidding me to do so?"

"No—but—to take the picture away with you—out into the world?"

"He can't hinder me, sweetheart," said Arnold tenderly; "but would you yourself hate to know that it was in my possession?"

"I? No!" was the girl's answer after short reflection; "if only—but I must ask Father about it."

"What a silly child you are!" said the young painter with a laugh; "even a princess would have no objection to an artist securing a sketch of her features for himself. No harm can come to you from it. But please don't run off like that, you wild creature; I am coming with you, you know—or do you want to leave me behind without my dinner? Have you forgotten about the church pictures?"

"Oh! yes, the pictures," said the girl, standing still and waiting for him; but Arnold, who had quickly tied up his portfolio again, was by her side in a moment, and they both continued their way toward the village far quicker than before.

The village, however, was much nearer than Arnold had supposed from the sound of the cracked bell, for what the young man from afar had taken for an alder grove proved to be, on their nearer approach, a row of fruit trees enclosed by a hedge. Closely hidden behind these, yet surrounded on the north and northeast by broad fields, lay the old village with its low church tower and its smoke-blackened cottages.

Here, too, it was that the pair first struck a firm, well-laid street, planted on either side with fruit trees. But over the village lowered a thick mist which Arnold had already perceived from afar, and it dimmed the bright sunshine, which fell upon the gray, old, weather-beaten roofs with a weird and yellowish light.

But Arnold scarcely had eyes for this. Gertrud, stepping out by his side, had meekly slipped her hand in his as they came to the first houses, and clasping it in her own she turned with him into the next street.

A strange feeling thrilled the lusty youth at the touch of her warm hand and almost involuntarily his eyes sought to meet those of the young maiden. But Gertrud did not look in his direction; with eyes fixed modestly on the ground, she conducted her guest to her father's house, and Arnold's attention, too, was at length taken up with the villagers he met, who all passed him by in silence and without a word of greeting.

He could not help noticing this at first, for in all the neighboring villages it would have been deemed a crime not to offer a stranger at least a "Good day" or "God bless you." Here no one thought of such a thing, and, just as in any large town, the people either passed by in silence and without showing any interest, or else stood here and there and looked after them; but no one spoke a word to them—not one of all the passers-by gave a greeting even to the girl.

And how strange the old houses looked, with their pointed gables ornamented with carved work, and their hard thatched roofs weatherworn and gray; and though it was Sunday, no window was polished bright, and the round panes set in leaden frames looked tarnished and dim, and showed on their dull surface shimmering rainbow colors.

Here and there a window would open as they walked by, and pleasant-faced girls or elderly worthy matrons would peep out. The curious dress of the people struck him also, differing essentially as it did from that of the village in the vicinity. And besides all this an almost soundless stillness reigned everywhere so that Arnold, to whom this silence at last became oppressive, said to his companion:

"Do you observe Sunday in your village so strictly that people when they meet one another haven't even a word of greeting to utter? If one didn't hear a dog barking now and then or a cock crowing, one might really think the whole place dumb and dead."

"It is dinnertime," said Gertrud quietly, "and people are not inclined to talk then; this evening you will find them all the noisier."

"Thank heaven!" exclaimed Arnold, "there are at least some children yonder playing in the street. I had begun to feel quite uncanny; I can tell you they spend Sunday quite differently in Bischofsroda."

"There's my father's house," said Gertrud in a low voice.

"But I can't thrust myself in upon him thus unexpectedly at dinnertime. I might be an unwelcome intruder, and I like to have friendly faces round me at meals.

"So show me rather where the inn is, my child, or let me find it myself, for probably Germelshausen is no exception to the rule of other villages. Generally the public house is quite close to the church, and if you take the church tower to guide you, you can't go far wrong."

"There you are right; that is exactly the case with us," said Gertrud quietly; "but they expect us already at home, and you need have no fear of getting an unfriendly reception."

"Expect us? Ah, you mean yourself and your Heinrich? Yes, Gertrud, if you would take me today in his place, then I would stay with you—until—until you yourself should tell me to go away again."

He had spoken these last words in

such feeling tones, almost against his will, the while gently pressing the hand which still held his, that Gertrud suddenly stopped, looked at him out of her big, grave eyes, and said:

"Would you really wish that?"

"A thousand times yes," cried the young painter, utterly carried away by the girl's wonderful beauty. But Gertrud made no further answer, and pursuing her way as if she was pondering over the words of her companion, she at length came to a halt in front of a tall house, which was approached by a flight of broad, stone steps, protected by iron railings. Speaking in her former shy and timid manner she resumed:

"This is where I live, kind sir, and if it would please you, come in with me to my father, who will no doubt be proud to see you at his table."

II

Before Arnold could return any answer to this invitation the mayor himself appeared in the doorway at the top of the steps, and a window was thrown open, revealing the kindly face of an old lady, who looked out and nodded to them.

"Why, Gertrud," exclaimed the farmer, "what a long time you have stayed out today, and look what a smart young fellow she has brought back with her!"

"My dear sir!"

"Please, no ceremony on the steps! The dumplings are ready; come in, or they'll get hard and cold."

"But that's not Heinrich," cried the old lady from the window. "Now, didn't I always say that he would never come back again?"

"All right, mother, all right," said the mayor, "this one will do very well instead"; and holding out his hand to the stranger, he went on: "A hearty welcome to Germelshausen, young gentleman, wherever the lass may have picked you up. And now come in to dinner and fall to to your heart's content; anything else we can talk of later."

He left the young painter no possible further chance to make any excuses, but vigorously shaking his hand, which Gertrud had released as soon as he had set foot on the stone steps, he took his arm with familiar kindness and conducted him into the spacious living room.

Although he was well acquainted with the habits of the German farmer, who shuts himself off from every breath of fresh air in his room, and not unfrequently even in summer keeps up a fire so as to produce the broiling heat he so delights in, yet what was most noticeable to Arnold at once was the musty, earthy atmosphere which pervaded the house.

The narrow entrance hall was likewise far from inviting. The plaster had fallen from the walls and appeared to have just been hastily swept to one side. The single dim window at the back of the hall hardly admitted the meager light, and the stairs which led to the upper story looked old and out of repair.

Little time, however, was given him to observe all this, for in the very next moment his hospitable host threw open the door of the parlor, and Arnold saw himself in a low but broad and spacious room, which was airy and fresh, with white sand sprinkled over the floor, and which with its large table in the center spread with a snow-white cloth contrasted pleasantly with the rest of the rather dilapidated arrangements of the house.

Besides the old lady, who now

had shut the window and moved her chair up to the table, there were also sitting in the corner a few red-cheeked children; and a buxom peasant woman, who also was wearing a costume utterly different from that of the neighboring villages, was just opening the door to admit the maid, who came in with a large dish.

And now the dumplings were smoking on the board and everyone made for the chairs, to partake of the welcome meal; but no one sat down, and the children, as it seemed to Arnold, cast almost anxious eyes on their father.

The latter advanced to his chair, and leaning his arms upon it, stared dumbly, silently, even gloomily upon the ground. Was he praying? Arnold saw that he kept his lips firmly pressed while his right hand hung down clenched by his side. In his features was no sign of prayer, only an obstinate yet irresolute defiance.

Gertrud then turned quietly to him and laid her hand on his shoulder, while the old lady stood speechless opposite to him, and looked at him with earnestly pleading eyes.

"Let us eat," growled the man, "it's no use, I fear"; and pushing his chair aside, nodded to his guest, dropped into his seat, and, seizing the huge ladle, served out helpings all round.

To Arnold the man's whole behavior was almost uncanny, nor could he feel comfortable amid the depression shown by the others. But the mayor was not the man to eat his dinner to the accompaniment of melancholy thoughts. In answer to his rap on the table the maid came in again, bearing bottles and glasses, and with the rich old wine which he now poured out, a very different and more cheerful state of mind soon prevailed among the company round the table.

The glorious beverage ran through Arnold's veins like liquid fire; never in his life had he tasted anything like it. Gertrud drank some too, and so did the old lady, who later seated herself at her spinning wheel in the corner and in a low voice sang a little song of the merry life in Germelshausen. The mayor himself seemed a different being.

He now became as cheerful and jovial as earlier he had been morose and silent, and Arnold himself could not escape the influence of the rich wine.

He could not precisely tell how it came about, but the mayor had taken a violin in his hand and was playing a merry dance, and Arnold with his arm about fair Gertrud's waist whirled with her round the room so madly that he upset the spinning wheel and the chair, bumped into the maid, who was trying to carry away the dinner things, and cut all sorts of merry capers, so that the others almost died of laughter to see him.

Suddenly there was complete silence in the room, and as Arnold looked round at the magistrate in astonishment, the latter pointed with his violin bow out of the window, and then laid the instrument back again in the wooden case from which he had taken it. And Arnold perceived that outside in the street a coffin was being carried by.

Six men dressed in white shirts were bearing it upon their shoulders, and behind them, quite alone, walked an old man, leading a little, fair-haired girl by the hand.

The old man walked along the street as one crushed with grief, but the little girl, who could hardly have been four years old, and probably had no idea who was lying in that black coffin, kept gaily nodding her head wherever she saw a face she knew, and laughed shrilly when two or three dogs scampered by and one of them ran up against the steps of the mayor's house and rolled over and over.

But the silence endured only as long as the coffin was in sight, and Gertrud drew up to the young man and said:

"Now rest a little while; you have been romping quite enough; otherwise, the heavy wine will get into your head more and more. Come, take your hat and let us go for a little walk together. By the time we get back it will be time to go to the inn, for there is a dance this evening."

"A dance? That's splendid," exclaimed Arnold, delighted; "I've come just at the right time. You'll give me the first dance, I hope, Gertrud?"

"Certainly, if you wish."

Arnold had already seized his hat and sketchbook.

"What do you want with the book?" asked the mayor.

"He sketches, Father," said Gertrud, "and he has already drawn me. Just have a look at the pictures."

Arnold opened the sketchbook and held out the picture to her father.

The farmer looked at it quietly for a while, without speaking.

"And do you want to take that home with you," he asked at length, "and perhaps frame it and hang it up in your room?"

"Why not, pray?"

"May he, Father?" asked Gertrud.

"If he does not stay with us," laughed the mayor, "I have no objection—but there's something wanting in the background."

"What?"

"Why, the funeral procession that passed a moment ago. Draw that on the paper, and you may take the picture with you."

"What! the funeral procession with Gertrud!"

"There's room enough," said the mayor obstinately; "you must put it in the sketch, or else I will not permit you to take away with you my lassie's portrait all by itself. In such solemn company no one can possibly think evil of it."

At this strange proposal to give the pretty maiden a funeral party as a guard of honor, Arnold laughingly shook his head. But the old man seemed to have made up his mind, and so, to humor him, he did as he wished. Later on he could quite easily rub out the dismal additional feature.

With practiced hand he drew on the paper the figures that had just passed by, though only from memory, and the whole family crowded round him as he worked, and watched with evident astonishment the rapid completion of the drawing.

"There, have I been successful?" cried Arnold at length, jumping up from his chair and holding out the picture at arm's length.

"Splendidly!" nodded the mayor; "I should never have thought you could finish it so quickly. Now, that will do; out you go with the lassie and have a look at the village; it may be a long while before you have a chance of seeing it again. Be back here by five o'clock sharp—we are having high jinks tonight and you must be there."

The musty room and the wine which had mounted to his head had begun to make Arnold feel heavy and oppressed. He longed to be out-of-doors, and a few minutes later he was striding along the street which led through the village, with fair Gertrud by his side.

As they made their way along there was not the same absence of noise as there had been before; children were playing in the road here and there, old people were sitting at their doors, looking at them, and the whole place with its quaint, ancient houses might have presented quite a pleasant appearance if only the sun had been able to pierce the thick brown smoke which hung like a cloud over the roofs.

"Is the moor or forest on fire hereabouts?" he asked the girl. "This sort of smoke does not hang over any other village and cannot come from the chimneys."

"It is earth vapor," said Gertrud quietly; "but have you never heard of Germelshausen?"

"Never."

"That is strange, and yet the village is old, oh! so old."

"The houses look like it, at any rate, and the people too have such a curious way with them, and their speech sounds quite differently from that of places near at hand. You go very little outside your own village, I expect?"

"Very little," said Gertrud curtly.

"And not a single swallow is left. They can't surely have flown away yet?"

"Oh, a long time ago," answered the girl apathetically; "in Germelshausen they never come now to build their nests. Perhaps they can't stand the earth vapor."

"But surely you don't have that always?"

"Yes, always."

"Then that is the reason why your fruit trees bear no fruit, and yet in Marisfeld this year they had to prop up the branches, so fruitful has the season been."

Gertrud said not a word in answer, and walked on in silence by his side straight through the village until they came to the extreme limit. On the way she gave a kindly nod to a child here and there or spoke a low word or two with one of the young girls—maybe about the evening's dance and the dresses they were to wear.

And as they talked, the girls cast sympathetic glances at the young painter, so that his heart warmed and saddened—he did not quite know why—and for all that he did not dare to ask Gertrud why it should be so.

They had now at length reached the last houses, and if it had been lively in the village itself, here at any rate everything was still and lonely and deathlike. The gardens looked as if they had not been walked in for years and years; grass was growing in the pathways, and it seemed especially noticeable to the young stranger that not a single fruit tree bore a single bit of fruit.

At this point some men met them, going back home from outside the village, and at once Arnold recognized them as the funeral party returning. They moved noiselessly past them into the village again, and almost involuntarily the pair turned their steps to the graveyard.

Arnold tried now to cheer up his companion, who seemed to him so very serious, by telling her about other places where he had been and what the great outer world was like. She had never seen a railway, never even heard of one, and listened with attention and astonishment to his explanations.

Nor had she any knowledge of the electric telegraph, and she knew just as little about all the other more modern inventions; so that the young artist could not understand how it was possible that there should be still living in Germany human beings so secluded, so absolutely cut off from the rest of the world and without the slightest connection with it.

Conversing thus, they reached the cemetery, and here the young stranger was immediately struck by the old-world appearance of the stones and monuments, simple and plain though they were as a general rule.

"Here is an old, old stone," he said, bending down to the nearest one and with difficulty deciphering the scrollwork upon it. "Anna Maria Berthold, maiden name Stieglitz, born 16th December, 1188, died 2nd December, 1224."

"That is my mother," said Gertrud solemnly, and the big, crystal tears filled her eyes and slowly trickled down on to her bodice.

"Your mother, dear child?" said Arnold in astonishment; "your great-great-grandmother perhaps it might have been."

"No," said Gertrud, "my own mother. Father married again, and the one at home is my stepmother."

"But surely it says died 1224?"

"What does the year matter?" said Gertrud mournfully. "It is sad enough to be thus parted from one's mother, and yet," she added sorrowfully under her breath, "perhaps it was well, very well that she was suffered to go to God beforehand."

Arnold bent down over the stone, shaking his head, and made a closer examination of the inscription, in case the first "2" in the date might be an "8," for in the old-time writing such a thing was not impossible, but the second "2" was exactly the same as the first, and it was as yet too soon to write 1884. Perhaps it was the stonemason who had made the mistake, and the girl was so deep in her memories of the departed that he did

not like to trouble her any further with questions that were perhaps displeasing to her.

He therefore left her by the gravestone before which she had sunk to her knees and was silently praying, and proceeded to examine some other monuments, but all of them without exception bore dates of many hundred years back, even as far back as A.D. 930 and 900. No more recent gravestone could be discovered, and yet the dead were even now laid to rest in this place, as the latest fresh grave betokened.

From the low churchyard wall there was a splendid view of the old village, and Arnold quickly availed himself of the opportunity of making a sketch of it. But over this place also lay the strange fog, though toward the wood he could see the sunlight falling bright and clear on the mountain slopes.

Then from the village came the sound of the old cracked bell again, and Gertrud, quickly rising from her knees and dashing the tears from her eyes, gently beckoned to the young man to follow her.

Arnold was quickly by her side.

"Now we must sorrow no more," she said with a smile; "the church bell is ringing the end of the service, and now for the dance. Up to the present you have no doubt imagined that the people of Germelshausen are nothing but kill-joys, but tonight you will think the contrary."

"But yonder is the church door," said Arnold, "and I can see nobody coming out."

"That is perfectly natural," laughed the girl, "for no one ever goes in, not even the priest. Only the old verger allows himself no rest, and still rings the service in and out."

"And do none of your people ever go to church?"

"No, neither to Mass nor to confession," said the girl quietly. "We have quarreled with the Pope, who lives among foreigners, and has forbidden it until we return to obedience."

"Why, I've never heard of such a thing in all my life."

"Yes, it is a long time ago," said the girl carelessly.

"Look, there's the verger all alone coming out of church and shutting the door; he never goes to the inn of an evening either, but sits all by himself at home."

"And does the priest go?"

"I should think so, and he is the jolliest of them all. He does not take things to heart."

"And how has all this come about?" asked Arnold, who was amazed not so much at the facts he had heard as at the girl's simplicity.

"It's a long story," Gertrud said, "and the priest has written it all down in a big, thick book. If you are interested, and if you understand Latin, you may read all about it there.

"But," she added by way of warning, "don't speak of it when Father is by, for he doesn't like it. Look, here come the boys and girls out-of-doors already; I must hurry off home now and dress, for I should not like to be the last."

"And the first dance, Gertrud?"

"I dance it with you; you have my promise."

The two walked quickly back to the village, which was now all astir with life, very different from what it was in the morning. Laughing groups of young people were standing about on all sides; the girls were all dressed up for the festival, and the young fellows too were in their best clothes.

while on the face of the inn, as they sped past, festoons of leaves were hanging from window to window, and formed a broad triumphal arch over the door.

Seeing that everyone was tricked out most resplendently, Arnold was unwilling to mingle with the merrymakers dressed in his traveling garb; so he unbuckled his knapsack in the mayor's house, took out of it his smart suit, and had just completed his toilet when Gertrud knocked at the door and called him.

And what a picture of loveliness the girl looked now in her simple yet rich gown, and how cordially she asked him to escort her, saying that her father and mother would not follow on till later!

"Yearning after her Heinrich cannot be depressing her spirits to any particular extent," was the youth's uppermost thought as he drew her arm through his and passed with her to the ballroom through the gathering dusk. But he refrained from giving utterance to such thoughts, for a strange, a wonderful feeling thrilled his breast, and his own heart throbbed violently as he felt the girl's heart beating against his arm.

"To think that tomorrow I must depart," he sighed softly to himself. Although he had not intended it, his words reached the ears of his companion, and she said with a smile:

"Don't trouble about that; we shall be together longer—longer perhaps than you like."

"And would you be glad, Gertrud, if I stayed with you?" asked Arnold, and as he spoke he felt the blood surging in tumultuous waves over forehead and temples.

"Of course I should," said the young girl simply: "you are nice and kind, and Father likes you too, of that I'm sure, and—Heinrich hasn't come, you know," she added in an undertone and somewhat angrily.

"Suppose he came tomorrow?"

"Tomorrow?" said Gertrud, looking at him gravely out of her great dark eyes; "between now and tomorrow lies a long, long night. Tomorrow! You will understand tomorrow what that word means. But today, let us not speak of it," she said abruptly, yet pleasantly; "today is a holiday, to which we have looked forward so long, oh! so long, and do not let us spoil it by gloomy thoughts.

"Here we are at the place; the boys will stare a good deal when they see me bringing a new partner."

Arnold was about to make some reply to her, but his words were drowned by the noisy music which rolled out from within the ballroom. Strange tunes, too, were the musicians playing, not one of which he recognized, and at first he was almost blinded by the flash of the many lights that sparkled before his eyes.

Gertrud led him into the center of the hall, where a bevy of young peasant girls stood chatting together, and not till then did she leave him to himself so that, until the real business of the dance began, he might look about him a little and make the acquaintance of the other young men.

III

At the first moment Arnold felt ill at ease among these many strangers; moreover, their strange costume and their strange speech repelled him, and though the harsh, unwonted accents came sweetly from Gertrud's lips, yet they grated on his ear when pronounced by others. The young fellows were all friendly disposed toward him, however, and one of them approached him, took him by the hand, and said:

"You have done wisely, sir, in choosing to bide with us. We lead a merry life, and the interval passes quickly enough."

"What do you mean by the interval?" asked Arnold, astonished not so much at the expression as because the youth pronounced so firmly his conviction that he had chosen to make the village his home. "Do you mean that I shall come back here?"

"But do you wish to go away?" asked the young peasant sharply.

"Tomorrow, yes, or the day after tomorrow; but I'll come back."

"Tomorrow; oh!" laughed the youth; "then that's all right. Well, we'll talk more about it tomorrow. But now come and I'll show you how we enjoy ourselves, for if you really want to go away tomorrow, you might not after all get a chance of seeing the fun."

The others looked at each other and laughed knowingly, while the young peasant took Arnold by the hand and conducted him all over the house, which was now packed full of a crowd of merrymakers. First they passed through rooms wherein sat cardplayers with great heaps of money lying before them. Next they came to a bowling alley, inlaid with shining flagstones.

In a third room, ring-throwing and other games were being played, and the young girls tripped in and out, laughing and singing and teasing the young men, till all of a sudden a flourish from the band, which up to now had been playing away merrily, gave the signal for the dance to commence, and Gertrud stood at Arnold's side and took his arm.

"Come, we must not be the last," said the lovely girl, "for as the mayor's daughter it is for me to open the ball."

"But what strange tune is that?" said Arnold; "I can't catch the time at all."

"Oh, you soon will," smiled Gertrud; "you'll catch the time in the first five minutes, and I'll tell you how."

With jubilant shouts the whole company, with the exception of the cardplayers, crowded into the ballroom, and Arnold was soon oblivious of everything else in the first blissful feeling of holding the wondrously beautiful maiden in his arms.

Again and again he danced with Gertrud, and no one else seemed to want to claim his partner from him, although the other girls often threw teasing remarks at him as they flew by.

One thing only struck him and alarmed him. Close by the inn stood the ancient church, and the shrill, discordant clang of the cracked bell could be distinctly heard in the ballroom. At the first stroke of the bell it was as if a magician's wand had smitten the dancers.

The music stopped playing in the middle of a beat, the merry surging crowd stood still and motionless, as if spellbound, and everyone silently counted the slow strokes one by one.

But as soon as the last sound died away, the animation and merriment broke out afresh. This was repeated at eight, at nine, at ten o'clock, and when Arnold would fain inquire what was the reason for such a strange proceeding, Gertrud laid her finger on her lips and at the same time looked so solemn and sad that he would not have troubled her further for all the world.

At ten o'clock there was a pause in the dancing, and the musicians, who must have had lungs of iron, headed the procession of young people down to the supper room.

There were merry doings there. The wine simply ran in streams, and Arnold, who could not be behindhand among all the others, reckoned up in his own mind what sort of hole this expensive evening would make in his modest pocket.

But Gertrud was sitting by his side, drinking with him out of the same glass, and how could he give way to any such misgivings? Even though her Heinrich should come tomorrow.

The first stroke of eleven o'clock rang out. Again the loud merriment of the revelers was silenced, again the same breathless listening to the long-drawn strokes.

A peculiar horror overcame him; he could not tell why; and the thought of his mother at home smote through his heart. He slowly raised his glass and drained it in a toast to his absent dear ones.

At the eleventh stroke the company sprang up from the table; the dancing was to begin again and they all scuttled back to the ballroom.

"Who was it you drank your last toast to?" asked Gertrud, as she laid her arm again in his.

Arnold hesitated before replying. Maybe Gertrud would only laugh at him if he told her. But no; she herself had prayed so fervently on that very afternoon by her own mother's grave—and so he said in a low voice:

"My mother."

Gertrud answered never a word, but walked in silence by his side up the stairs. Her laughter had ceased also, and before they took their places for the dance again she asked him:

"Do you love your mother so much?"

"More than life itself."

"And does she love you?"

"Does not a mother love her child?"

"And what if you never went back home to her?"

"Poor Mother!" said Arnold, "her heart would break."

"The dance is just starting again," cried Gertrud quickly; "come along, we mustn't miss a moment more."

So wilder than ever the dance began. The young men, fired by the strong wine, shouted and hurrahed, and shrieked, and such a din arose as threatened to drown the music.

Arnold did not now feel so happy in all this uproar, and Gertrud too had become serious and silent. But with all the others the merriment seemed only to increase, and during a pause the mayor came up to them, gave the young man a hearty slap on the shoulder, and said, laughing:

"That's right, Mr. Painter, shake a merry leg tonight; we shall have plenty of time to have a good long rest. Nay, then, Gertie, why pull such a solemn face? Does that fit in with the dance this day? Merry's the word—there, they're off again! Now I must look up my old woman and trip the last dance with her. Take your places; the bandsmen are fairly bursting their cheeks again." And with a huzzah he plunged through the crowd of revelers.

Arnold was embracing Gertrud once more for a fresh dance when the latter suddenly broke away from him, gripped his arm, and whispered softly: "Come!"

Arnold had no time to ask her whither, for she slipped from his grasp and sped away toward the door.

"Whither away, Gertie?" some of her playmates called out to them.

"Coming back in a moment," came the sound of her curt answer, and a few seconds later she was standing with Arnold outside before the house in the sharp night air.

"Where do you propose to go, Gertrud?"

"Come!"

Again she caught his arm and led him through the village, past her father's house, into which she dashed and presently emerged with a small bundle.

"What is the meaning of this?" asked Arnold in alarm.

"Come!" was the only word she said in answer, and past the houses she strode with him until they left the outermost wall of the village behind them. So far they had followed the broad, firm, hard-trodden highway; now Gertrud turned off the road to the left and mounted a little, low hill from the top of which could be seen the brilliantly lighted windows and doors of the inn.

Here she came to a halt, held out her hand to Arnold, and said tenderly:

"My greetings to your mother; farewell!"

"Gertrud," cried Arnold, astonished, aghast, "do you wish to send me away from you thus, now, in the middle of the night? Has any word of mine offended you?"

"No, Arnold," said the girl, calling him by his Christian name for the first time. "Just . . . just because I love you, you must go away."

"But I cannot let you go away from me back to the village like this, all alone and in the dark," pleaded Arnold. "Girl, you don't know how much I love you, how utterly and entirely you have won my heart in these few hours. You know not . . ."

"Say no more," she interrupted him quickly, "we will not say good-by. When the clock has struck twelve —it can hardly want ten minutes yet—return to the inn door; there I shall be expecting you."

"And until then . . . !"

"Stay just where you are. Promise me not to take one step to right or left till the clock has struck the last stroke of twelve."

"I promise, Gertrud; but then . . ."

"Then come," she said, holding out her hand in farewell, and would have left him.

"Gertrud!" cried Arnold, in a pleading, anguished voice.

Gertrud stood a moment as if in hesitation, then suddenly she turned toward him, threw her arms around his neck; and Arnold felt the icy lips of the lovely maiden pressed on his. It was but for a moment; in the next instant she had torn herself away and was flying toward the village. And Arnold in amazement at her strange behavior, yet mindful of his promise, remained standing just where she had left him.

Now for the first time he saw how the weather had changed in these few hours. The wind was howling through the trees, the sky was overcast with heavy racing clouds, and one or two large drops of rain proclaimed the approach of a storm.

Through the darkness of the night the lights glowed bright from the inn, and when the wind came roaring across he could hear in broken waves of sound the riotous blare of the instruments—but not for long. Only for a few moments had he been standing in his place when the clock in the old church tower began to strike. In that same instant the music ceased or was drowned in the howling storm, which raged so violently over the hill slope that Arnold was obliged to stoop down to the ground in order not to lose his balance.

Before him on the ground he felt the bundle which Gertrud had fetched out of the house—his own knapsack and sketchbook—and affrighted, he stood upright again. The clock had finished striking, the hurricane roared past over his head, but nowhere in the village was there any longer a light to be seen. The dogs which but a short while ago had been barking and howling were silent, and a thick, damp mist was rising up from the hollow.

"The time is up," muttered Arnold to himself, hoisting his knapsack on his back, "and I must see Gertrud once again; I cannot part from her like this. The dance is over; the dancers will now be going home, and if the mayor will not put me up for the night I can stay at the inn. Besides, in the darkness I shouldn't find my way through the forest."

He cautiously went down the gentle slope which he and Gertrud had ascended together, in order to strike the broad white road which would bring him to the village, but in vain did he grope about for it among the bushes below.

The ground was soft and swampy, and in his thin boots he sank in up to the ankles; there was everywhere a tangle of alder bushes growing just where he had imagined the road to be. He could not possibly have crossed it in the dark; he could not have failed to feel it the moment he stepped on it; and besides, he knew that the village wall ran right across it—this at any rate he could not miss.

But it was in vain that with anguished haste he sought for it; the ground became more soft, more swampy the farther he advanced, the undergrowth became thicker and everywhere beset with thorns, which tore his clothes and scratched his hands till they bled.　　.

Had he wandered off to the right or to the left and beyond the village? He feared lest he should lose his bearings still more completely, and came to a halt on a fairly dry spot, determined to wait there until the old clock should strike one.

But it did not strike, not a dog barked, no sound of human voice reached him, and with great difficulty, wet to the skin and shivering with cold, he toiled back again to the higher ground of the hill slope where Gertrud had left him.

From this spot he tried, indeed, a few more times to penetrate the thicket and find the village, but in vain. Tired to death, and a prey to a peculiar horror, he at last avoided the low, dark, weird hollow and sought the shelter of a tree, there to spend the night.

And how slowly for him did the hours pass by! For shivering as he was with cold, he was not able to steal from that long night even one moment's sleep. And he was forever straining his ears into the darkness, as again and again he thought he heard the rasping sound of the bell, only to find again and again that he had been mistaken.

At last the first glow of light began to dawn out of the far east. The clouds had dispersed, the sky was once more clear and bright with stars, and the awakening birds twittered softly in the gloomy trees.

Brighter and lighter grew the golden horizon; already he could clearly discern the treetops round about him; but it was in vain that his eye sought the view of the old brown church tower and the weather-worn roofs. Nothing but a wilderness of alderbushes, dotted here and there with a few stunted willows, stretched out before him. No road was to be seen leading to the right or to the left, no sign of human habitation in the vicinity.

The day broke clearer and clearer. The earliest sunbeams fell upon the broad green expanse that spread out before his gaze; and Arnold, who was at a loss to solve the riddle, wandered some considerable distance back into the valley. He must, he thought, have lost his way in the dark, without knowing it, while he was seeking for the place, and had got too far away. He was now firmly determined to find it again.

At length he came to the stone near which he had drawn Gertrud's picture. This spot he would have recognized again out of thousands, for the old lilac tree with its stiff branches indicated it only too clearly.

He now knew exactly from what direction he had come and where Germelshausen must lie; so he paced rapidly back along the valley, keeping closely to the same track which he and Gertrud had followed yesterday. Over there also he recognized the bend in the slope over which had hung the murky fog, and only the alder bushes still separated him from the nearest houses.

Now he had reached it; he pressed on and—found himself once more in the very same swampy morass in which he had waded about the night before.

Completely at a loss and not trusting his own senses, he was for forcing a way through at this point, but the filthy swamp ooze at length compelled him to make for dry ground again, and there he wandered helplessly backward and forward.

The village had disappeared, and that was the end of it.

Several hours had perhaps been consumed in this fruitless search, and his weary limbs at last refused to serve him any longer. He could go no further; before anything else he must rest. What had been the use of his vain quest? At the first village he came across he could easily find a guide to conduct him to Germelshausen, and then he could not miss the road again.

Dead tired, he flung himself down under a tree—and how utterly ruined was his best suit! This, however, did not trouble him now; he produced his sketchbook and out of it he took Gertrud's portrait. With bitter pain his eyes fastened on the dear, sweet features of the maiden, who, as he realized to his great alarm, had already taken too firm a hold upon his heart.

Then he heard behind him a rustling among the leaves—a dog began to bark; and quickly springing to his feet, he was aware of an old woodsman standing not far away from him and curiously observing the strange figure who was so decently dressed and yet presented such a wild appearance.

"Greeting!" exlaimed Arnold, heartily pleased to meet a human being, and quickly thrusting the picture back into the portfolio. "You could not have been more welcome if I had invited you here, Herr Forester, for I think I have lost my way."

"Hm," said the old man, "if you have been lying here in the bush all night, I should think so too, and hardly half an hour's walk over yonder to Dillstedt and a good inn. Heavens! what a sight you are, for all the world as if you had been dragged neck and crop out of thorns and mud!"

"Are you quite familiar with the forest here?" asked Arnold, who before all things wanted to know where he really was.

"I should think I was," laughed the woodsman as he struck a light and lighted his pipe again.

"What is the name of the nearest village?"

"Dillstedt—straight over there. When you get on to that little hill yonder, you can easily see it lying below you."

"And how far is it from here to Germelshausen?"

"To where?" cried the woodsman, removing his pipe in horror from his lips.

"To Germelshausen."

"God help me!" said the old man, casting a scared look about him; "the forest I know well enough, but how many fathoms deep down below the earth the 'cursed village' lies, God alone knows—nor is it any business of ours."

"The 'cursed village'?" cried Arnold in astonishment.

"Germelshausen—yes," said the woodsman. "Just there in the swamp, where now grow the old willows and alders, it is said to have stood hundreds and hundreds of years ago. Later on it sank away, no man knows why or whither; and the story goes that every hundred years on a certain day it is raised up again to the light of heaven, but I should not wish any Christian man to chance to be there then.

"But, man alive! camping out in the bush last night does not seem to have agreed with you. You look as white as a ghost. There now, just you have a sip out of this flask;

it will do you good—now have a good pull!"

"Thank you."

"Tut, tut, that wasn't half enough —take a proper, first-class pull at it. That's right; that's the real stuff to take. And now make haste and get across to the inn, and into a warm bed."

"In Dillstedt?"

"Why, of course: there's none nearer."

"What about Germelshausen?"

"Be good enough not to mention the place again, especially here on the spot where we are standing. Let the dead rest, and above all those who do not even enjoy rest, but keep on rising again unexpectedly amongst us."

"But only yesterday the village was still standing here," cried Arnold, who had almost lost his trust in his own senses. "I was inside it—eating and drinking and dancing there!"

The woodsman calmly looked the young man up and down, and then said with a smile:

"But it went by some other name, didn't it? Probably you have come straight over from Dillstedt. There was a dance there yesterday evening, and it's not everybody can stand the strong beer that the landlord brews at present."

By the way of answer Arnold opened his portfolio and drew out the drawing that he had made from the churchyard.

"Do you know that village?"

"No," said the woodsman shaking his head; "there's not such a flat tower as that in the whole countryside."

"That is Germelshausen," cried Arnold; "and do the peasant girls in this neighborhood dress as this girl does here?"

"Um—no! and what's that queer-looking funeral procession you have put in the picture?"

Arnold returned no answer. He thrust the sheets back again into the portfolio, and a strange feeling of pain thrilled through him.

"You can't miss the road to Dillstedt," said the woodsman good-naturedly, for a dark suspicion now occurred to him that the stranger might perhaps not be quite right in the head. "But if you would like, I will accompany you till we come to where we can see the place; that won't take me much out of my way."

Arnold declined with many thanks. "I'll find my way over there all right. And so it is only once in every hundred years that they say the village comes up again?"

"So people say," answered the woodsman, "but who can say if it is true?"

Arnold had taken up his knapsack again.

"God be wi' you!" he said, holding out his hand to the woodsman.

"Many thanks," answered he; "where are you going now?"

"To Dillstedt."

"That's right—when you get over the slope you'll come to the broad highroad again."

Arnold turned away, and slowly proceeded on his way. Only when he had reached the top of the slope which commanded a view over the whole of the valley did he pause once again and look back.

"Farewell, Gertrud!" he murmured softly, and as he walked over the hill, the big crystal tears were streaming from his eyes.

Giovanni Verga

1840-1922

ALTHOUGH he lived more than fourscore years, Giovanni Verga's period of creative writing was very short. In his prime he was Italy's foremost novelist and short-story writer, but the works which gave him that position were all written between 1880 and 1889. Like so many young men with a literary bent, Verga left home at an early age and went to the city to seek his fame. Florence was then the cultural center of Italy. There Verga came under the influence of the literary circle that frequented the famous *salotti* of the Countess Maffei. He wrote, but not well and not successfully. It was not until he left Florence and returned to his home in the countryside of Sicily that he found real inspiration. He now wrote of the peasants with whom he had grown up, stories of local habits and of old customs. *Vita dei campi* (published in English as *Under the Shadow of Etna*), from which "The Saint Joseph's Ass" is taken, and *Cavalleria Rusticana*, more charming as a story than as an opera, are the books on which his reputation was made.

With the new generation, which turned to d'Annunzio, Verga fell out of fashion. For thirty years he was all but forgotten. There was a belated revival of interest when on his eightieth birthday the government made him a senator, and when he died two years later, his funeral cortege extended for miles. D. H. Lawrence's translation of his stories as *Little Novels of Sicily*, published in 1923, reintroduced Verga to the English-reading world.

The Saint Joseph's Ass

BY GIOVANNI VERGA

THEY had bought him at the fair at Buccheri when he was quite a foal, when as soon as he saw a she-ass he went up to her to find her teats, for which he got a good many bangs on the head and showers of blows upon the buttocks, and caused a great shouting of "Gee back!" Neighbor Neli, seeing him lively and stubborn as he was, a young creature that licked his nose after it had been hit, giving his ears a shake, said, "This is the chap for me!" And he went straight to the owner, holding in his pocket his hand which clasped the thirty-five shillings.

"It's a fine foal," said the owner, "and it's worth more than five-and-thirty shillings. Never mind if he's got that black-and-white skin, like a magpie. I'll just show you his mother, whom we keep there in the bough shelter because the foal has always got his nose at the teats. You'll see a fine black beast there; she works for me better than a mule, and has brought me more young ones than she has hairs on her back. Upon my soul, I don't know where that magpie jacket has come from, on the foal. But he's sound in the bone, I tell you! And you don't value men according to their faces. Look what a chest and

legs like pillars! Look how he holds his ears! An ass that keeps his ears straight up like that, you can put him in a cart or in the plow as you like, and make him carry ten quarters of buckwheat better than a mule, as true as this is holy day today! Feel his tail, if you and all your family couldn't hang on to it!"

Neighbor Neli knew it better than he; but he wasn't such a fool as to agree, and stood on his own, with his hand in his pocket, shrugging his shoulders and curling his nose, while the owner led the colt round in front of him.

"Hm!" muttered neighbor Neli, "with that hide on him, he's like Saint Joseph's ass. Those colored animals are all Jonahs, and when you ride through the village on their backs everybody laughs at you. What do you want me to make you a present of, for Saint Joseph's ass?"

Then the owner turned his back on him in a rage, shouting that if he didn't know anything about animals, or if he hadn't got the money to pay with, he'd better not come to the fair and make Christians waste their time, on the blessed day that it was.

Neighbor Neli let him swear, and

From *Little Novels of Sicily* by Giovanni Verga, translated by D. H. Lawrence. By permission of The Viking Press, Inc. Copyright, 1925, by Thomas Seltzer, Inc.

went off with his brother, who was pulling him by his jacket sleeve, and saying that if he was going to throw away his money on that ugly beast he deserved to be kicked.

However, on the sly they kept their eye on the Saint Joseph's ass, and on its owner who was pretending to shell some broad beans, with the halter rope between his legs, while neighbor Neli went wandering round among the groups of mules and horses, and stopping to look, and bargaining for first one and then the other of the best beasts, without ever opening the fist which he kept in his pocket with the thirty-five shillings, as if he'd got the money to buy half the fair. But his brother said in his ear, motioning toward the ass of Saint Joseph, "That's the chap for us!"

The wife of the owner of the ass from time to time ran to look what had happened, and finding her husband with the halter in his hand, she said to him, "Isn't the Madonna going to send us anybody today to buy the foal?"

And her husband answered every time: "Not so far! There came one man to try for him, and he liked him. But he drew back when he had to pay for him, and has gone off with his money. See him, that one there, in the white stocking cap, behind the flock of sheep. But he's not bought anything up to now, which means he'll come back."

The woman would have liked to sit down on a couple of stones, just close to her ass, to see if he would be sold. But her husband said to her: "You clear out! If they see we're waiting, they'll never come to bargain."

Meanwhile the foal kept nuzzling with his nose between the legs of the she-asses that passed by, chiefly because he was hungry, and his master, the moment the young thing opened his mouth to bray, fetched him a bang and made him be quiet, because the buyers wouldn't want him if they heard him.

"It's still there," said neighbor Neli in his brother's ear, pretending to come past again to look for the man who was selling broiled chick-peas. "If we wait till Ave Maria we can get him for five shillings less than the price we offered."

The sun of May was hot, so that from time to time, in the midst of the shouting and swarming of the fair, there fell a great silence over all the fairground, as if there was nobody there, and then the mistress of the ass came back to say to her husband: "Don't you hold out for five shillings more or less, because there's no money to buy anything in with, this evening; and then you know the foal will eat five shillings' worth in a month, if he's left on our hands."

"If you're not going," replied her husband, "I'll fetch you a kick you won't forget!"

So the hours of the fair rolled by, but none of those who passed before the ass of Saint Joseph stopped to look at him; for, sure enough, his master had chosen the most humble position, next the low-price cattle, so as not to make him show up too badly beside the beautiful bay mules and the glossy horses! It took a fellow like neighbor Neli to go and bargain for the Saint Joseph's ass, which set everybody in the fair laughing the moment they saw it. With having waited so long in the sun the foal let his head and his ears drop, and his owner had seated himself gloomily on the stones, with his hands also dangling between his knees, and the halter in his hands, watching here and there the long shadows, which began to form in the plain as the sun went down, from the legs of all the beasts which had not found a buyer. Then Neli and his brother, and another friend whom they had picked up for the occasion, came walking that way, looking into the air, so that the owner of the ass also twisted his head away to show he wasn't sitting there waiting for them; and the friend of neighbor Neli said like this, looking vacant, as if the idea had just come to him:

"Oh, look at the ass of Saint Joseph! Why don't you buy him, neighbor Neli?"

"I asked the price of him this morning; he's too dear. Then I should have everybody laughing at me with that black-and-white donkey. You can see that nobody would have him, so far."

"That's a fact, but the color doesn't matter, if a thing is any use to you."

And he asked of the owner: "How much do you expect us to make you a present of, for that Saint Joseph's donkey?"

The wife of the owner of the ass of Saint Joseph, seeing that the bargaining had started again, came edging softly up to them, with her hands clasped under her short cloak.

"Don't mention such a thing!" neighbor Neli began to shout, running away across the plain. "Don't mention such a thing to me, I won't hear a word of it."

"If he doesn't want it, let him go without it," answered the owner. "If he doesn't take it, somebody else will. It's a sad man who had nothing left to sell, after the fair!"

"But I mean him to listen to me, by the blessed devil I do!" squealed the friend. "Can't I say my own fool's say like anybody else?"

And he ran to seize neighbor Neli by the jacket, and he came back to speak a word in the ear of the ass's owner, who now wanted at any cost to go home with his little donkey; so the friend threw his arms round his neck, whispering: "Listen! five shillings more or less, if you don't sell it today; you won't find another softy like my pal here to buy your beast, which isn't worth a cigar."

And he embraced the ass's mistress also, talking in her ear, to get her on his side. But she shrugged her shoulders and replied with a sullen face: "It's my man's business. It's nothing to do with me. But if he lets you have it for less than forty shillings he's a simpleton, in all conscience! It cost us more!"

"I was a lunatic to offer thirty-five shillings this morning," put in neighbor Neli. "You see now whether you've found anybody else to buy it at that price. There's nothing left in all the fair but three or four scabby sheep and the ass of Saint Joseph. Thirty shillings now, if you like."

"Take it," suggested the ass's mistress to her husband, with tears in her eyes. "We haven't a penny to buy anything tonight, and Turiddu has got the fever on him again; he needs some sulphate."

"All the devils!" bawled her husband. "If you don't get out, I'll give you a taste of the halter!"

"Thirty-two-and-six, there!" cried the friend at last, shaking him hard by the jacket collar. "Neither you nor me! This time you've got to take my word, by all the saints in paradise! And I don't ask as much as a glass of wine. You can see the sun's gone down. Then what are you waiting for, the pair of you?"

And he snatched the halter from the owner's hand, while neighbor Neli, swearing, drew out of his pocket the fist with the thirty-five shillings, and gave them him without looking at them, as if he was tearing out his own liver. The friend drew aside with the mistress of the ass, to count the money on a stone, while the owner of the ass rushed through the fair like a young colt, swearing and punching himself on the head.

But then he permitted himself to go back to his wife, who was very slowly and carefully counting over again the money in the handkerchief, and he asked, "Is it right?"

"Yes, it's quite right; Saint Gaetano be praised! Now I'll go to the chemist."

"I've fooled them! I'd have given it him for twenty shillings, if I'd had to; those colored donkeys are all Jonahs."

And neighbor Neli, leading the little donkey behind him down the slope, said: "As true as God's above I've stolen his foal from him! The color doesn't matter. Look what legs, like pillars, neighbor. He's worth forty shillings with your eyes shut."

"If it hadn't been for me," replied the friend, "you wouldn't have done a thing. Here, I've still got two-and-six of yours. And if you like, we'll go and drink your donkey's health with it."

And now the colt stood in need of all his health to earn back the thirty-two-and-six he had cost, and the straw he ate. Meanwhile he took upon himself to keep gamboling behind neighbor Neli, trying to bite his jacket in fun, as if he knew it was the jacket of his new master,

and he didn't care a rap about leaving forever the stable where he had lived in the warmth, near his mother, rubbing his muzzle on the edge of the manger, or butting and capering with the ram, or going to rouse up the pig in its corner. And his mistress, who was once more counting the money in the handkerchief in front of the druggist's counter, she didn't either once think of how she had seen the foal born, all black and white with his skin as glossy as silk, and he couldn't stand on his legs yet, but lay nestling in the sun in the yard, and all the grass which he had eaten to get so big and stout had passed through her hands. The only one who remembered her foal was the she-ass, who stretched out her neck, braying toward the stable door, but when she no longer had her teats swollen with milk, she too forgot about the foal.

"Now this creature," said neighbor Neli, "you'll see he'll carry me ten quarters of buckwheat better than a mule. And at harvest I'll set him threshing."

At the threshing the colt, tied in a string with the other beasts, old mules and broken-down horses, trotted round over the sheaves from morning till night, till he was so tired he didn't even want to open his mouth to bite at the heap of straw when they had put him to rest in the shade, now that a little wind had sprung up, so that the peasants could toss up the grain into the air with broad wooden forks to winnow it, crying, *Viva Maria!*

Then he let his muzzle and his ears hang down, like a grown-up ass, his eye spent, as if he was tired of looking out over the vast white campagna which fumed here and there with the dust from the threshing floors, and it seemed as if he was made for nothing else but to be let die of thirst and made to trot round on the sheaves. At evening he went back to the village with full saddle-bags, and the master's lad went behind him, pricking him between the legs, along the hedges of the byway that seemed alive with the twittering of the tits and the scent of catmint and of rosemary, and the donkey would have liked to snatch a mouthful, if they hadn't made him trot all the time, till the blood ran down his legs, and they had to take him to the vet; but his master didn't care, because the harvest had been a good one, and the colt had earned his thirty-two-and-six. His master said: "Now he's done his work, and if I sell him for twenty shillings I've still made money by him."

The only one who was fond of the foal was the lad who made him trot along the little road, when they were coming home from the threshing floor, and he cried while the farrier was burning the creature's legs with a red-hot iron, so that the colt twisted himself up, with his tail in the air and his ears as erect as when he had roved round the fairground, and he tried to get free from the twisted rope which pressed his lips, and he rolled his eyes with pain almost as if he had human understanding when the farrier's lad came to change the red-hot irons, and his skin smoked and frizzled like fish in a frying pan. But neighbor Neli shouted at his son: "Silly fool! what are you crying for? He's done his work now, and seeing that the harvest has gone well, we'll sell him and buy a mule, which will be better for us."

Some things children don't understand; and after they had sold the colt to Farmer Cirino from Licodia,

neighbor Neli's son used to go to visit it in the stable, to stroke its nose and its neck, and the ass would turn to snuff at him as if its heart were still bound to him, whereas donkeys are made to be tied up where their master wishes, and they change their fate as they change their stable. Farmer Cirino from Licodia had bought the Saint Joseph's ass cheap, because it still had the wound in the pastern; and the wife of neighbor Neli, when she saw the ass going by with its new master, said: "There goes our luck; that black-and-white hide brings a jolly threshing floor; and now times go from bad to worse, so that we've even sold the mule again."

Farmer Cirino had yoked the ass to the plow, with the old horse that went like a jewel, drawing out his own brave furrow all day long, for miles and miles, from the time when the larks began to trill in the dawn-white sky till when the robins ran to huddle behind the bare twigs that quivered in the cold, with their short flight and their melancholy chirping, in the mist which rose like a sea. Only, seeing that the ass was smaller than the horse, they had put him a pad of straw on the saddle, under the yoke, and he went at it harder than ever, breaking the frozen sod, pulling with all his might from the shoulder. "This creature saves my horse for me, because he's getting old," said Farmer Cirino. "He's got a heart as big as the plain of Catania, has that ass of Saint Joseph! And you'd never think it."

And he said to his wife, who was following behind him clutched in her scanty cloak, parsimoniously scattering the seed: "If anything should happen to him, think what a loss it would be! We should be ruined, with all the season's work in hand."

And the woman looked at the work in hand, at the little stony, desolate field, where the earth was white and cracked, because there had been no rain for so long, the water coming all in mist, the mist that rots the seed; so that when the time came to hoe the young corn it was like the devil's beard, so sparse and yellow, as if you'd burned it with matches. "In spite of the way we worked that land!" whined Farmer Cirino, tearing off his jacket. "That donkey puts his guts into it like a mule! He's the ass of misfortune, he is."

His wife had a lump in her throat when she looked at that burned-up cornfield, and only answered with the big tears that came to her eyes. "It isn't the donkey's fault. He brought a good year to neighbor Neli. It's us who are unlucky."

So the ass of Saint Joseph changed masters once more, for Farmer Cirino went back again with his sickle from the cornfield; there was no need to reap it that year, in spite of the fact that they'd hung images of the saints on to the cane hedge, and had spent ninepence having it blessed by the priest. "The devil is after us!" Farmer Cirino went swearing through those ears of corn that stood up straight like feathers, which even the ass wouldn't eat; and he spat into the air at the blue sky that had not a drop of water in it. Then neighbor Luciano the carter, meeting Farmer Cirino leading home the ass with empty saddlebags, asked him: "What do you want me to give you for Saint Joseph's ass?"

"Give me what you like. Curse him and whoever made him," replied Farmer Cirino. "Now we haven't got bread to eat, nor barley to give to the beast."

"I'll give you fifteen shillings because you're ruined; but the ass isn't worth it, he won't last above six months. See what a poor sight he is!"

"You ought to have asked more," Farmer Cirino's wife began to grumble after the bargain was concluded. "Neighbor Luciano's mule has died, and he hasn't the money to buy another. If he hadn't bought the Saint Joseph's ass he wouldn't know what to do with his cart and harness; and you'll see that donkey will bring him riches."

The ass then learned to pull the cart, which was too high on the shafts for him, and weighed so heavily on his shoulders that he wouldn't have lasted even six months, scrambling his way up the steep, rough roads, when it took all neighbor Luciano's cudgeling to put a bit of breath into his body; and when he went downhill it was worse, because all the load came down on top of him, and pressed on him so much that he had to hold on with his back curved up in an arch, with those poor legs that had been burned by fire, so that people seeing him began to laugh, and when he fell down it took all the angels of paradise to get him up again. But neighbor Luciano knew that he pulled his ton and a half of stuff better than a mule, and he got paid two shillings a half ton. "Every day the Saint Joseph's ass lives it means six shillings I earned," he said, "and he costs me less to feed than a mule." Sometimes people toiling up on foot at a snail's pace behind the cart, seeing that poor beast digging his hoofs in with no strength left, and arching his spine, breathing quick, his eye hopeless, suggested: "Put a stone under the wheel, and let that poor beast get his wind." But neighbor Luciano replied: "If I let him go his own pace he'll never earn me any six shillings a day. I've got to mend my own skin with his. When he can't do another stroke I'll sell him to the lime man, for the creature is a good one and will do for him; and it's not true a bit that Saint Joseph's asses are Jonahs. I got him for a crust of bread from Farmer Cirino, now he's come down and is poor."

Then the Saint Joseph's ass fell into the hands of the lime man, who had about twenty donkeys, all thin skeletons just ready to drop, but which managed nevertheless to carry him his little sacks of lime, and lived on mouthfuls of weeds which they could snatch from the roadside as they went. The lime man didn't want him because he was all covered with scars worse than the other beasts, and his legs seared with fire, and his shoulders worn out with the collar, and his withers gnawed by the plow saddle, and his knees broken by his falls, and then that black-and-white skin which in his opinion didn't go at all with his other black animals. "That doesn't matter," replied Luciano. "It'll help you to know your own asses at a distance." And he took off another ninepence from the seven shillings which he had asked, to close the bargain. But even the mistress who had seen him born would no longer have recognized the Saint Joseph's ass, he was so changed, as he went with his nose to the ground and his ears like an umbrella, under the little sacks of lime, twisting his behind at the blows from the boy who was driving the herd. But the mistress herself had also changed by then, with the bad times there had

been, and the hunger she had felt, and the fevers that they'd all caught down on the plain, she, her husband, and her Turiddu, without any money to buy sulphate, for one hasn't got a Saint Joseph's ass to sell every day, not even for thirty-five shillings.

In winter, when work was scarce, and the wood for burning the lime was rarer and farther to fetch, and the frozen little roads hadn't a leaf on their hedges, or a mouthful of stubble along the frozen ditchside, life was harder for those poor beasts; and the owner knew that the winter would carry off half of them for him; so that he usually had to buy a good stock of them in the spring. At night the herd lay in the open, near the kiln, and the beasts did the best for themselves, pressing close up to one another. But those stars that shone like swords pierced them in their vulnerable parts, in spite of their thick hides, and all their sores and galls burned again and trembled in the cold as if they could speak.

However, there are plenty of Christians who are no better off, and even haven't got that rag of a cloak in which the herd boy curled himself up to sleep in front of the furnace. A poor widow lived close by—in a hovel even more dilapidated than the lime kiln, so that the stars pierced through the roof like swords, as if you were in the open, and the wind made the few rags of coverlets flutter. She used to do washing, but it was a lean business, because folk washed their own rags, when they were washed at all, and now that her boy was grown she lived by going down to the village to sell wood. But nobody had known her husband, and nobody knew where she got the wood she sold;

though her boy knew, because he went to glean it here and there, at the risk of being shot at by the estate keepers. "If you had a donkey," said the lime man, who wanted to sell the Saint Joseph's ass because it was no longer any good to him, "you could carry bigger bundles to the village, now that your boy is grown."

The poor woman had a shilling or two tied in a corner of a handkerchief, and she let the lime man get them out of her, because they said that "old stuff goes to die in the house of the crazy."

At least the poor Saint Joseph's ass lived his last days a little better; because the widow cherished him like a treasure, thanks to the pennies he had cost her, and she went out at nights to get him straw and hay, and kept him in the hut beside the bed, so that he helped to keep them all warm, like a little fire, he did, and in this world one hand washes the other. The woman, driving before her the ass laden with wood like a mountain, so that you couldn't see his ears, went building castles in the air; and the boy foraged round the hedges and ventured into the margins of the wood to get the load together, till both mother and son imagined themselves growing rich at the trade; till at last the baron's estate keeper caught the boy in the act of stealing boughs and tanned his hide for him thoroughly with a stick. To cure the boy the doctor swallowed up all the pence in his handkerchief, the stock of wood, and all there was to sell, which wasn't much; so that one

night when the boy was raving with fever, his inflamed face turned toward the wall, and there wasn't a mouthful of bread in the house, the mother went out raving and talking to herself as if she had got the fever as well; and she went and broke down an almond tree close by, though it didn't seem possible that she could have managed to do it, and at dawn she loaded it on the ass to go and sell it. But under the weight, as he tried to get up the steep path, the donkey kneeled down really like Saint Joseph's ass before the Infant Jesus, and couldn't get up again.

"Holy spirits," murmured the woman, "oh, carry that load of wood for me, you yourselves."

And some passers-by pulled the ass by the rope and hit his ears to make him get up.

"Don't you see he's dying," said a carter at last, and so the others left him in peace, since the ass had eyes like a dead fish, and a cold nose, and shivers running over his skin.

The woman thought of her son in his delirium, with his face red with fever, and she stammered: "Now what shall we do? Now what shall we do?"

"If you want to sell him with all the wood I'll give you two shillings for him," said the carter, who had his wagon empty. And as the woman looked at him with vacant eyes, he added, "I'm only buying the wood, because that's all the ass is worth!" And he gave a kick at the carcass, which sounded like a burst drum.

Robert Louis Stevenson

1850-1894

DURING his lifetime and for many years following his death Robert Louis Stevenson was the most beloved of writers, and far and away the most attractive figure in the literary world of his generation. "The most inspiriting, the most fascinating human being that I have ever known," Edmund Gosse said.

Stevenson contracted tuberculosis at an early age and spent a good part of his life traveling in search of health. Born in Edinburgh, he was graduated there as a civil engineer and later admitted to the bar. But Scotland, which he so dearly loved, was the one country that his fragile health could not stand up against. Every year he stayed there he became worse. He tried France and Germany and eventually America. (While in California he married the woman with whom he had long been in love—an American woman of forceful personality, eleven years older than he, and married when he met her. After her divorce they lived in the mining camp described in *The Silverado Squatters.*) In the course of the years he went to Saranac, the New Jersey coast, Davos, and the French Riviera. Finally he bought a schooner, and with his wife and stepson cruised in warm waters on a long last journey that ended in Samoa, where he later died.

At no time could Stevenson work more than a few hours of a few consecutive days, and most of his writing had to be done in bed. But he was indefatigable, and his output—essays, stories, novels, poetry, travel books—is both considerable and brilliant. The full charm of his personality, so inseparable from his writing, comes through most vividly in his letters, collected and published after his death.

In Samoa the natives called Stevenson Tusitala (Teller of Tales). They loved him dearly, and buried him, at his own request, high on a mountain peak.

"A Lodging for the Night" was his first published story, and one of his most successful.

A Lodging for the Night

BY ROBERT LOUIS STEVENSON

It was late in November, 1456. The snow fell over Paris with rigorous, relentless persistence; sometimes the wind made a sally and scattered it in flying vortices; sometimes there was a lull, and flake after flake descended out of the black night air, silent, circuitous, interminable. To poor people, looking up under moist eyebrows, it seemed a wonder where it all came from. Master Francis Villon had propounded an alternative that afternoon at a tavern window: was it only Pagan Jupiter plucking geese upon Olympus? or were the holy angels moulting? He was only a poor Master of Arts, he went on; and as the question somewhat touched upon divinity, he durst not venture to conclude. A silly old priest from Montargis, who was among the company, treated the young rascal to a bottle of wine in honor of the jest and grimaces with which it was accompanied, and swore on his own white beard that he had been just such another irreverent dog when he was Villon's age.

The air was raw and pointed, but not far below freezing; and the flakes were large, damp, and adhesive. The whole city was sheeted up. An army might have marched from end to end and not a footfall given the alarm. If there were any belated birds in heaven, they saw the island like a large white patch, and the bridges like slim white spars, on the black ground of the river. High up overhead the snow settled among the tracery of the cathedral towers. Many a niche was drifted full; many a statue wore a long white bonnet on its grotesque or sainted head. The gargoyles had been transformed into great false noses, drooping towards the point. The crockets were like upright pillows swollen on one side. In the intervals of the wind, there was a dull sound of dripping about the precincts of the church.

The cemetery of St. John had taken its own share of the snow. All the graves were decently covered; tall white housetops stood around in grave array; worthy burghers were long ago in bed, benightcapped like their domiciles; there was no light in all the neighborhood but a little peep from a lamp that hung swinging in the church choir, and tossed the shadows to and fro in time to its oscillations. The clock was hard on ten when the patrol went by with halberds and a lantern, beating their hands; and they saw nothing suspicious about the cemetery of St. John.

Yet there was a small house, backed up against the cemetery wall, which was still awake, and awake to evil purpose, in that snoring district. There was not much to betray it from without; only a stream of warm vapor from the chimney top, a patch where the snow melted on the roof, and a few half-obliterated footprints at the door. But within, behind the shuttered windows, Master Francis Villon the poet, and some of the thievish crew with whom he consorted, were keeping the night alive and passing round the bottle.

A great pile of living embers diffused a strong and ruddy glow from the arched chimney. Before this straddled Dom Nicolas, the Picardy monk, with his skirts picked up and his fat legs bared to the comfortable warmth. His dilated shadow cut the room in half; and the firelight only escaped on either side of his broad person, and in a little pool between his outspread feet. His face had the beery, bruised appearance of the continual drinker's; it was covered with a network of congested veins, purple in ordinary circumstances, but now pale violet, for even with his back to the fire the cold pinched him on the other side. His cowl had half fallen back, and made a strange excrescence on either side of his bull neck. So he straddled, grumbling, and cut the room in half with the shadow of his portly frame.

On the right, Villon and Guy Tabary were huddled together over a scrap of parchment; Villon making a ballade which he was to call the "Ballade of Roast Fish," and Tabary spluttering admiration at his shoulder. The poet was a rag of a man, dark, little, and lean, with hollow cheeks and thin black locks. He carried his four-and-twenty years with feverish animation. Greed had made folds about his eyes, evil smiles had puckered his mouth. The wolf and pig struggled together in his face. It was an eloquent, sharp, ugly, earthly countenance. His hands were small and prehensile, with fingers knotted like a cord; and they were continually flickering in front of him in violent and expressive pantomime. As for Tabary, a broad, complacent, admiring imbecility breathed from his squash nose and slobbering lips: he had become a thief, just as he might have become the most decent of burgesses, by the imperious chance that rules the lives of human geese and human donkeys.

At the monk's other hand, Montigny and Thevenin Pensete played a game of chance. About the first there clung some flavor of good birth and training, as about a fallen angel; something long, lithe, and courtly in the person; something aquiline and darkling in the face. Thevenin, poor soul, was in great feather: he had done a good stroke of knavery that afternoon in the Faubourg St. Jacques, and all night he had been gaining from Montigny. A flat smile illuminated his face; his bald head shone rosily in a garland of red curls; his little protuberant stomach shook with silent chucklings as he swept in his gains.

"Doubles or quits?" said Thevenin.

Montigny nodded grimly.

"*Some may prefer to dine in state,*" wrote Villon, "*on bread and cheese on silver plate. Or, or—help me out, Guido!*"

Tabary giggled.

"Or parsley on a golden dish," scribbled the poet.

The wind was freshening without; it drove the snow before it, and sometimes raised its voice in a victorious whoop, and made sepulchral grumblings in the chimney. The cold was growing sharper as the night went on. Villon, protruding his lips, imitated the gust with something between a whistle and a groan. It was an eerie, uncomfortable talent of the poet's, much detested by the Picardy monk.

"Can't you hear it rattle in the gibbet?" said Villon. "They are all dancing the devil's jig on nothing, up there. You may dance, my gallants, you'll be none the warmer! Whew! what a gust! Down went somebody just now! A medlar the fewer on the three-legged medlar tree!—I say, Dom Nicolas, it'll be cold tonight on the St. Denis Road?" he asked.

Dom Nicolas winked both his big eyes, and seemed to choke upon his Adam's apple. Montfaucon, the great grisly Paris gibbet, stood hard by the St. Denis Road, and the pleasantry touched him on the raw. As for Tabary, he laughed immoderately over the medlars; he had never heard anything more lighthearted; and he held his sides and crowed. Villon fetched him a fillip on the nose, which turned his mirth into an attack of coughing.

"Oh, stop that row," said Villon, "and think of rhymes to 'fish.'"

"Doubles or quits," said Montigny doggedly.

"With all my heart," quoth Thevenin.

"Is there any more in that bottle?" asked the monk.

"Open another," said Villon. "How do you ever hope to fill that big hogshead, your body, with little things like bottles? And how do you expect to get to heaven? How many angels, do you fancy, can be spared to carry up a single monk from Picardy? Or do you think yourself another Elias—and they'll send the coach for you?"

"Hominibus impossible," replied the monk as he filled his glass.

Tabary was in ecstasies.

Villon filliped his nose again.

"Laugh at my jokes, if you like," he said.

"It was very good," objected Tabary.

Villon made a face at him. "Think of rhymes to 'fish,'" he said. "What have you to do with Latin? You'll wish you knew none of it at the great assizes, when the devil calls for Guido Tabary, clericus—the devil with the humpback and redhot fingernails. Talking of the devil," he added in a whisper, "look at Montigny!"

All three peered covertly at the gamester. He did not seem to be enjoying his luck. His mouth was a little to a side; one nostril nearly shut, and the other much inflated. The black dog was on his back, as people say, in terrifying nursery metaphor; and he breathed hard under the gruesome burden.

"He looks as if he could knife him," whispered Tabary, with round eyes.

The monk shuddered, and turned his face and spread his open hands to the red embers. It was the cold that thus affected Dom Nicolas, and not any excess of moral sensibility.

"Come now," said Villon—"about this ballade. How does it run so far?" And beating time with his hand, he read it aloud to Tabary.

They were interrupted at the fourth rhyme by a brief and fatal movement among the gamesters.

The round was completed, and Thevenin was just opening his mouth to claim another victory, when Montigny leaped up, swift as an adder, and stabbed him to the heart. The blow took effect before he had time to utter a cry, before he had time to move. A tremor or two convulsed his frame; his hands opened and shut, his heels rattled on the floor; then his head rolled backward over one shoulder with the eyes wide open, and Thevenin Pensete's spirit had returned to Him who made it.

Everyone sprang to his feet; but the business was over in two two's. The four living fellows looked at each other in rather a ghastly fashion; the dead man contemplating a corner of the roof with a singular and ugly leer.

"My God!" said Tabary; and he began to pray in Latin.

Villon broke out into hysterical laughter. He came a step forward and ducked a ridiculous bow at Thevenin, and laughed still louder. Then he sat down suddenly, all of a heap, upon a stool, and continued laughing bitterly as though he would shake himself to pieces.

Montigny recovered his composure first.

"Let's see what he has about him," he remarked, and he picked the dead man's pockets with a practiced hand, and divided the money into four equal portions on the table. "There's for you," he said.

The monk received his share with a deep sigh, and a single stealthy glance at the dead Thevenin, who was beginning to sink into himself and topple sideways off the chair.

"We're all in for it," cried Villon, swallowing his mirth. "It's a hanging job for every man jack of us that's here—not to speak of those who aren't." He made a shocking gesture in the air with his raised right hand, and put out his tongue and threw his head on one side, so as to counterfeit the appearance of one who has been hanged. Then he pocketed his share of the spoil, and executed a shuffle with his feet as if to restore the circulation.

Tabary was the last to help himself; he made a dash at the money, and retired to the other end of the apartment.

Montigny stuck Thevenin upright in the chair, and drew out the dagger, which was followed by a jet of blood.

"You fellows had better be moving," he said, as he wiped the blade on his victim's doublet.

"I think we had," returned Villon, with a gulp. "Damn his fat head!" he broke out. "It sticks in my throat like phlegm. What right has a man to have red hair when he is dead?" And he fell all of a heap again upon the stool, and fairly covered his face with his hands.

Montigny and Dom Nicolas laughed aloud, even Tabary feebly chiming in.

"Crybaby," said the monk.

"I always said he was a woman," added Montigny, with a sneer. "Sit up, can't you?" he went on, giving another shake to the murdered body. "Tread out that fire, Nick!"

But Nick was better employed; he was quietly taking Villon's purse, as the poet sat limp and trembling on the stool where he had been making a ballade not three minutes before. Montigny and Tabary dumbly demanded a share of the booty, which the monk silently promised as he passed the little bag into the bosom of his gown. In many ways an artistic nature unfits a man for practical existence.

No sooner had the theft been accomplished than Villon shook himself, jumped to his feet, and began helping to scatter and extinguish the embers. Meanwhile Montigny opened the door and cautiously peered into the street. The coast was clear; there was no meddlesome patrol in sight. Still it was judged wiser to slip out severally; and as Villon was himself in a hurry to escape from the neighborhood of the dead Thevenin, and the rest were in a still greater hurry to get rid of him before he should discover the loss of his money, he was the first by general consent to issue forth into the street.

The wind had triumphed and swept all the clouds from heaven. Only a few vapors, as thin as moonlight, fleeted rapidly across the stars. It was bitter cold; and by a common optical effect, things seemed almost more definite than in the broadest daylight. The sleeping city was absolutely still; a company of white hoods, a field full of little alps, below the twinkling stars. Villon cursed his fortune. Would it were still snowing! Now, wherever he went, he left an indelible trail behind him on the glittering streets; wherever he went he was still tethered to the house by the cemetery of St. John; wherever he went he must weave, with his own plodding feet, the rope that bound him to the crime and would bind him to the gallows. The leer of the dead man came back to him with a new significance. He snapped his fingers as if to pluck up his own spirits, and choosing a street at random, stepped boldly forward in the snow.

Two things preoccupied him as he went: the aspect of the gallows at Montfaucon in this bright, windy phase of the night's existence, for one; and for another, the look of the dead man with his bald head and garland of red curls. Both struck cold upon his heart, and he kept quickening his pace as if he could escape from unpleasant thoughts by mere fleetness of foot. Sometimes he looked back over his shoulder with a sudden nervous jerk; but he was the only moving thing in the white streets, except when the wind swooped round a corner and threw up the snow, which was beginning to freeze, in spouts of glittering dust.

Suddenly he saw, a long way before him, a black clump and a couple of lanterns. The clump was in motion, and the lanterns swung as though carried by men walking. It was a patrol. And though it was merely crossing his line of march he judged it wiser to get out of eyeshot as speedily as he could. He was not in the humor to be challenged, and he was conscious of making a very conspicuous mark upon the snow. Just on his left hand there stood a great hotel, with some turrets and a large porch before the door; it was half ruinous, he remembered, and had long stood empty; and so he made three steps of it, and jumped into the shelter of the porch. It was pretty dark inside, after the glimmer of the snowy streets, and he was groping forward with outspread hands, when he stumbled over some substance which offered an indescribable mixture of resistances, hard and soft, firm and loose. His heart gave a leap, and he sprang two steps back and stared dreadfully at the obstacle. Then he gave a little laugh of relief. It was only a woman, and she dead. He knelt beside her to make sure upon this latter point. She was freezing cold, and rigid like a stick. A little ragged finery fluttered in the

wind about her hair and her cheeks
had been heavily rouged that same
afternoon. Her pockets were quite
empty; but in her stocking, underneath the garter, Villon found two
of the small coins that went by the
name of whites. It was little enough;
but it was always something; and
the poet was moved with a deep
sense of pathos that she should have
died before she had spent her
money. That seemed to him a dark
and pitiable mystery; and he looked
from the coins in his hand to the
dead woman, and back again to the
coins, shaking his head over the
riddle of man's life. Henry V of England, dying at Vincennes just after
he had conquered France, and this
poor jade cut off by a cold draught
in a great man's doorway, before she
had time to spend her couple of
whites—it seemed a cruel way to
carry on the world. Two whites
would have taken such a little while
to squander; and yet it would have
been one more good taste in the
mouth, one more smack of the lips,
before the devil got the soul, and the
body was left to birds and vermin.
He would like to use all his tallow
before the light was blown out and
the lantern broken.

While these thoughts were passing through his mind, he was feeling, half mechanically, for his purse.
Suddenly his heart stopped beating;
a feeling of cold scales passed up
the back of his legs, and a cold
blow seemed to fall upon his scalp.
He stood petrified for a moment;
then he felt again with one feverish
movement; and then his loss burst
upon him, and he was covered at
once with perspiration. To spend-
thrifts money is so living and actual
—it is such a thin veil between them
and their pleasures! There is only
one limit to their fortune—that of

time; and a spendthrift with only a
few crowns is the Emperor of Rome
until they are spent. For such a person to lose his money is to suffer the
most shocking reverse, and fall from
heaven to hell, from all to nothing,
in a breath. And all the more if he
has put his head in the halter for
it; if he may be hanged tomorrow
for that same purse, so dearly
earned, so foolishly departed! Villon
stood and cursed; he threw the two
whites into the street; he shook his
fist at heaven; he stamped, and was
not horrified to find himself tramp-
ling the poor corpse. Then he began
rapidly to retrace his steps towards
the house beside the cemetery. He
had forgotten all fear of the patrol,
which was long gone by at any rate,
and had no idea but that of his lost
purse. It was in vain that he looked
right and left upon the snow; nothing
was to be seen. He had not dropped
it in the streets. Had it fallen in the
house? He would have liked dearly
to go in and see; but the idea of the
grisly occupant unmanned him. And
he saw besides, as he drew near,
that their efforts to put out the fire
had been unsuccessful; on the contrary, it had broken into a blaze,
and a changeful light played in the
chinks of door and window, and revived his terror for the authorities
and Paris gibbet.

He returned to the hotel with the
porch, and groped about upon the
snow for the money he had thrown
away in his childish passion. But
he could only find one white; the
other had probably struck sideways
and sunk deeply in. With a single
white in his pocket, all his projects
for a rousing night in some wild
tavern vanished utterly away. And it
was not only pleasure that fled
laughing from his grasp; positive dis-
comfort, positive pain, attacked him

as he stood ruefully before the porch. His perspiration had dried upon him; and although the wind had now fallen, a binding frost was setting in stronger with every hour, and he felt benumbed and sick at heart. What was to be done? Late as was the hour, improbable as was success, he would try the house of his adopted father, the chaplain of St. Benoît.

He ran there all the way, and knocked timidly. There was no answer. He knocked again and again, taking heart with every stroke; and at last steps were heard approaching from within. A barred wicket fell open in the iron-studded door, and emitted a gush of yellow light.

"Hold up your face to the wicket," said the chaplain from within.

"It's only me," whimpered Villon.

"Oh, it's only you, is it?" returned the chaplain; and he cursed him with foul unpriestly oaths for disturbing him at such an hour, and bade him be off to hell, where he came from.

"My hands are blue to the wrist," pleaded Villon; "my feet are dead and full of twinges; my nose aches with the sharp air; the cold lies at my heart. I may be dead before morning. Only this once, Father, and before God, I will never ask again!"

"You should have come earlier," said the ecclesiastic coolly. "Young men require a lesson now and then." He shut the wicket and retired deliberately into the interior of the house.

Villon was beside himself; he beat upon the door with his hands and feet, and shouted hoarsely after the chaplain.

"Wormy old fox!" he cried. "If I had my hand under your twist, I would send you flying headlong into the bottomless pit."

A door shut in the interior, faintly audible to the poet down long passages. He passed his hand over his mouth with an oath. And then the humor of the situation struck him, and he laughed and looked lightly up to heaven, where the stars seemed to be winking over his discomfiture.

What was to be done? It looked very like a night in the frosty streets. The idea of the dead woman popped into his imagination, and gave him a hearty fright; what had happened to her in the early night might very well happen to him before morning. And he so young! and with such immense possibilities of disorderly amusement before him! He felt quite pathetic over the notion of his own fate, as if it had been someone else's, and made a little imaginative vignette of the scene in the morning when they should find his body.

He passed all his chances under review, turning the white between his thumb and forefinger. Unfortunately he was on bad terms with some old friends who would once have taken pity on him in such a plight. He had lampooned them in verses; he had beaten and cheated them; and yet now, when he was in so close a pinch, he thought there was at least one who might perhaps relent. It was a chance. It was worth trying at least, and he would go and see.

On the way, two little accidents happened to him which colored his musings in a very different manner. For, first, he fell in with the track of a patrol, and walked in it for some hundred yards, although it lay out of his direction. And this spirited him up; at least he had confused his trail; for he was still possessed with the idea of people tracking him all about Paris over the snow, and collaring him next morning before he was awake. The other matter affected him quite differently. He passed a street corner, where, not so long before, a woman and her child had been devoured by wolves. This was just the kind of weather, he reflected, when wolves might take it into their heads to enter Paris again; and a lone man in these deserted streets would run the chance of something worse than a mere scare. He stopped and looked upon the place with an unpleasant interest—it was the center where several lanes intersected each other; and he looked down them all, one after another, and held his breath to listen, lest he should detect some galloping black things on the snow or hear the sound of howling between him and the river. He remembered his mother telling him the story and pointing out the spot, while he was yet a child. His mother! If he only knew where she lived, he might make sure at least of shelter. He determined he would inquire upon the morrow; nay, he would go and see her, too, poor old girl! So thinking, he arrived at his destination—his last hope for the night.

The house was quite dark, like its neighbors; and yet after a few taps, he heard a movement overhead, a door opening, and a cautious voice asking who was there. The poet named himself in a loud whisper, and waited, not without some trepidation, the result. Nor had he to wait long. A window was suddenly opened, and a pailful of slops splashed down upon the doorstep. Villon had not been unprepared for something of the sort, and had put himself as much in shelter as the nature of the porch admitted; but for all that, he was deplorably drenched below the waist. His hose began to freeze almost at once.

Death from cold and exposure stared him in the face; he remembered he was of phthisical tendency, and began coughing tentatively. But the gravity of the danger steadied his nerves. He stopped a few hundred yards from the door where he had been so rudely used, and reflected with his finger to his nose. He could only see one way of getting a lodging and that was to take it. He had noticed a house not far away, which looked as if it might be easily broken into, and thither he betook himself promptly, entertaining himself on the way with the idea of a room still hot, with a table still loaded with the remains of supper, where he might pass the rest of the black hours and whence he should issue, on the morrow, with an armful of valuable plate. He even considered on what viands and what wines he should prefer; and as he was calling the roll of his favorite dainties, roast fish presented itself to his mind with an odd mixture of amusement and horror.

"I shall never finish that ballade," he thought to himself; and then, with another shudder at the recollection, "Oh, damn his fat head!" he repeated fervently, and spat upon the snow.

The house in question looked dark at first sight; but as Villon made a preliminary inspection in search of the handiest point of attack, a little twinkle of light caught his eye from behind a curtained window.

"The devil!" he thought. "People awake! Some student or some saint, confound the crew. Can't they get drunk and lie in bed snoring like their neighbors! What's the good of curfew, and poor devils of bell ringers jumping at a rope's end in bell towers? What's the use of day, if people sit up all night? The gripes to them!" He grinned as he saw where his logic was leading him. "Every man to his business, after all," added he, "and if they're awake, by the Lord, I may come by a supper honestly for once, and cheat the devil."

He went boldly to the door and knocked with an assured hand. On both previous occasions, he had knocked timidly and with some dread of attracting notice; but now when he had just discarded the thought of a burglarious entry, knocking at a door seemed a mighty simple and innocent proceeding. The sound of his blows echoed through the house with thin, phantasmal reverberations, as though it were quite empty; but these had scarcely died away before a measured tread drew near, a couple of bolts were withdrawn, and one wing was opened broadly, as though no guile or fear of guile were known to those within. A tall figure of a man, muscular and spare, but a little bent, confronted Villon. The head was massive in bulk, but finely sculptured; the nose blunt at the bottom, but refining upward to where it joined a pair of strong and honest eyebrows; the mouth and eyes surrounded with delicate markings, and the whole face based upon a thick white beard, boldly and squarely trimmed. Seen as it was by the light of a flickering hand lamp, it looked perhaps nobler than it had a right to do; but it was a fine face, honorable, rather than intelligent, strong, simple, and righteous.

"You knock late, sir," said the old man in resonant, courteous tones.

Villon cringed, and brought up many servile words of apology; at a crisis of this sort, the beggar was uppermost in him, and the man of genius hid his head with confusion.

"You are cold," repeated the old man, "and hungry? Well, step in." And he ordered him into the house with a noble enough gesture.

"Some great seigneur," thought Villon, as his host, setting down the lamp on the flagged pavement of the entry, shot the bolts once more into their places.

"You will pardon me if I go in front," he said, when this was done; and he preceded the poet upstairs into a large apartment, warmed with a pan of charcoal and lit by a great lamp hanging from the roof. It was very bare of furniture: only some gold plate on a sideboard; some folios; and a stand of armor between the windows. Some smart tapestry hung upon the walls, representing the crucifixion of our Lord in one piece, and in another a scene of shepherds and shepherdesses by a running stream. Over the chimney was a shield of arms.

"Will you seat yourself," said the old man, "and forgive me if I leave you? I am alone in my house tonight, and if you are to eat I must forage for you myself."

No sooner was his host gone than Villon leaped from the chair on which he had just seated himself, and began examining the room, with the stealth and passion of a cat. He weighed the gold flagons in his hand, opened all the folios, and investigated the arms upon the shield, and the stuff with which the seats were lined. He raised the window curtains, and saw that the windows were set with rich stained glass in figures, so far as he could see, of martial import. Then he stood in the middle of the room; drew a long breath and retaining it with puffed cheeks, looked round and round him, turning on his heels, as if to impress every feature of the apartment on his memory.

"Seven pieces of plate," he said. "If there had been ten, I would have risked it. A fine house, and a fine old master, so help me all the saints!"

And just then, hearing the old man's tread returning along the corridor, he stole back to his chair, and began humbly toasting his wet legs before the charcoal pan.

His entertainer had a plate of meat in one hand and a jug of wine in the other. He sat down the plate upon the table, motioning Villon to draw in his chair, and going to the sideboard, brought back two goblets, which he filled.

"I drink to your better fortune," he said gravely, touching Villon's cup with his own.

"To our better acquaintance," said the poet, growing bold. A mere man of the people would have been awed by the courtesy of the old seigneur, but Villon was hardened in that matter; he had made mirth for great lords before now, and found them as black rascals as himself. And so he devoted himself to the viands with a ravenous gusto, while the old man, leaning backward, watched him with steady, curious eyes.

"You have blood on your shoulder, my man," he said.

Montigny must have laid his wet hand upon him as he left the house. He cursed Montigny in his heart.

"It was none of my shedding," he stammered.

"I had not supposed so," returned his host quietly. "A brawl?"

"Well, something of that sort," Villon admitted with a quaver.

"Perhaps a fellow murdered?"

"Oh, no, not murdered," said the poet, more and more confused. "It was all fair play—murdered by acci-

dent. I had no hand in it, God strike me dead!" he added fervently.

"One rogue the fewer, I dare say," observed the master of the house.

"You may dare to say that," agreed Villon, infinitely relieved. "As big a rogue as there is between here and Jerusalem. He turned up his toes like a lamb. But it was a nasty thing to look at. I dare say you've seen dead men in your time, my lord?" he added, glancing at the armor.

"Many," said the old man. "I have followed the wars, as you imagine."

Villon laid down his knife and fork, which he had just taken up again.

"Were any of them bald?" he asked.

"Oh, yes; and with hair as white as mine."

"I don't think I should mind the white so much," said Villon. "His was red." And he had a return of his shuddering and tendency to laughter, which he drowned with a great draught of wine. "I'm a little put out when I think of it," he went on. "I knew him—damn him! And then the cold gives a man fancies— or the fancies give a man cold, I don't know which."

"Have you any money?" asked the old man.

"I have one white," returned the poet, laughing. "I got it out of a dead jade's stocking in a porch. She was as dead as Caesar, poor wench, and as cold as a church, with bits of ribbon sticking in her hair. This is a hard world in winter for wolves and wenches and poor rogues like me."

"I," said the old man, "am Enguerrand de la Feuillèe, seigneur de Brisetout, bailly du Patatrac. Who and what may you be?"

Villon rose and made a suitable reverence. "I am called Francis Villon," he said, "a poor Master of Arts of this university. I know some Latin, and a deal of vice. I can make chansons, ballades, lais, virelais, and roundels, and I am very fond of wine. I was born in a garret, and I shall not improbably die upon the gallows. I may add, my lord, that from this night forward I am your lordship's very obsequious servant to command."

"No servant of mine," said the knight; "my guest for this evening, and no more."

"A very grateful guest," said Villon politely, and he drank in dumb show to his entertainer.

"You are shrewd," began the old man, tapping his forehead, "very shrewd; you have learning; you are a clerk; and yet you take a small piece of money off a dead woman in the street. Is it not a kind of theft?"

"It is a kind of theft much practiced in the wars, my lord."

"The wars are the field of honor," returned the old man proudly. "There a man plays his life upon the cast; he fights in the name of his lord the king, his Lord God, and all their lordships the holy saints and angels."

"Put it," said Villon, "that I were really a thief, should I not play my life also, and against heavier odds?"

"For gain but not for honor."

"Gain?" repeated Villon with a shrug. "Gain! The poor fellow wants supper, and takes it. So does the soldier in a campaign. Why, what are all these requisitions we hear so much about? If they are not gain to those who take them, they are loss enough to the others. The men-at-arms drink by a good fire, while the burgher bites his nails to buy them wine and wood. I have seen a good many plowmen swinging on trees about the country; ay, I have seen thirty to one elm, and a very poor figure they made; and when I asked someone how all these came to be hanged, I was told it was because they could not scrape together enough crowns to satisfy the men-at-arms."

"These things are a necessity of war, which the low-born must endure with constancy. It is true that some captains drive overhard; there are spirits in every rank not easily moved by pity; and, indeed, many follow arms who are no better than brigands."

"You see," said the poet, "you cannot separate the soldier from the brigand; and what is a thief but an isolated brigand with circumspect manners? I steal a couple of mutton chops, without so much as disturbing people's sleep; the farmer grumbles a bit, but sups none the less wholesomely on what remains. You come up blowing gloriously on a trumpet, take away the whole sheep, and beat the farmer pitifully into the bargain. I have no trumpet; I am only Tom, Dick, or Harry; I am a rogue and a dog, and hanging's too good for me—with all my heart; but just ask the farmer which of us he prefers, just find out which of us he lies awake to curse on cold nights."

"Look at us two," said his lordship. "I am old, strong, and honored. If I were turned from my house tomorrow, hundreds would be proud to shelter me. Poor people would go out and pass the night in the streets with their children, if I merely hinted that I wished to be alone. And I find you up, wandering homeless, and picking farthings off dead women by the wayside! I fear no man and nothing; I have seen you tremble and lose countenance at a word. I wait God's summons contentedly in my own house, or, if it please the king to call me out again, upon the field of battle. You look for the gallows; a rough, swift death, without hope or honor. Is there no difference between these two?"

"As far as to the moon," Villon acquiesced. "But if I had been born lord of Brisetout, and you had been the poor scholar Francis, would the difference have been any the less? Should not I have been warming my knees at this charcoal pan, and would not you have been groping for farthings in the snow? Should not I have been the soldier, and you the thief?"

"A thief?" cried the old man. "I a thief! If you understood your words, you would repent them."

Villon turned out his hands with a gesture of inimitable impudence. "If your lordship had done me the honor to follow my argument!" he said.

"I do you too much honor in submitting to your presence," said the knight. "Learn to curb your tongue when you speak with old and honorable men, or someone hastier than I may reprove you in a sharper fashion." And he rose and paced the lower end of the apartment, struggling with anger and antipathy. Villon surreptitiously refilled his cup, and settled himself more comfortably in the chair, crossing his knees and leaning his head upon one hand and the elbow against the back of the chair. He was now replete and warm, and he was in nowise frightened for his host, having gauged him as justly as was possible between two such different characters. The night was far spent, and in a very comfortable fashion after

all; and he felt morally certain of a safe departure on the morrow.

"Tell me one thing," said the old man, pausing in his walk. "Are you really a thief?"

"I claim the sacred right of hospitality," returned the poet. "My lord, I am."

"You are very young," the knight continued.

"I should never have been so old," replied Villon, showing his fingers, "if I had not helped myself with these ten talents. They have been my nursing mothers and my nursing fathers."

"You may still repent and change."

"I repent daily," said the poet. "There are few people more given to repentance than poor Francis. As for change, let somebody change my circumstances. A man must continue to eat, if it were only that he may continue to repent."

"The change must begin in the heart," returned the old man solemnly.

"My dear lord," answered Villon, "do you really fancy that I steal for pleasure? I hate stealing, like any other piece of work or of danger. My teeth chatter when I see a gallows. But I must eat, I must drink, I must mix in society of some sort. What the devil! Man is not a solitary animal—*Cui Deus fæminam tradit.* Make me king's pantler—make me abbot of St. Denis; make me bailly of the Patatrac; and then I shall be changed indeed. But as long as you leave me the poor scholar Francis Villon, without a farthing, why, of course, I remain the same."

"The Grace of God is all-powerful."

"I should be a heretic to question it," said Francis. "It has made you lord of Brisetout and bailly of the Patatrac; it has given me nothing but the quick wits under my hat and these ten toes upon my hands. May I help myself to wine? I thank you respectfully. By God's grace, you have a very superior vintage."

The lord of Brisetout walked to and fro with his hands behind his back. Perhaps he was not yet quite settled in his mind about the parallel between thieves and soldiers; perhaps Villon had interested him by some cross-thread of sympathy; perhaps his wits were simply muddled by so much unfamiliar reasoning; but whatever the cause, he somehow yearned to convert the young man to a better way of thinking, and could not make up his mind to drive him forth again into the street.

"There is something more than I can understand in this," he said at length. "Your mouth is full of subtleties, and the devil has led you very far astray; but the devil is only a very weak spirit before God's truth, and all his subtleties vanish at a word of true honor, like darkness at morning. Listen to me once more. I learned long ago that a gentleman should live chivalrously and lovingly to God, and the king, and his lady; and though I have seen many strange things done, I have still striven to command my ways upon that rule. It is not only written in all noble histories, but in every man's heart if he will take care to read. You speak of food and wine, and I know very well that hunger is a difficult trial to endure; but you do not speak of other wants; you say nothing of honor, of faith to God and other men, of courtesy, of love without reproach. It may be that I am not very wise—and yet I think I am—but you seem to me like one who has lost his way and made a great error in life. You are attend-ing to the little wants, and you have totally forgotten the great and only real ones, like a man who should be doctoring toothache on the Judgment Day. For such things as honor and love and faith are not only nobler than food and drink, but indeed I think we desire them more, and suffer more sharply for their absence. I speak to you as I think you will most easily understand me. Are you not, while careful to fill your belly, disregarding another appetite in your heart, which spoils the pleasure of your life and keeps you continually wretched?"

Villon was sensibly nettled under all this sermonizing.

"You think I have no sense of honor!" he cried. "I'm poor enough, God knows! It's hard to see rich people with their gloves, and you blowing in your hands. An empty belly is a bitter thing, although you speak so lightly of it. If you had had as many as I, perhaps you would change your tune. Anyway I'm a thief—make the most of that—but I'm not a devil from hell, God strike me dead. I would have you to know I've an honor of my own, as good as yours, though I don't prate about it all day long, as if it was a God's miracle to have any. It seems quite natural to me; I keep it in its box till it's wanted. Why now, look you here, how long have I been in this room with you? Did you not tell me you were alone in the house? Look at your gold plate! You're strong, if you like, but you're old and unarmed, and I have my knife. What did I want but a jerk of the elbow and here would have been you with the cold steel in your bowels, and there would have been me, clinking in the streets, with an armful of golden cups! Did you suppose I hadn't wit enough to see that? And

I scorned the action. There are your damned goblets, as safe as in a church; there are you, with your heart ticking as good as new; and here am I, ready to go out again as poor as I came in, with my one white that you threw in my teeth! And you think I have no sense of honor—God strike me dead!"

The old man stretched out his right arm. "I will tell you what you are," he said. "You are a rogue, my man, an impudent and blackhearted rogue and vagabond. I have passed an hour with you. Oh! believe me, I feel myself disgraced! And you have eaten and drunk at my table. But now I am sick of your presence; the day has come, and the night-bird should be off to his roost. Will you go before, or after?"

"Which you please," returned the poet, rising. "I believe you to be strictly honorable." He thoughtfully emptied his cup. "I wish I could add you were intelligent," he went on, knocking on his head with his knuckles. "Age! age! the brains stiff and rheumatic."

The old man preceded him from a point of self-respect; Villon followed, whistling, with his thumbs in his girdle.

"God pity you," said the lord of Brisetout at the door.

"Good-by, Papa," returned Villon with a yawn. "Many thanks for the cold mutton."

The door closed behind him. The dawn was breaking over the white roofs. A chill, uncomfortable morning ushered in the day. Villon stood and heartily stretched himself in the middle of the road.

"A very dull old gentleman," he thought. "I wonder what his goblets may be worth."

Maurice Hewlett
1861-1923

MAURICE HEWLETT is in a class by himself, part of no trend
and creating no trend. He was a medievalist, a lecturer on
medieval art, living in a house that dated back to 1350, and
visiting the ancient cities of Italy for a part of every year.
He "used other men's art and wisdom as a springboard," he
said of himself. His best stories are those excursions into the
rich, dark shadows of the Middle Ages with all their romance
and pageantry, the richer and the more romantic for his
scholarly and original mind. His prose has the texture of
tapestry.

But Maurice Hewlett was no escapist: he lived very much
in the present. He considered himself a worker of the English
countryside, and in his later years moved into a workman's
cottage. During World War I he built planes for the British,
made a fortune, and gave it all away, while his wife, a vicar's
daughter whom he married in 1888, became, surprisingly
enough, an aviatrix. . . . *Little Novels of Italy* (published
in 1899), from which "Quattrocentisteria" comes, is probably his most popular book.

Quattrocentisteria

(HOW SANDRO BOTTICELLI SAW SIMONETTA IN THE SPRING)

BY MAURICE HEWLETT

I

UP AT Fiesole, among the olives and chestnuts which cloud the steeps, the magnificent Lorenzo was entertaining his guests on a morning in April. The olives were just whitening to silver; they stretched in a trembling sea down the slope. Beyond lay Forence, misty and golden; and round about were the mossy hills, cut sharp and definite against a grape-blue sky, printed with starry buildings and sober ranks of cypress. The sun, catching the mosaics of San Miniato and the brazen cross on the façade, made them shine like sword blades in the quiver of the heat between. For the valley was just a lake of hot air, hot and murky—"fever weather," said the people in the streets—with a glaring summer sun let in between two long spells of fog. 'Twas unnatural at that season, via; but the blessed saints sent the weather and one could only be careful what one was about at sundown.

Up at the Villa, with brisk morning airs rustling overhead, in the cool shades of trees and lawns, it ' was pleasant to lie still, watching these things, while a silky young exquisite sang to his lute a not-too-audacious ballad about Selvaggia, or Becchina and the saucy Prior of Sant' Onofrio. He sang well too, that dark-eyed boy; the girl at whose feet he was crouched was laughing and blushing at once; and, being very fair, she blushed hotly. She dared not raise her eyes to look into his, and he knew it and was quietly measuring his strength—it was quite a comedy! At each wanton refrain he lowered his voice to a whisper and bent a little forward. And the girl's laughter became hysterical; she was shaking with the effort to control herself. At last she looked up with a sort of sob in her breath and saw his mocking smile and the gleam of the wild beast in his eyes. She grew white, rose hastily, and turned away to join a group of ladies sitting apart. A man with a heavy, rather sullen face and a bush of yellow hair falling over his forehead in a wave was standing aside, watching all this. He folded his arms and scowled under his big brows; and when the girl moved away his eyes followed her.

The lad ended his song in a broad

sarcasm amid bursts of laughter and applause. The Magnificent, sitting in his carved chair, nursed his sallow face and smiled approval. "My brother boasts his invulnerability," he said, turning to his neighbor, "let him look to it, Messer Cupido will have him yet. Already, we can see, he has been let into some of the secrets of the bower." The man bowed and smiled deferentially. "Signor Giuliano has all the qualities to win the love of ladies, and to retain it. Doubtless he awaits his destiny. The Wise Man has said that 'Beauty . . .'" The young poet enlarged on his text with some fire in his thin cheeks, while the company kept very silent. It was much to their liking; even Giuliano was absorbed; he sat on the ground, clasping one knee between his hands, smiling upwards into vacancy, as a man does whose imagination is touched. Lorenzo nursed his sallow face and beat time to the orator's cadences with his foot; he, too, was abstracted and smiling. At the end he spoke; "Our Marsilio himself has never said nobler words, my Agnolo. The mantle of the Attic prophet has descended indeed upon this Florence. And Beauty, as thou sayest, is from heaven. But where shall it be found here below, and how discerned?" The man of the heavy jowl was standing with folded arms, looking from under his brows at the group of girls. Lorenzo saw everything; he noticed him. "Our Sandro will tell us it is yonder. The Star of Genoa shines over Florence and our poor little constellations are gone out. *Ecco*, my Sandro, gravest and hardiest of painters, go summon Madonna Simonetta and her handmaidens to our symposium. Agnolo will speak further to us of this sovereignty of Beauty."

The painter bowed his head and moved away.

A green alley vaulted with thick ilex and myrtle formed a tapering vista where the shadows lay misty blue and pale shafts of light pierced through fitfully. At the far end it ran out into an open space and a splash of sunshine. A marble Ganymede with lifted arms rose in the middle like a white flame. The girls were there, intent upon some commerce of their own, flashing hither and thither over the grass in a flutter of saffron and green and crimson. Simonetta—Sandro could see—was a little apart, a very tall, isolated figure, clear and cold in a recess of shade, standing easily, resting on one hip with her hands behind her. A soft, straight robe of white clipped her close from shoulder to heel; the lines of her figure were thrust forward by her poise. His eye followed the swell of her bosom, very gentle and girlish, and the long folds of her dress falling thence to her knee. While she stood there, proud and remote, a chance beam of the sun shone on her head so that it seemed to burn. "Heaven salutes the Queen of Heaven—Venus Urania!" With an odd impulse he stopped, crossed himself, and then hurried on.

He told his errand to her; having no eyes for the others.

"Signorina—I am to acquaint her serenity that the divine poet Messer Agnolo is to speak of the sovereign power of beauty; of the Heavenly Beauty whereof Plato taught, as it is believed."

Simonetta arched a slim neck and looked down at the obsequious speaker, or at least he thought so. And he saw how fair she was, a creature how delicate and gracious, with gray eyes frank and wide, and full red lips where a smile (nervous and a little wistful, he judged, rather than defiant) seemed always to hover. Such clear-cut, high beauty made him ashamed; but her coloring (for he was a painter) made his heart beat. She was no ice-bound shadow of deity then! but flesh and blood; a girl—a child, of timid, soft contours, of warm roses and blue veins laced in a pearly skin. And she was crowned with a heavy wealth of red-gold hair, twisted in great coils, bound about with pearls, and smoldering like molten metal where it fell rippling along her neck. She dazzled him, so that he could not face her or look further. His eyes dropped. He stood before her moody, disconcerted.

The girls, who had dissolved their company at his approach, listened to what he had to say, linked in knots of twos and threes. They needed no excuses to return; some were philosophers and poetesses; some had left their lovers in the ring round Lorenzo. So they went down the green alley still locked by the arms, by the waist or shoulders. They did not wait for Simonetta. She was a Genoese, and proud as the snow. Why did Giuliano love her? Did he love her, indeed? He was bewitched then, for she was cold, and a brazen creature in spite of it. How dare she bare her neck so! Oh! 'twas Genoese. *"Uomini senza fede e donne senza vergogna,"* they quoted as they ran.

And Simonetta walked alone down the way with her head high; but Sandro stepped behind, at the edge of her trailing white robe. . . .

. . . The poet was leaning against an ancient alabaster vase, soil-stained, yellow with age and its long sojourn in the loam, but with traces of its carved garlands clinging to it still. He fingered it lovingly as he talked. His oration was concluding,

and his voice rose high and tremulous; there were sparks in his hollow eyes. . . . "And as this sovereign Beauty is queen of herself, so she is subject to none other, owns to no constraining custom, fears no reproach of man. What she wills, that has the force of a law. Being Beauty, her deeds are lovely and worshipful. Therefore Phryne, whom men, groping in darkness and the dull ways of earth, dubbed courtesan, shone in a court of law before the assembled nobles of Athens, naked and undismayed in the blaze of her fairness. And Athens discerned the goddess and trembled. Yes, and more; even as Aphrodite, whose darling she was, arose pure from the foam, so she too came up out of the sea in the presence of a host, and the Athenians, seeing no shame, thought none, but, rather, reverenced her the more. For what shame is it that the body of one so radiant in clear perfections should be revealed? Is then the garment of the soul, her very mold and image, so shameful? Shall we seek to know her essence by the garment of a garment, or hope to behold that which really is in the shadows we cast upon shadows? Shame is of the brute dullard who thinks shame. The evil ever sees Evil glaring at him. Plato, the golden-mouthed, with the soul of pure fire, has said the truth of this matter in his *De Republica*, the fifth book, where he speaks of young maids sharing the exercise of the palaestra, yea, and the Olympic contests even! For he says, 'Let the wives of our wardens bare themselves, for their virtue will be a robe; and let them share the toils of war and defend their country. And for the man who laughs at naked women exercising their bodies for high reasons, his laughter is a fruit of unripe wisdom, and he himself knows not what he is about; for that is ever the best of sayings that the useful is the noble and the hurtful the base.' " . . .

There was a pause. The name of Plato had had a strange effect upon the company. You will have said they had suddenly entered a church and had felt all lighter interests sink under the weight of the dim, echoing nave. After a few moments the poet spoke again in a quieter tone, but his voice had lost none of the unction which had enriched it. . . . "Beauty is queen; by the virtue of Deity, whose image she is, she reigns, lifts up, fires. Let us beware how we tempt Deity lest we perish ourselves. Actaeon died when he gazed unbidden upon the pure body of Artemis; but Artemis herself rayed her splendor upon Endymion, and Endymion is among the immortals. We fall when we rashly confront Beauty, but that Beauty who comes unawares may nerve our souls to wing to heaven." He ended on a resonant note and then, still looking out over the valley, sank into his seat. Lorenzo, with a fine humility, got up and kissed his thin hand. Giuliano looked at Simonetta, trying to recall her gaze, but she remained standing in her place, seeing nothing of her companions. She was thinking of something, frowning a little and biting her lip, her hands were before her; her slim fingers twisted and locked themselves nervously, like a tangle of snakes. Then she tossed her head, as a young horse might, and looked at Giuliano suddenly, full in the eyes. He rose to meet her with a deprecating smile, cap in hand—but she walked past him, almost brushing him with her gown, but never flinching her full gaze, threaded her way through the group to the back, behind the poet, where Sandro was. He had seen her coming, indeed he had watched her furtively throughout the oration, but her near presence disconcerted him again—and he looked down. She was strongly excited with her quick resolution; her color had risen and her voice faltered when she began to speak. She spoke eagerly, running her words together.

"*Ecco*, Messer Sandro," she whispered, blushing. "You have heard these sayings . . . Who is there in Florence like me?"

"There is no one," said Sandro simply.

"I will be your Lady Venus," she went on breathlessly. "You shall paint me, rising from the sea foam. . . . The Genoese love the sea." She was still eager and defiant; her bosom rose and fell unchecked.

"The Signorina is mocking me; it is impossible; the Signorina knows it."

"Eh, Madonna! is it so shameful to be fair—Star of the Sea as your poets sing at evening? Do you mean that I dare not do it? Listen then, Signor Pittore; tomorrow morning at Mass time you will come to the Villa Vespucci with your brushes and pans and you will ask for Monna Simonetta. Then you will see. Leave it now; it is settled." And she walked away with her head high and the same superb smile on her red lips. Mockery! She was in dead earnest; all her child's feelings were in hot revolt. These women who had whispered to each other, sniggered at her dress, her white neck and her free carriage; Giuliano who had presumed so upon her candor—these prying, censorious Florentines—she would strike them dumb with her amazing loveliness. They sang her a goddess that she might be flattered and suffer their company: she would show herself a goddess indeed—the star of her shining Genoa, where men were brave and silent and maidens frank like the sea. Yes, and then she would withdraw herself suddenly and leave them forlorn and dismayed.

As for Sandro, he stood where she had left him, peering after her with a mist in his eyes. He seemed to be looking over the hillside, over the city glowing afar off gold and purple in the hot air, to Mont' Oliveto and the heights, where a line of black cypresses stood about a low white building. At one angle of the building was a little turret with a belvedere of round arches. The tallest cypress just topped the windows. There his eyes seemed to rest.

II

At Mass time Sandro, folded in his shabby green cloak, stepped into the sun on the Ponte Vecchio. The morning mists were rolling back under the heat; you began to see the yellow line of houses stretching along the turbid river on the far side, and frowning down upon it with blank, mud-stained faces. Above, through steaming air, the sky showed faintly blue and a campanile to the right loomed pale and uncertain like a ghost. The sound of innumerable bells floated over the still city. Hardly a soul was abroad; here and there a couple of dusty peasants were trudging in with baskets of eggs and jars of milk and oil; a boat passed down to the fishing, and the oar knocked sleepily in the rowlock as she cleared the bridge. And above, on the heights of Mont' Oliveto, the tapering forms of cypresses were faintly outlined— straight bars of shadow—and the level ridge of a roof ran lightly back into the soft shroud.

Sandro could mark these things as he stepped resolutely on to the bridge, crossed it, and went up a narrow street among the sleeping houses. The day held golden promise; it was the day of his life! Meantime the mist clung to him and nipped him; what had fate in store? What was to be the issue? In the Piazza Santo Spirito, gray and hollow-sounding in the chilly silences, his own footsteps echoed solemnly as he passed by the door of the great ragged church. Through the heavy darkness within light flickered faintly and went; service was not begun. A drab crew of cripples lounged on the steps, yawning and shivering, and two country girls were strolling to the Mass with brown arms round each other's waists. When Sandro's footfall clattered on the stones they stopped by the door, looking after him, and laughed to see his dull face and muffled figure. In the street beyond he heard a bell jingling, hasty, incessant; and soon a white-robed procession swept by him, fluttering vestments, tapers, and the Host under a canopy, silk and gold. Sandro snatched at his cap and dropped on his knees in the road, crouching low and muttering under his breath as the vision went past. He remained kneeling for a moment after it had gone, then crossed himself—forehead, breast, lip—and hurried forward. . . . He stepped under the archway into the Court. There was a youth with a cropped head and swarthy neck lounging there, teasing a spaniel. As the steps sounded on the flags he looked up; the old green cloak and clumsy shoes of the visitor did not interest him; he turned his back and went on with his game.

Sandro accosted him—Was the Signorina at the house? The boy went on with his game. "Eh, Diavolo! I know nothing at all," he said.

Sandro raised his voice till it rang round the courtyard. "You will go at once and inquire. You will say to the Signorina that Sandro di Mariano Filipepi the Florentine painter is here by her orders; that he waits her pleasure below."

The boy had got up; he and Sandro eyed each other for a little space. Sandro was the taller and had the glance of a hawk. So the porter went. . . .

. . . Presently with throbbing brows he stood on the threshold of Simonetta's chamber. It was the turret room of the villa and its four arched windows looked through a leafy tracery over towards Florence. Sandro could see down below him in the haze the glitter of the Arno and the dusky dome of Brunelleschi cleave the sward of the hills like a great burnished bowl. In the room itself there was tapestry, the Clemency of Scipio, with courtiers in golden cuirasses and tall plumes, and peacocks and huge Flemish horses—a rich profusion of crimson and blue drapery and stout-limbed soldiery. On a bracket, above a green silk curtain was a silver statuette of Madonna and the Bambino Gesu, with a red lamp flickering feebly before. By the windows a low divan heaped with velvet cushions and skins. But for a coffer and a prayer desk and a curtained recess which enshrined Simonetta's bed, the room looked wind-swept and bare.

When he entered Simonetta was standing by the window, leaning her hand against the ledge for support. She was draped from top to toe in a rose-colored mantle which shrouded her head like a nun's wimple and then fell in heavy folds to the ground. She flushed as he came, but saluted him with a grave inclination. Neither spoke. The silent greeting, the full consciousness in each of their parts, gave a curious religious solemnity to the scene—like some familiar but stately Church mystery. Sandro busied himself mechanically with his preparations—he was a lover and his pulse chaotic, but he had come to paint—and when these were done, on tiptoe, as it were, he looked timidly about him round the room, seeking where to pose her. Then he motioned her with the same reverential, preoccupied air, silent still, to a place under the silver Madonna. . . .

. . . There was a momentary quiver of withdrawal. Simonetta blushed vividly and drooped her eyes down to her little bare foot peeping out below the lines of the rosy cloak. The cloak's warmth shone on her smooth skin and rayed over her cheeks. In her flowery loveliness she looked diaphanous, ethereal; and yet you could see what a child she was, with her bright audacity, her ardor and her willfulness flushing and paling about her like the dawn. There she stood trembling on the brink. . . .

Suddenly all her waywardness shot into her eyes; she lifted her arms and the cloak fell back like the shard of a young flower; then, delicate and palpitating as a silver reed, she stood up in the soft light of the morning, and the sun, slanting in between the golden leaves and tendrils, kissed her neck and shrinking shoulder.

Sandro stood facing her, moody and troubled, fingering his brushes and bits of charcoal; his shaggy brows were knit, he seemed to be breathing hard. He collected himself with an effort and looked up at her as she stood before him shrinking, awe-struck, panting at the thing she had done. Their eyes met, and the girl's distress increased; she raised her hand to cover her bosom; her breath came in short gasps from parted lips, but her wide eyes still looked fixedly into his, with such blank panic that a sudden movement might really have killed her. He saw it all; she! there at his mercy. Tears swam and he trembled. Ah! the gracious lady! what divine condescension! what ineffable courtesy! But the artist in him was awakened almost at the same moment; his looks wandered in spite of her piteous candor and his own nothingness. Sandro the poet would have fallen on his face with an *"Exi a me, nam peccator sum."* Sandro the painter was different—no mercy there. He made a snatch at a carbon and raised his other hand with a kind of command—"Holy Virgin! what a line! Stay as you are, I implore you: swerve not one hair's breadth and I have you forever!" There was conquest in his voice.

So Simonetta stood very still, hiding her bosom with her hand, but never took her watch off the enemy. As he ran blindly about doing a hundred urgent indispensable things— noting the light, the line she made, how her arm cut across the folds of the curtain—she dogged him with staring, fascinated eyes, just as a hare, crouching in her form, watches a terrier hunting round her and waits for the end.

But the enemy was disarmed. Sandro the passionate, the lover, the brooding devotee, was gone; so was *la bella* Simonetta the beloved, the behymned. Instead, here was a fretful painter, dashing lines and broad smudges of shade on his paper, while before him rose an exquisite, slender, swaying form, glistening carnation and silver, and, over all, the maddening glow of red-gold hair. Could he but catch those velvet shadows, those delicate, glossy, reflected lights! Body of Bacchus! How could he put them in! What a picture she was! Look at the sun on her shoulder! and her hair— Christ! how it burned! It was a curious moment. The girl who had never understood or cared to understand this humble lover guessed now that he was lost in the artist. She felt that she was simply an effect and she resented it as a crowning insult. Her color rose again, her red lips gathered into a pout. If Sandro had but known, she was his at that instant. He had but to drop the painter, throw down his brushes, set his heart and hot eyes bare—to open his arms and she would have fled into them and nestled there; so fierce was her instinct just then to be loved, she, who had always been loved! But Sandro knew nothing and cared nothing. He was absorbed in the gracious lines of her body, the lithe long neck, the drooping shoulder, the tenderness of her youth; and then the grand open curve of the hip and thigh on which she was poised. He drew them in with a free hand in great sweeping lines, eagerly, almost angrily; once or twice he broke his carbon and— body of a dog!—he snatched at another.

This lasted a few minutes only: even Simonetta, with all her maiden tremors still feverishly acute, hardly noticed the flight of time; she was so hot with the feeling of her wrongs, the slight upon her victorious fairness. Did she not know how fair she was? She was getting very angry;

she had been made a fool of. All Florence would come and gape at the picture and mock her in the streets with bad names and coarse gestures as she rode by. She looked at Sandro. Santa Maria! how hot he was! His hair was drooping over his eyes! He tossed it back every second! And his mouth was open, one could see his tongue working! Why had she not noticed that great mouth before? 'Twas the biggest in all Florence. O! why had he come? She was frightened, remorseful, a child again, with a trembling pathetic mouth and shrinking limbs. And then her heart began to beat under her slim fingers. She pressed them down into her flesh to stay those great masterful throbs. A tear gathered in her eye; larger and larger it grew, and then fell. A shining drop rested on the round of her cheek and rolled slowly down her chin to her protecting hand, and lay there half hidden, shining like a raindrop between two curving petals of a rose.

It was just at that moment the painter looked up from his work and shook his bush of hair back. Something in his sketch had displeased him; he looked up frowning, with a brush between his teeth. When he saw the tearstained, distressful, beautiful face it had a strange effect upon him. He dropped nerveless, like a wounded man, to his knees, and covered his eyes with his hands. "Ah Madonna! for the pity of heaven forgive me! forgive me! I have sinned, I have done thee fearful wrong; I, who still dare to love thee." He uncovered his face and looked up radiant: his own words had inspired him. "Yes," he went on, with a steadfast smile, "I, Sandro, the painter, the poor devil of a painter, have seen thee and I dare to love!" His triumph was short-

lived. Simonetta had grown deadly white, her eyes burned, she had forgotten herself. She was tall and slender as a lily, and she rose, shaking, to her height.

"Thou presumest strangely," she said, in a slow still voice. "Go! Go in peace!"

She was conqueror. In her calm scorn, she was like a young immortal, some cold victorious Cynthia whose chastity had been flouted. Sandro was pale too: he said nothing and did not look at her again. She stood quivering with excitement, watching him with the same intent alertness as he rolled up his paper and crammed his brushes and pencils into the breast of his jacket. She watched him still as he backed out of the room and disappeared through the curtains of the archway. She listened to his footsteps along the corridor, down the stair. She was alone in the silence of the sunny room. Her first thought was for her cloak; she snatched it up and veiled herself, shivering as she looked fearfully round the walls. And then she flung herself on the piled cushions before the window and sobbed piteously, like an abandoned child.

The sun slanted in between the golden leaves and tendrils and played in the tangle of her hair. . . .

III

At ten o'clock on the morning of April the twenty-sixth, a great bell began to toll: two beats heavy and slow, and then silence, while the air echoed the reverberation, moaning. Sandro, in shirt and breeches, with bare feet spread broad, was at work in his garret on the old bridge. He stayed his hand as the strong tone struck, bent his head and said a prayer: *"Miserere ei, Domine; requiem eternam dona, Domine"*; the words came out of due order as if he was very conscious of their import. Then he went on. And the great bell went on; two beats together, and then silence. It seemed to gather solemnity and a heavier message as he painted. Through the open window a keen draft of air blew in with dust and a scrap of shaving from the Lung' Arno down below; it circled round his workshop, fluttering the sketches and rags pinned to the walls. He looked out on a bleak landscape. San Miniato in heavy shade, and the white houses by the river staring like dead faces. A strong breeze was abroad; it whipped the brown water and raised little curling billows, ragged and white at the edges, and tossed about snaps of surf. It was cold. Sandro shivered as he shut to his casement; and the stiffening gale rattled at it fitfully. Once again it thrust it open, bringing wild work among the litter in the room. He made fast with the rain driving in his face. And above the howling of the squall he heard the sound of the great bell, steady and unmoved as if too full of its message to be put aside. Yet it was coming to him athwart the wind.

Sandro stood at his casement and looked at the weather—beating rain and yeasty water. He counted, rather nervously, the pulses between each pair of the bell's deep tones. He was impressionable to circumstances, and the coincidence of storm and passing bell awed him. . . . "Either the God of Nature suffers or the fabric of the world is breaking" —he remembered a scrap of talk wafted towards him (as he stood in attendance) from some humanist at Lorenzo's table only yesterday,

above the light laughter and snatches of song. That breakfast party at the Camaldoli yesterday! What a contrast—the even spring weather with the sun in a cloudless sky, and now this icy dead morning with its battle of wind and bell, fighting, he thought—over the failing breath of some strong man. Man! God, more like. "The God of Nature suffers," he murmured as he turned to his work. . . .

Simonetta had not been there yesterday. He had not seen her, indeed, since that nameless day when she had first transported him with the radiance of her bare beauty and then struck him down with a level gaze from steel-cold eyes. And he had deserved it, he had—she had said— "presumed strangely." Three more words only had she uttered and he had slunk out from her presence like a dog. What a goddess! Venus Urania! So she, too, might have ravished a worshiper as he prayed, and, after, slain him for a careless word. Cruel? No, but a goddess. Beauty had no laws; she was above them. Agnolo himself had said it, from Plato. . . . Holy Michael! What a blast! Black and desperate weather. . . . "Either the God of Nature suffers." God shield all Christian souls on such a day! . . .

One came and told him Simonetta Vespucci was dead. Some fever had torn at her and raced through all her limbs, licking up her life as it passed. No one had known of it— it was so swift! But there had just been time to fetch a priest; Fra Matteo, they said, from the Carmine, had shrived her ('twas a bootless task, God knew, for the child had babbled so, her wits wandered, look you), and then he had performed the last office. One had fled to tell the Medici. Giuliano was wild with grief; 'twas as if he had killed her instead of the spring ague—but then, people said he loved her well! And our Lorenzo had bid them swing the great bell of the Duomo—Sandro had heard it perhaps?—and there was to be a public procession and a Requiem sung at Santa Croce before they took her back to Genoa to lie with her fathers. Eh! Bacchus! She was fair and Giuliano had loved her well. 'Twas natural enough then. So the gossip ran out to tell his news to more attentive ears, and Sandro stood in his place, intoning softly, "Te Deum Laudamus."

He understood it all. There had been a dark and awful strife—earth shuddering as the black shadow of death swept by. Through tears now the sun beamed broad over the gentle city where she lay lapped in her mossy hills. "Lux eterna lucet ⁓i," he said with a steady smile; atque lucebit," he added after a pause. He had been painting that day an agonizing Christ, red and languid, crowned with thorns. Some of his own torment seems to have entered it, for, looking at it now, we see, first of all, wild eyeballs staring with the mad earnestness, the purposeless intensity of one seized or "possessed." He put the panel away and looked about for something else, the sketch he had made of Simonetta on that last day. When he had found it, he rolled it straight and set it on his easel. It was not the first charcoal study he had made from life, but a brush drawing on dark paper, done in sepia wash and the lights in white lead. He stood looking into it with his hands clasped. About half a braccia high, faint and shadowy in the pale tint he had used, he saw her there victim rather than goddess.

Standing timidly and wistfully, shrinking rather, veiling herself, maidenlike, with her hands and hair, with lips trembling and dewy eyes, she seemed to him now an immortal who must needs suffer for some great end; live and suffer and die; live again, and suffer and die. It was a doom perpetual like Demeter's, to bear, to nurture, to lose and to find her Persephone. She had stood there immaculate and apprehensive, a wistful victim. Three days before he had seen her thus; and now she was dead. He would see her no more.

Ah! Yes, once more he would see her. . . .

They carried dead Simonetta through the streets of Florence with her pale face uncovered and a crown of myrtle in her hair. People thronging there held their breath, or wept to see such still loveliness; and her poor parted lips wore a patient little smile, and her eyelids were pale violet and lay heavy to her cheek. White, like a bride, with a nosegay of orange-blossom and syringa at her throat, she lay there on her bed with lightly folded hands and the strange aloofness and pre-occupation all the dead have. Only her hair burned about her like a molten copper; and the wreath of myrtle leaves ran forward to her brows and leaped beyond them into a tongue.

The great procession swept forward; black brothers of Misericordia, shrouded and awful, bore the bed or stalked before it with torches that guttered and flared sootily in the dancing light of day. They held the pick of Florence, those scowling shrouds—Giuliano and Lorenzo, Pazzi, Tornabuoni, Soderini or Pulci; and behind, old Cattaneo, battered with storms, walked heavily, swinging his long arms and looking into the day's face as if he would try another fall with Death yet. Priests and acolytes, tapers, banners, vestments and a great silver crucifix, they drifted by, chanting the dirge for Simonetta; and she, as if for a sacrifice, lifted up on her silken bed, lay couched like a white flower edged with the color of flame. . . .

. . . Santa Croce, the great church, stretched forward beyond her into distances of gray mist and cold spaces of light. Its bare vastness was damp like a vault. And she lay in the midst listless, heavy-lidded, apart, with the half smile, as it seemed, of some secret mirth. Round her the great candles smoked and flickered, and Mass was sung at the High Altar for her soul's repose. Sandro stood alone, facing the shining altar but looking fixedly at Simonetta on her couch. He was white and dry—parched lips and eyes that ached and smarted. Was this the end? Was it possible, my God! that the transparent, unearthly thing lying there so prone and pale was dead? Had such loveliness aught to do with life or death? Ah! sweet lady, dear heart, how tired she was, how deadly tired! From where he stood he could see with intolerable anguish the somber rings round her eyes and the violet shadows on the lids, her folded hands and the straight, meek line to her feet. And her poor wan face with its wistful pitiful little smile was turned half aside on the delicate throat, as if in a last appeal —"Leave me now, O Florentines, to my rest. I have given you all I had: ask no more. I was a young girl, a child; too young for your eager strivings. You have killed me with your play; let me be now, let me sleep!" Poor child! Poor child!

Sandro was on his knees with his face pressed against the pulpit and tears running through his fingers as he prayed. . . .

As he had seen her, so he painted. As at the beginning of life in a cold world, passively meeting the long trouble of it, he painted her a rapt Presence floating evenly to our earth. A gray, translucent sea laps silently upon a little creek and, in the hush of a still dawn, the myrtles and sedges on the water's brim are quiet. It is a dream in half tones that he gives us, gray and green and steely blue; and just that, and some homely magic of his own, hint the commerce of another world with man's discarded domain. Men and women are asleep, and as in an early walk you may startle the hares at their play, or see the creatures of the darkness—owls and night hawks and heavy moths—flit with fantastic purpose over the familiar scene, so here it comes upon you suddenly that you have surprised Nature's self at her mysteries; you are let into the secret; you have caught the spirit of the April woodland as she glides over the pasture to the copse. And that, indeed, was Sandro's fortune. He caught her in just such a propitious hour. He saw the sweet wild thing, pure and undefiled by touch of earth; caught her in that pregnant pause of time ere she had lighted. Another moment and a buxon nymph of the grove would fold her in a rosy mantle, colored as the earliest wood anemones are. She would vanish, we know, into the daffodils or a bank of violets. And you might tell her presence there, or in the rustle of the myrtles, or coo of doves mating in the pines; you might feel her genius in the scent of the earth or the kiss of the West wind; but you could only see her in mid-April, and you should look for her over the sea. She always comes with the first warmth of the year.

But daily, before he painted, Sandro knelt in a dark chapel in Santa Croce, while a blue-chinned priest said Mass for the repose of Simonetta's soul.